ENEMIES

A NOVEL

BY

JT HINE

ISBN: 978-1-7331755-8-6 (print)
978-1-7331755-9-3 (eBook)

Book design: ebooklaunch.com
Editor: Kerry Genova, Writer's Resource, Inc.
First edition: February 2022

Dedication

To Daniel

"Everyone wants to play the violin,
but every quartet needs a viola."

ACKNOWLEDGMENTS

Many people helped to bring this story to you, most of them unwittingly by enriching my life with their experiences. More specifically, I am grateful to the beta readers: Renata Celin, Patricia Stumpp, Leah Janeckzo, Selene Genovesi, and Riccardo Schiaffino.

I am also grateful to Margot Lee Shetterly for writing *Hidden Figures* in 2016, which would have pleased my character Mary Ardwood greatly.

The editor was Kerry Genova of Writers' Resource, Inc. Kim Olson proofread the manuscript.

Daniel Hine provided the musical selections mentioned in the story.

Contents

1. Quantico

SANDRA FOCUSED ON HIS CHEST. He would telegraph any moves there first; the rest she could get in her peripheral vision. She had learned that much, wrestling with Walter before her older brother shipped out to Vietnam.

She sensed more than saw her opponent infinitesimally jerk his right hand to make a swing. Before his arm moved, she leaped into him, grabbing his neck and raising her right knee to his lower abdomen. Her inertia threw him on his back. As she pushed back with her left leg, she drove her opposite fist into his sternum. While he lay stunned, she dropped from a standing position and rolled him, bringing his wrists behind his back.

The instructor's whistle stopped the drill.

"That's enough for today. Hit the showers!"

Sandra looked around to see that they were the only ones in a finished match: he down, she on top and in control.

Reaching down, she pulled him up. Their classmates picked up their gear at the edge of the practice mat and headed off, joking and chatting.

"Jeez, Sandra." He rubbed his chest and Adam's apple. "That hurt!"

"Sorry, Roy. I only tried to push off."

"I'll be okay —"

"What are you two doing?" Sergeant Mosely appeared behind him, staring hard at her.

"Sir?"

"How did Mister Yu here end up on the floor?"

"I put him there, sir. Just like you taught us."

"Trying to hurt him?"

"No, sir. If I were, I would have kneed his groin, and I would have either put out his eyes or broken his nose instead of grabbing his neck."

Roy shook his shoulders. "She *is* fast, Sergeant."

"Clean up, both of you." He grinned. "Miss Billingsley, I see you took notes on attitude. Next week I'll give you someone bigger."

Roy and Sandra hoisted their bags and left the gym. While he peeled off to the student locker room, she walked up the stairs to the administration wing. To accommodate its only female trainee, the FBI Academy had outfitted the only ladies' restroom in the building with a shower. No storage yet, so she carried everything she needed for the day in her duffel bag.

The last class of the day was on fingerprinting, or, precisely, the many ways to collect fingerprint evidence. Last week they had learned how to take prints on the heavy paper forms, using rollers and ink. Today, they practiced dusting for prints to obtain the best quality on different surfaces.

It was almost six o'clock when Roy fed onto Interstate 95 toward Washington. He took her to the bus stop in Arlington.

"Give my best to Millie and the kids."

"Sure thing. Pick you up tomorrow at one." He drove quickly away; she knew he was a little late for dinner. She had met Roy's family the first weekend after she started the weekly training.

The unpublicized program to train nontraditional recruits was the secret project of a few top-ranking special agents at FBI Headquarters. They wanted the Bureau to be ready when the Equal Employment Opportunity Bill stuck in Congress finally became law, which they expected at any time. The initial cohort included some financial analysts, two black police officers, a Chinese-American detective from New York, and Sandra. The weekend classes would be followed by field exercises next summer. The men would receive their badges. No one was sure what would happen to Sandra.

She walked to the Chinese restaurant on Braddock Road. Except for the nights at the Yu house, she had eaten there every Saturday night since starting her commute to Quantico.

As she ate her Sichuan chicken, she opened her copy of *Cristo si è fermato a Eboli.* In Rome, she had read Frances Frenaye's translation. In the original Italian, Carol Levi's year in exile was a completely different experience. The heat, the dust, and the rugged wisdom of the people of Lucania, as seen through a Northerner's eyes, came through in a way that she had not understood in English.

From the first time Joe Lockhart had walked into her office and rattled off Italian to someone on her desk phone, she had wanted to learn the language better. Now she was taking intermediate Italian and fourth-year Italian literature at the George Washington University. The courses also gave her an understanding that helped in her art history major.

After supper, she walked to the bus stop. She missed the 8:30 bus and waited a half hour for the next one, finishing another chapter while sitting on the bench at the stop.

Just before midnight, she stepped off the bus at Dupont Circle. The bus had broken down crossing the river, and it took an hour for a replacement to arrive. *They can't build that subway soon enough!* After twenty years of planning and talk, construction on the Washington Metrorail had only started two years ago.

As she crossed the small park in the center of the Circle, she heard someone step out of the bushes in the shadows. She tensed up just before a hand clamped down on her right shoulder and pushed her off the path to the grass behind some oleanders.

She tried to roll but found her legs caught. Her assailant gripped her ankles, flipping her on her back like a fish on a table.

He spread her legs and moved his hands to her arms as he kneeled on her legs. He was tall and heavy.

The smell of oil, gasoline, sweat, and beer threatened to close her throat. Rising panic and a sense of helplessness choked her. *This was not how it felt in training.*

He fell flat on her, pushing the air out of her chest, then lifted himself, still holding her wrists down. Sandra felt his hand leave her left wrist as he reached for his belt buckle. She formed a fist and drove it up toward his head. He snapped his hand over her wrist again and slammed her arm back down.

He dropped on her again and again, crushing her pubic area each time. *God, he's heavy!* She could feel her vision narrowing. She struggled to focus.

The third time, she twisted, catching him on her shoulder. That put him off-balance. As he fell to the side, she turned more until he fell next to her. His left hand loosened on her wrist. Pulling her hand out, she drove her right elbow into his chest. He gasped, then growled.

By then, her legs were coming free. She pushed, using the momentum to put a fist to his temple.

"Bitch!" He punched her with his left fist. The pain stabbed her side like a baseball bat. She fell again, her left hand still pinned.

She had to keep her right hand moving. She bounced her fist in an arc from his head down between his legs. He bellowed as she connected with his testicles. Sandra rolled right as fast as she could.

He grabbed her left ankle, stopping her movement.

"Help!" she screamed as loudly as she could.

Suddenly, there was silence. The man ran from the scene.

"What the hell?" A pair of teenagers came around the bush. One lanky, the other slightly overweight and only shoulder high to his friend.

"Mitch!" said the short one. "Go get the cops. Over there at the coffee shop!" Mitch disappeared. "You okay, miss?"

Sandra paused to catch her breath. "I'm not sure."

Two policemen appeared.

"Are you injured, miss?" asked the older one.

"I – I don't think so."

"Let's get into the light."

They led her to a bench under a streetlight. She recovered her composure as a small crowd gathered. One of the policemen shooed them away.

"Can you tell us what happened?"

Sandra described the assault and provided what little detail she could about the size and shape of her attacker. In the dark, she was unable to determine his features. All she remembered was his smell.

"What are you doing walking here?"

"Going home. I live right there." She pointed.

"You shouldn't be out by yourself at this hour."

"Excuse me?"

"It's not safe here. We get at least three calls a week for assaults here. Not all the women think to scream."

Sandra considered their faces.

"So, is anyone trying to stop this guy?"

"Like I said, you shouldn't be here alone."

Rage replaced confusion and surprise. She forced herself to keep her tone calm.

"No statement, no search for evidence, no call in?"

"He didn't hurt you, did he?"

"Not that he didn't want to, and I'll have the bruises."

"Well, we can't really do much. He ran, and there aren't any witnesses."

Sandra bit her lip. *This isn't going anywhere.* She made a mental note of their names and badge numbers.

"Thank you, officers. Have a nice evening. I'll walk home now if you don't mind."

"Good night, miss."

The Piranesi print she bought in Rome fell to the floor when she slammed the door entering her apartment.

A large, black bruise was spreading on the right side of her rib cage. Lighter contusions showed on her ankles and wrists. The soreness on her mons pubis had cleared up. She saw no other exterior damage.

Her state of mind was something else. She swung to rage, fear, shock and back to rage. She desperately wanted to talk to someone: Dad, Mom, any of her brothers, but her family had already made known their opinion of her living by herself in Washington DC.

She thought of Joe, but the only number she had was his grandparents' house in Richmond. He was still settling in at the University of Virginia, and he had not called to give her a number in Charlottesville. But thinking about him did ease her mood.

He had held a door for her the summer before, and they had recognized each other at a nightclub in Rome, Italy, a couple of months later. Sandra had skipped grades three and six in school, and Joe had lost a year after his father died, so they were the same age. It was a lovely evening, ending with a ride home on his Vespa 50 scooter.

Then in the spring, Jason Joseph Lockhart, Jr. had walked into her office in the Embassy Annex, and their world changed. Working with her boss, Special Agent Jim Redwood of the FBI, Joe had helped the Italian government foil a coup attempt by neofascists in the military. Retired General Ettore Arcibaldo, the coup leader, swore vengeance on the American teenager, but by the time Sandra left Rome, he seemed mainly concerned with his upcoming trial and with maintaining his position as the leader of his political party.

As she lay in bed, she shuffled around to find a position that did not make her bruises complain. She tried to focus on happy memories of Vespa rides, dancing, and dinners in Rome, of hiding Joe in her apartment in the Via della Giuliana, and his all-too-brief visit on his way to Richmond last week.

Still, it was tough to get to sleep.

ରୀ ରୀ ରୀ

The next morning, she was still stewing over the attack. Not wanting to keep her own company, she walked to the diner up the street. Darlene was working mornings this month. The sassy Jamaican waitress and Sandra had struck up something of a friendship.

She arrived just before the families began arriving on their way to church.

"Hi, Darlene. I don't feel like making breakfast."

The waitress eyed her as she poured black coffee into the mug on the table. "You don't look so hot either. Bad night?"

Sandra sighed and told her about the assault. And being blown off by the police.

"What time was that?"

"Not that late, about midnight."

"Bad timing, girl."

"Not you too!"

"You don't understand. It's the end of their shift. When I work nights here, the police come in about eleven thirty and hope that nothing keeps them from turning over at the station on time and going home."

"But I was attacked! Isn't that serious?"

Darlene frowned at her, long and hard. "Lemme tell you something, Sandra. If it was a man, those two would be going home at three a.m. And a white man? Maybe at dawn."

"So, I'm on my own at night?"

"Ain't we always?" Darlene cocked her head and raised an eyebrow. "What'll you have, honey?"

"I may kill someone this afternoon. Make it steak and eggs and the waffles."

"Atta girl. Be right back."

ଓଓଓ

At one p.m., she was waiting at the bus stop in Arlington when Roy stopped.

"Did you walk into a door?"

"No. That's from fighting a monster last night."

"You were attacked?"

"Just a block from my apartment. The cops blew it off. They probably didn't want to be late for turnover."

"Don't I know how that works! I can't count the number of times I dragged home late because of something that came up at the last minute. Something I do not miss about my days on the beat." Roy had just made sergeant in the NYPD before applying to the FBI program. He was also majoring in criminology and accounting at George Mason College.

"I thought they were blowing me off because I'm a woman."

He glanced at her and nodded. "There's that too. The Bureau is even worse in case you haven't noticed."

"I have. Maybe that is why I thought as I did instead of the getting-home-late thing."

"Do you want me to drive you all the way in? We could talk to Millie about it."

"Thank you, Roy. Let me figure out this one without getting concessions for my sex. Now, I'm so angry, I could injure someone if they cross me."

"Ask Sarge about it. I'll bet he says you need more moves to go with that attitude he likes." Roy grinned. She relaxed.

"I'll do that."

Sunday afternoon was spent in the classroom, but Sandra sought out Sergeant Moseley in his office. He gave her the name and address of a buddy who had fought in Vietnam with him.

That night, the phone rang as she let herself into the apartment.

"*Ciao, bella. Come stai?*" Hi, beautiful, how are you?

"Joe!" Dropping her duffel bag, she sat on the floor.

"Take this down before I forget to give it to you." She reached for a pencil from the table and wrote the number of the pay phone on the second floor of McCormick Hall.

"I've never said this to anyone before, but I have really missed you."

"I missed you too. How have you been?"

"Good and bad." She told him about the weekend training and the assault in Dupont Circle. "I'm going to find a self-defense course this week. That will be the last guy who ever gets so close."

"Including me?"

"You know what I mean, silly. How was your first week at *the* university?"

"I'm sore from so much running, but my roommate ran cross-country in high school. He's teaching me how to pace myself."

"What are the classes like?"

"Only naval science so far, which I like a lot. Move-in Day is next weekend, and then we'll see what the schedule is. I have to go, Sandra. There's a line for the phone. I'll call you tomorrow from someplace where we can talk."

"Do that. Thanks for calling. And be safe."

"You too. Bye." They hung up.

2. ORIENTATION

"BYE, GRANDPA, *Grandmaman*. See you soon!" After closing the door, Joe stood back. He waved, then watched as Brigadier General Matthew J. Ardwood, US Army (retired), backed the car out and drove up the alley to McCormick Road.

The silhouettes of his grandparents reminded him of how his parents would have looked: he erect, hair almost brushing the roof, and she only a little shorter, her hair elegantly coiffed in a practical style, her frame slender and athletic. For a moment, he missed his mother. Then he sighed and hoisted his duffel bag to his shoulder.

The complex of dormitories spread away from the historic Academical Village of the University of Virginia like a sprawling suburb. Built in the early fifties to accommodate the massive influx of veterans using their GI Bill of Rights benefits, it typified American college residential construction of the era: big blocks of brick buildings, with long corridors that held two- and four-man rooms and common showers and bathrooms at either end. At UVA, however, the brick matched the nineteenth-century bricks originally used by Thomas Jefferson: true dimensions (2x4x6 inches) and baked from clay available only in Central and Southern Virginia.

The magnolias, oaks and poplars growing among the structures made Joe feel as if he were in a park instead of a college campus. *Call it the Grounds here*, he reminded himself, *not the campus*. Taking a big breath of clean air, he climbed to his room on the second floor of McCormick Hall.

As he walked into his room, he saw that someone had added to the pile of personal effects. There were four beds, and Joe had put his suitcase, typewriter, and his box of office supplies on one of the two nearest the window. Someone else had begun covering the opposite lower bed.

"Early check-in too?" a very lightly accented voice said from behind him. The vowels were clean, without the diphthongs typical of middle American speech. Joe turned to see a student with coal-black eyes and bronze skin standing in the doorway. His black hair was shiny, the curliness carefully controlled and combed back. Only a little shorter than Joe, with a sharp nose and high cheekbones. The eyes reflected the smile. Joe grinned too.

"Yeah. We get to pick the best beds." He stuck out his hand. "Joe Lockhart."

"Diego de la Torre." The handshake was firm, confident.

"*Encantado.*" Pleased to meet you.

"*¿Habla español?*" Diego's eyes widened with delight.

"Just a few courteous phrases. Where are you from?"

"Central Valley California. You?"

"Rome, but my grandparents live in Richmond, so I'm claiming Virginia as my residence."

Diego stood back to appraise his new roommate.

"You don't look heavy enough for football."

"NROTC Special Orientation." Naval Reserve Officer Training Corps.

"Me too." The Californian gave him a friendly slap on the upper arm. "Contract or regular?"

Joe smiled. "Contract. I didn't find out about the regular option until it was too late to apply."

"That may be good. Give you a chance to see if you like it, even though you must pay your tuition this year. You can convert in June, I think."

"Are you a regular?"

"Yes. There was no way I was going to the Naval Academy. My congressman makes political appointments, and my senators have their quotas filled. I applied for next year, so I may still go if I don't decide to stay here."

They unpacked their gear in companionable silence. Both men had less stuff than the dressers and closets would hold, so it did not take long.

Diego slammed the last drawer shut on his side. "You know where Maury Hall is?"

"Grandpa showed me, coming here. Down that way and a right turn after the Lawn." Going to the window, he pointed to the left up the street toward the original part of the university.

"We got two hours. You want some supper?"

"Sure. Let's check out the cafeteria next door, so we can figure out how the meal plan works." They headed downstairs.

The heat of the day radiated from the bricks of their building as the shadows began to lengthen. The tops of the trees rippled in an evening breeze that the buildings blocked at ground level.

In the dining rooms next to McCormick Hall, they found more choices than they had experienced in their high school cafeterias. Joe took the spaghetti and some roast chicken, while Diego chose steak and fries. The pasta was overcooked to Joe's taste, but he was hungry and not inclined to criticize anything on his first day.

They capped off supper with vanilla ice cream cones, which they ate before the treat could melt. At McCormick Road, they turned left.

"Isn't this fantastic?" said Diego, sweeping a hand across the view.

They stood at the south side of the Lawn, opposite the imposing Palladian structure called the Rotunda. Wide stairs led up to a classical portico and a broad façade. From either side of the Rotunda, ten facing residences, the Pavilions, bracketed the Lawn. A portico of arches and columns covered the walkways in front of the ten Pavilions and the ground-level student apartments connecting them. A row of similar apartments, the West and East Ranges, ran behind the pavilions, with private gardens in the space between. Fourth-year undergraduates occupied the Lawn rooms; graduate students lived in the ranges.

"Think we'll live on the Lawn someday?"

"It's supposed to be an honor," said Joe. "I don't know how honorable it will feel in the winter, with the only bathroom at the end of that exposed walkway and no heat."

"No heat?"

"Nope. My grandfather said that the university keeps the Academical Village exactly as it was in 1826.

Each apartment has only a fireplace in it. Yet it takes a high grade point average and all sorts of endorsements to be selected to live here for your fourth year."

"Well, we won't have to worry about that for a while. Did your grandfather go to UVA?"

"No, VMI, the Virginia Military Institute in Lexington. But the family is from Richmond, and between friends and relatives, they came here often. After he retired, he taught in the Government Department for a while. The Army ROTC unit invites him to give a guest lecture each year."

Located between the East Range and the Hospital, Maury Hall was not nearly as imposing as the other buildings. Erected during the Second World War, the cube of plastered concrete sported modest decoration and large windows. A pair of seven-foot-tall anchors flanking the steps to the main entrance proudly shouted the building's purpose to the world. Lights were coming on inside as they pushed open the front door.

&&&

"Reveille, amigo. All hands on deck!"

With a groan, Joe pushed his head under his pillow. His classmate shook his shoulders.

"Oh God, Diego. It's still dark."

"Of course. The run starts at dawn. You gonna sleep in for your last day of NSO?"

"No." He sighed. "That's a thought worth waking up for. Everything has ached for two weeks, man."

"Maybe cut back the late-night phone calls to Sandra." Diego lifted the coffee maker from the hotplate on his side of the room. "*¿Café?*"

"*Sí, gracias.*"

Joe heaved himself out of bed and turned to make it. Donning his bathrobe, he trotted down to the bathroom. When he returned, Diego handed him a mug of hot black coffee. Dark and strong, like the Italian espresso he grew up with.

"I gotta send your mother something for Christmas. Where does she find this coffee?"

"A *torrefacción* in Salinas. We've had a coffee roaster on that corner for two hundred and fifty years."

After some stretching, Joe donned his running gear: Navy-issue blue shorts and a gray tee-shirt. They would come back to change before the first naval science class.

They jogged to Maury Hall because the midshipmen needed to warm up before the run. At exactly five forty-five, they fell into formation in front of the building. The drill sergeant, a Marine named Henry, barked them to attention, then ordered a double-time march, running to the Lawn and along the length of the Academical Village. The Army ROTC unit came up behind them, followed by the Air Force. Each unit was singing its own chant at a volume designed to wake up any students in their little rooms.

"I love doing that," said Diego. An angry fourth-year flipped them the finger as he staggered blearily to the toilets.

"Me too." Joe was taking more breaths than his friend. "I'll bet they're glad this is the last day too."

The three services split up as they ran past the Rotunda. The Navy group turned left down McCormick Road and picked up speed. As they started the climb up Observatory Hill, sweat poured from half the faces in the formation, including Joe's.

"Didn't you run in high school?" asked Diego.

"Four-forty and four-forty hurdles. Only two meets in the spring. Not much of a sports program."

"That's just a long sprint. No wonder this wears you out."

"I'll get used to it, but I wish we had had cross-country. That would have been more useful."

Diego put his hand on Joe's back. "Imagine lengthening your stride, and breathe at some interval that matches the pace, even if you pant on every step."

Joe focused on his pace and his breathing. The rhythm of the forced march fell somewhere between sixty and ninety steps per minute. He had been falling behind and catching up, wearing himself out. He nodded as he found a spot where he exhaled every third step. By the time they turned back downhill, he was exhaling every fourth step, and going into the last mile, he could talk almost normally.

"Gracias, amigo."

"De nada. We'll make a runner of you yet."

"I miss my bike. Riding that scooter got me out of shape last year."

"There's a shop on Elliewood Avenue."

"Do you want one too?"

"Sure. Then maybe we could see something besides the Corner after class."

"Cut the grab-ass, girls!" Sergeant Henry shouted. "Peterson!"

Peterson called out in his booming bass "I once knew a girl in Kalamazoo…" The men matched the beat of the lusty limerick, calling out "Whon, too, thuree, fower!" between irreverent or raunchy verses. As they approached the central Grounds, Peterson switched to the more acceptable lyrics about the lineage of students from Virginia Tech, VMI, North Carolina, and other rival sports teams. Some of the other early check-ins, mostly football players and graduate students, cheered and waved as the middies ran by.

They had a half hour to run back to McCormick Hall, shower, don their "white works" uniforms and report back to Maury Hall. It seemed that they had been running or trotting everywhere. The shapeless, white cotton imitation of a sailor's uniform looked terrible even clean, but it was comfortable in the summer.

"At least no O-course today," said Joe as they jogged past Old Cabell Hall at the end of the Lawn. They had run the Obstacle Course every other day and needed the day in between to recover.

"And from now on, we'll only do this every weekend."

"I was thinking of Sandra while we were running."

"So, Peterson's limericks make you think of her?" Diego smiled and wiggled his eyebrows.

"No, dummy; what she would think of it."

"Probably take offense and dump you."

"Not so sure. As far as I can tell, she's tougher than most of us."

"How so?"

"She grew up on a farm with four brothers. Lived alone in Rome for more than a year. She's the only woman at the FBI Academy."

"The FBI doesn't have female agents."

"Not yet, but the Equal Employment Opportunity Act will pass eventually, and it will change all that. The

Bureau is training some non-traditional agents, and Sandra is in the first cohort.

"The drill instructor is Force Recon like Henry. I bet she can sing dirtier than Peterson." Force Reconnaissance is the Marine Corps' Special Forces.

"I gotta meet this woman. She sounds amazing."

"I can agree with you on that."

The morning consisted of three classes. Another uniform change at lunch, this time into Service Dress White, the uniform for more formal occasions. Today was their last day and their swearing-in. About three-quarters of the men had family close enough to come for the event, and the upperclassmen would be back for it. The only upperclassmen that they knew were Peterson and three other rising third-year midshipmen who had helped run NSO.

Before the assembly in the small auditorium of Maury Hall, the new ROTC midshipmen lined up to sign the papers committing them to service. The regulars, like Diego, received a "full ride," meaning tuition, fees, room and board paid by the US Navy, plus a small stipend that barely covered their uniforms. In return, they would owe the country five years as commissioned officers. If they left the program before two years, they would have to complete a two-year obligation as enlisted men. Contract midshipmen such as Joe were only obligated to finish the year. The government only paid for their uniforms.

"How do you feel about it?" he asked as Diego signed.

"Same terms as the Naval Academy. Annapolis and a career are still my plan, remember."

Upperclassmen and enlisted staff escorted the parents to their seats. The front rows were roped off for the new candidates.

After they settled in, Sergeant Henry called out, "Attention on deck!"

Every man jumped to his feet and stood at attention. Joe thought, *Why does he always wait until we sit down before he does that?* From his position in the center of the room, Joe saw Henry standing tight-lipped at the foot of the steps. The drill sergeant's eyes did not match the rest of his expression. *He enjoys this.*

Behind him, he heard some parents and other civilians sitting down irregularly. Henry's show had made them forget that they did not have to stand. Some remained standing with the midshipmen.

Captain Norwood and his two assistants walked to the stage. The captain wore five rows of ribbons on his chest and the crossed swords of the brand-new Surface Warfare Officer device above them. Lieutenant-Commander Mills boasted two rows and pilot's wings. Major Jackson wore three rows, plus marksman medals. He had commanded the same Force Recon unit in which Sergeant Henry had served.

Looking at his commanding officer, Joe could not imagine living through World War II, Korea *and* Vietnam. Then he realized that his father had also spent almost his entire adult life at war, patching up Norwood's shipmates and countless others. Joe's paternal grandparents had died while the naval surgeon was in North Africa, and his older brother had sold the house in Ilion, New York. Returning homeless from the war, the Yankee doctor had answered an ad to work at the Medical

College of Virginia in Richmond. There, he met the brilliant doctor who became his wife and Joe's mother.

To Joe, Jason Lockhart was mainly a surgeon, working at Saint Mary's Hospital. A tall man who could carry his son and a suitcase as easily as two bags of groceries. He was also an amazing tennis player, the only one who could keep up with his partner, former national champion Nancy Ardwood.

Until today, Joe had understood war the way he understood his lessons. He had studied history in some detail, but the reality had hovered in the distance. He vaguely remembered his father in uniform coming home from Korea, but reading Captain Norwood's biography had made the Korean War come alive.

Now he was about to become a member of this group of men, and he felt a choking sensation in his throat. He imagined his father in the operating room of the hospital ship *USS Haven* (AH-12), blood up to his elbows as the corpsmen wheeled the most desperate marines and sailors from triage to his table. Captain Norwood earned the star on his Purple Heart (second award) when a shell hit his ship off Inchon. The first Purple Heart was for something in World War II, but the citation was still classified.

The Commanding Officer went to the lectern.

"At ease. Ladies and gentlemen, please be seated."

The midshipmen sat with a single whoosh. Joe felt a jab in his ribs.

"You okay?" Diego whispered. Feeling his eyes well, Joe avoided blinking to keep tears from falling. Slowly, he regained control.

"Yeah. What we're doing just hit me."

"Just now?"

"Tell you later."

Captain Norwood made a short speech about duty and priorities. Joe sneaked a look around. His classmates stared at the man speaking, specifically at his chest, a map of the military history of the United States in the second half of the twentieth century. *Not just men*, Joe thought, *heroes. Who the hell do I think I am?*

Though he hardly listened as the captain administered the Oath of Office, Joe would never forget the paragraph that he had signed earlier, and he repeated the words with the others:

"Having been appointed a Midshipman in the United States Naval Reserve, I solemnly swear that I will support and defend the Constitution of the United States against all enemies, foreign and domestic; that I will bear true faith and allegiance to the same; that I take this obligation freely, without any mental reservation or purpose of evasion; and that I will well and faithfully discharge the duties of the office on which I am about to enter, so help me God."

"Welcome aboard, midshipmen. Tomorrow is Move-in Day, but you have already moved in. Now you are more than university students. You are officers and gentlemen in the United States Navy. Do us proud, on Grounds and everywhere you go. Any questions?"

Silence. They knew that they could ask the officers and men anything, anytime.

"Attention on deck!" The midshipmen shot to their feet as the official party left the stage and departed the auditorium. Sergeant Henry smiled. "Congratulations, gentlemen. Dismissed!"

Joe caught Diego's arm as they eased out of their

chairs to the aisle.

"Got anywhere to go, amigo?"

"No, why?"

"Come meet my grandparents."

"They're the ones from Richmond?"

"Only grandparents I have."

"If you're sure." Diego looked hesitant.

"Relax, man. He's career Army. He was stationed at Fort Ord, so he even knows your neck of the woods better than I."

"Fort Ord? Neat-o." Diego lengthened his stride.

"Over there." It was hard to miss Matthew Ardwood's silver hair above the crowd.

After hugging his grandparents, Joe turned to his friend. "General Ardwood, Midshipman Diego de la Torre."

The general gave him a warm, strong grip. "*Encantado. ¿Esta su padre Don Carlos de Salinas?*"

Diego's jaw dropped, but he pulled it back up. "*Sí, señor general, y soy muy honorado.* I'm surprised that you know my father."

"Your family's reputation for the finest produce and beef is well-known. Fort Ord buys direct, you know." He nodded to the door, and they joined the flow out the door.

"I'm stunned, sir."

"Join us for dinner, and we can surprise you some more."

"Grandpa, should we risk spilling something on our whites? I only have the one set."

"I'll have them bring an extra big napkin for you. You're not ashamed, are you?"

"No, sir!" they said together.

"Good. I booked a table at the Clifton Inn. It's not an undergraduate hangout, but the diners there would be delighted to have two new officers in their midst."

Dinner in the 1799 restaurant was not quite the Ostaria dell'Orso in Rome, but it was the best food that Joe had eaten since arriving in America.

"Thanks, Grandpa. This is almost as good as home."

"Thank your grandmother for the idea. She remembered the places you and Nancy took us to and figured that you were either starving or dying of culture shock by now."

"Merci, Grandmaman." Annabelle Ardwood reached next to her and gave her grandson a hug.

After a pleasant silence enjoying the moment, her husband turned to Diego.

"Please let us be your East Coast base. For example, stay with us for the short holidays like Thanksgiving and fall break."

"That would be wonderful, sir, but I'm almost a stranger."

"Not hardly. Don Carlos is more than a farmer in Salinas, and I have followed you since you were born."

Diego stared, then dropped his gaze. "I don't understand, sir."

"Carlos de la Torre and I go back farther than Fort Ord. I pinned his second lieutenant bars on him at Guadalcanal."

"Omigod! I never knew. Papa would never talk about the war. He just said he enlisted and served in the Pacific. He wouldn't even tell me his unit. I didn't know he was an officer."

General Ardwood considered the young Californian

in silence, then said, "I hope you are not disappointed. Many of us who fought in that war won't talk about it. Talking brings back the terror. Some are ashamed of what they had to do, but most are still trying to deal with the horrors. I'll call him and ask permission to share more with you. He is a friend, and he might let me tell you more. It might help him, too, to open up with you. You're a serving officer yourself now."

Diego was mostly silent and thoughtful as they drove back to McCormick Hall. After hugs and handshakes, the Ardwoods drove to Richmond while the two friends walked up to their room, Diego still deep in thought.

"Hey, roomie, if you're going to sit in a trance like that, maybe you should get undressed and go to bed. Then you can pretend to sleep too."

"I just can't understand it." Diego seemed to be talking to himself.

Joe removed the buttons from his Service Dress White blouse, putting them and his shoulder boards in a small box. He took off the white shoes and trousers.

"Don't make yourself have to launder the uniform already."

Diego looked up at him blankly, then began the same routine. They applied white polish to their shoes and stretched out the cotton trousers on hangars. Laundering the uniforms involved very hot water, bleach, starch, and ironing, so they tried to wear them twice between each wash if possible.

After their showers, brushing and flossing, Diego sat on the bed and stared again.

"Talk to me, amigo."

Diego looked up sadly. "I never knew. He was so upset whenever I talked about wanting to join the service. I think that I wanted this career partly to get back at him. Most of the time, he would just storm out and stew in silence for a long time."

Joe sat on his bed. He looked across at his friend.

"What if you could find out more? This is a major research university, after all."

"Where would we start?"

"You may be the cross-country jock, but I'm the bookworm. For starters, we know his unit, and we know he was at Guadalcanal."

Diego looked blank. "Unit?"

"If Colonel Ardwood gave him his commission, he had to be in the Twenty-Seventh Regiment of the Twenty-Fifth Infantry Division. Anyone earning a battlefield commission probably earned a medal or two. Let's look in the Army war records."

"They have that stuff here?"

"Alderman is a Federal Depository. It has copies of everything in the Library of Congress."

Diego's face began to lighten up. "Have you been there?"

"Once, to find the card catalogs and the periodicals. They have phone directories and hometown newspapers. I was looking up people I knew around the country."

"You think they'd have the *Salinas Californian?*"

"Maybe. We can check it out if you like."

"And look up the Twenty-fifth Division."

"That too." Joe met Diego's smile with his own. "You know about bands of brothers being created in war?"

"Yes?"

"If my grandfather is a friend of your papa after all this time, we might be some kind of cousins!"

"Weird thought, but fun."

"What time does Move-In start here?"

"Eight thirty."

"Grandpa said it's a zoo, and the families will be lining up at dawn, trying to park by the curb. Let's get up early."

"I don't have a problem with that. You're the sleepyhead."

Diego laughed as Joe's pillow slammed into the wall over his bunk.

3. THE GEORGE WASHINGTON UNIVERSITY

MONDAY MORNING after the attack at Dupont Circle, Sandra struggled to focus and to keep a poker face. Professor White more than annoyed her. She did not mind an occasional joke, but the forty-something man at the front of the room did not seem to have anything relevant to say. After the third dumb blonde joke, she tuned him out and slipped her copy of *Forensic Sciences* to her desk. There was nothing about business law that White was going to say that she had not read. The article on the investigation of art forgeries was more interesting, and it was relevant to her art history class.

Maureen nudged her left elbow. Sandra looked up to see Professor White looking at her.

"Well, Miss Billingsley?" From his smirk and the polite chuckles of her classmates, she knew he had cracked another bad joke.

"Well, like, what, sir?" She batted her eyelashes and twirled her blond ponytail. The frat boys on the other side of the room burst out laughing, while the women on either side of her covered their mouths and giggled. Maureen had written "B&E" on her notepad.

Speechless for a moment, White struggled to regain his composure. "B&E, Miss Billingsley."

"Breaking and entering, sir?"

"Of course. Which is the crime?"

"Neither, sir. It takes both to constitute a crime, implying destruction and trespass." She waited for White to speak, but he looked at the clock and left the room.

"What was that all about?" Sandra asked Maureen as they gathered their books.

"He just made another blonde joke and was going to demonstrate the point." She sighed. "When you quoted from the text, he couldn't handle it."

"What an idiot. Does he think we're illiterate?"

"No, just female. He thinks we don't belong here."

"This is going to be a long semester."

In the afternoon, Sandra enrolled in a martial arts studio for lessons three times a week. The dojo was beyond Rock Creek in Georgetown, an easy walk for her.

She expected the trim and fit men she saw, but not the number of women. Most were well-heeled spouses of government bureaucrats, congressmen, or executives. She also saw three schoolteachers and one policewoman.

Without anyone saying anything, she knew she was not alone. That felt very empowering.

⇒⇒⇒

The following Saturday morning, Sandra locked her "new" bike to the rack in front of George Washington High School and walked to the bus stop nearby.

Roy rolled up at exactly 8 a.m.

"Did you find a new route? This is actually more convenient for me than the Braddock Road stop."

"No, I got a bicycle, and I'm parking it at the high school," she said, pointing across the street.

"Cool. Aren't you worried about its being stolen?"

"That's why I got a used ten-speed that doesn't look worth stealing. If it disappears, I won't be out much."

"Not enough exercise on the confidence course?"

Sandra laughed. "A bike is faster and more reliable. I've been spending three hours a day on the bus, more when it breaks down, which was twice just this week. Especially on Saturday and Sunday, I can't afford that."

"Good point." Roy took the ramp for I-95, and they continued to Quantico in companionable silence.

ᏝᏝᏝ

"Yu and Schwartz! Billingsley and Jefferson! Taylor and Ruggiano! Face off!"

Sandra took her position next to Roy and considered the two-hundred-pound, six-foot-two mass of muscle across from her. Like a mantra, she recited Sarge's words to herself, "Leverage. Leverage. Leverage." Sometimes, Sarge Robinson sounded like an investment counselor, but his mnemonics worked. On her second lesson, she had taken down all the men that she had been paired with.

Leroy Jefferson was something else. A seasoned officer who had grown up on the streets of Northeast Washington, he had been known to break up small riots singlehandedly. His reputation had preceded him to the Academy, and his scowl was as intimidating as his size.

But just before Sergeant Mosely blew his whistle, Jefferson smiled.

He's not taking this seriously, Sandra thought.

31

She walked slowly toward Leroy as he ran across the mat. He put out his arms as if to pick her up.

Jumping forward, she grabbed his right arm and let him plow past her. A snap-and-pull yanked the arm back, driving him to the floor.

She hung on to his arm, letting his inertia fling her up and over his back. Before he could react, she crossed his arms behind his back.

When he tried to raise himself, Sandra rode him like a bronco.

The whistle stopped the action.

Sandra slid over and jumped up, offering a hand to Leroy.

"No hard feelings, I hope?"

"Well, I was pissed, but next time, I won't cut you any slack."

"Good idea, Mister Jefferson." Sergeant Mosely appeared behind him. "I won't let you do it this weekend, though." He looked out at the six. "Rotate to the right one place. Now!"

Sandra brought down the other four men, except for Roy, who surprised her with a feint and a kick.

They had wrestled to a stalemate when the whistle stopped them.

"I knew I would need some home-grown ingredients for this stew." He grinned.

They bowed to each other, which caused the others to pause and stare.

"Okay, you two. This ain't your neighborhood dojo," Mosely barked but also smiled.

"Sorry, sir – felt sort of natural."

The drill instructor came closer to Roy and Sandra. "Robinson said you've only had two lessons."

"Yes, sir."

"Keep working. You're a quick study." He turned to Roy. "And I guess you had some extra training too?"

"Just some kung fu. Dad made us take it in high school."

Mosely turned back to the others. "You six watch. Next six!"

Roy and Sandra walked to the bleachers with the others.

"You're the first European-American I've gone against that didn't fold with that kick. I was still figuring out which way to throw you at the end."

"I'm glad he stopped us. I was contemplating something that Millie would not appreciate."

Roy laughed. They settled in to study their classmates' techniques.

That night, Sandra applied the Tiger Balm Joe had given her to her arms and legs. Pulling down people who outweighed her by up to eighty pounds was something she would need to train for.

ধধধ

For the three-day Columbus Day weekend, the FBI Academy closed classes. Sandra studied for midterms on Saturday. Sunday after church at Saint Thomas on Eighteenth Street, she bundled up in the crisp sunshine and lashed her small duffel bag to the back of her bike.

She pedaled to the National Gallery of Art. There, she took in a traveling exhibit of Dutch Masters. Some of the paintings had been the subjects of term papers her freshman year. In the lobby was a poster advertising another exhibition on loan from the Borghese Museum in Rome. She looked forward to that one.

Outside, she bought lunch at a food cart and went to the Lincoln Memorial to eat it. Then she cycled the length of the National Mall and back, stopping at the National Archives to see the Declaration of Independence. As the shadows lengthened, she biked over the Potomac River to Arlington, where Roy and Millie Yu lived off Mount Vernon Avenue.

"Ooh, that smells wonderful," she said when Roy opened the door. She squatted down to shake hands with little Annie, who was peeking out from behind her father. The girl gave Sandra a bear hug, then ran to her room. Sandra stood. "She's so sweet."

"Until there are chores," he said with an eye roll.

Because Sandra was a friend and a frequent visitor, the meal was a casual affair. The Yus had sold their apartment in New York for enough money to buy a large house in the Virginia suburb. The guest room had its own bathroom. They insisted she stay overnight whenever she came for dinner, so she did not need to ride home late at night.

"Roy will become a full-time special agent after this summer," said Millie over dessert, "but I'm still not clear on what happens to you. Don't you have to finish at GW?"

"Yes, but no one knows after that. The people running the program expect the Bureau will need to recruit women agents if the EEO bill becomes law. They want to be ready, but there are a lot of attitudes to overcome. I don't mind finishing school while they figure it out."

"That seems so strange."

"I was an FBI employee when I applied, so they can put me in an office or something else until they want to give me a badge. But they won't have to start me through training when the public expects to see female agents quickly."

"The key is keeping her in some kind of FBI status," said Roy. "It also gives her cover. There are people at Headquarters who would go crazy if they found out what our young GS-5 is really doing weekends." They chuckled.

With the dishes cleared, Annie brought out her violin. Sandra had given Roy her viola the day before. With Millie on piano and Roy on cello, they played chamber music until it was Annie's bedtime. When the parents came back to the living room, Sandra was looking happily out the window.

"That was fun. I haven't been able to play with someone since I left home. Annie is so talented."

"Her age surprises people, but she did start Suzuki two years ago. Kids learn fast."

As Sandra stretched out in the queen-sized bed, the darkness and the silence of the Virginia countryside reminded her of home. Much as she enjoyed the excitement and cultural offerings in Rome and Washington, she missed the quiet and peace of the farm in Ohio. Grateful for the generosity of her friends, she drifted off to sleep.

4. MOVE-IN DAY

JOE FINISHED DRYING the coffee cups and starting the new percolator with a fresh load of coffee, while Diego made sure that the closets each had a free half open for their new roommates. They could hear the noise from the sidewalks spread up the stairways and into the hall.

Diego stuck a wedge under their door to hold it open. A moment later, a skinny, pale, black-haired boy appeared, holding two suitcases. Behind him came a tall, heavyset boy with a sunburned nose.

"This room 214?" said the second one, looking at Joe.

"This is it. The upper bunks are available. The left side gets the afternoon sun. I'm Joe."

"Steve. What's he doing here?"

"Our roommate, Diego."

"That's bullshit. Ain't rooming with no nigger!"

"He isn't a Negro, and you owe him an apology."

"Leave it, Joe." Diego touched his elbow.

Joe eyed the two new boys, who had set down their suitcases.

"Before I have a chance to shake hands and offer him coffee, he's spouting bigoted insults. He doesn't even know who you are."

"And I don't care," said Steve. "He can get out and find another room."

"Doesn't work that way, Steve. We've been here for two weeks, and we're staying."

"What do you think, Matt? Do we take this shit from a nigger-lover?"

"Nope. Let's throw them out."

While Matt went for Diego, Steve advanced on Joe, punching him hard in the stomach. The pain took his breath away as he fell backward, his head crashing into the wall by his bed. As the darkness tried to close in, he had a picture of the unarmed combat drills at the gym and felt a rising fury. The shadows changed into a red haze.

Only vaguely aware of Diego to his left, Joe grabbed the edge of his mattress and threw himself to his feet in one motion. His momentum took him face to face with Steve. With his head tucked slightly, he heard the crack of two hard skulls hitting. Driving his fists into Steve's solar plexus, he pushed off with his legs, shoving both to the floor, sliding out into the corridor. A woman screamed.

The haze receded as Joe stood and got his bearings. Steve was not moving. A wall of parents and students had formed around their room. Most gaped in amazement. Some grinned with excitement like the crowd at a cock-fight.

"What's going on here?" The resident assistant for their floor worked through the spectators. Jack stood six-foot-two and had already established his street cred with the football players who got drunk last week and started fighting.

Steve stirred. Joe reached down to give him a hand up.

"Don't touch him, Joe." Jack bent over Steve. "Don't move. Make sure nothing's broken."

Steve scowled. "Nothing but this nigger-lover's face when I finish with him." He struggled to his feet.

"Don't you do anything. What's your name?"

"Dixon."

"Room 214?"

"Not if you think we're rooming with a nigger and his buddy."

"Dixon, we don't use language like that here. Where's your roommate, Joe?"

"Right here, Jack." Diego came out, pushing Matt in front of him. He had Matt's hands locked behind him. "This one can't keep his hands to himself."

Jack looked around. "Did anyone here see how this started?"

"I did." Ed Schlesinger, an Air Force ROTC across the hall. "These two showed up to move in. Diego and Joe had the door wedged open and welcomed them in. This one started right out with the insults, then punched Joe in the chest, knocking him to the far wall. The other one went at Diego, but then I couldn't see because Joe was flying through the door with the big guy."

Jack looked around. "Anyone else?" Silence. "Where are your parents?"

"Over at the Alumni Club."

"So, are you both legacies?"

"Yeah, and we want them out of our room."

"We'll see about that. First, take your suitcases down to Accommodations, then go find your parents. Clearly, a switch is needed here."

"What about these two? My dad is going to sue."

"No one is going to sue anyone. We have our own disciplinary system here. I'll go downstairs with you. Now! We're blocking the others moving in."

As Steve and Matt gathered their things and left, Jack turned to Joe and Diego.

"NROTC, right?" They nodded. "Don't be surprised if you're on the carpet first thing Monday. From what I heard, Captain Norwood takes a dim view of his men fighting in the residence halls." Then he was gone.

"Oh shit! We're in for it now," said Joe, running his hand over the bruise on his chest. "Can they throw us out of the program for this?"

"Yes, but I wouldn't expect them to do that."

"Why not?"

"I have a hunch about the skipper and Sarge. Some scuffle probably happens every year, though I would have expected a fight on the Corner with some Army cadets, not our roommates."

Diego turned on the coffee maker. "Want some coffee?"

"Sure. We made it for company."

Joe felt behind his head, which was beginning to hurt; his hand came back bloody. Then he noticed the patch of blood on the wall. "I didn't feel that before. How bad is it?"

Diego examined the back of Joe's head. "Mostly a bruise now, but there's a little scrape, and head wounds always bleed like hell. Let me clean it up."

He winced when Diego took a wet washcloth to the wound.

"Got some iodine?"

"Nope."

"How about some whiskey?

Laughing made his head hurt.

"I think we'll need a first aid kit if these are the kind of neighbors we'll have."

"I agree."

While Joe cleaned the blood off the paint, Diego poured coffee. They sat on their desk chairs and waited for Jack to come back.

"What happened with you and Matt?"

"Nothing much. He came at me like Steve. I let him go through and pulled his arm behind him. Then I locked up his hands, and we watched you explode from the floor and knock Steve through the door. That was pretty dramatic, amigo."

"You mean, he never touched you?"

"Of course not."

"Can you show me?"

Diego had Joe come at him the way Steve had charged him. As Diego stepped neatly aside, Joe felt his right arm pull behind him, and Diego swinging on it to position himself behind Joe. He was barely aware of what happened when his left arm was pulled back, and a firm grip held both hands pinned in the small of his back.

"Where did you learn that?"

"Where else? Growing up. When I started getting in trouble for hurting the other kids in school and the gringos who tried to pick on me in town, Papa told me to learn how to disable them without inflicting damage. 'Don't leave evidence for the cops to make it your fault,'" he said.

"Your father taught you?"

"No, he let us figure it out. We had learned quickly how to neutralize bullies, but doing it without breaking things or drawing blood was different. My brothers and sisters all had to learn."

"Your sisters?"

"Of course. They got more trash from the crackers than we did. That and the farm work made them tough. Probably like your Sandra."

"If we're thrown out on Monday, I'll ask Mom to hire you as my bodyguard."

"I hope I won't need a side job as a security guard to stay here." Diego gave him a friendly slap.

With a knock on the door, Jack let himself in. They stood and looked at him expectantly.

"Sit down, fellas. I'm not your drill sergeant." With a smile, he said, "that started quite a ruckus, you know."

"We didn't start it!"

"Relax. I didn't mean the fight. When their parents got to Accommodations, the two fathers went ballistic. Hollering about the old school going to hell, and nastier epithets than their sons used."

"So, are they coming back?"

"No. Next thing you know, we had a riot of parents screaming at the counter at the Accommodations Office as the staff tried to notify prospective roommates of the changes to room assignments. In all the noise, no one wanted to listen to the fact that you're not a Negro, Diego."

"I should have used more sunscreen as a baby."

Jack laughed. "I like your spirit. Under the circumstances, I would have done worse than what Joe did today."

"So, who's going to room with us?" asked Joe.

"No one. The Housing Director decided that it would be cheaper to absorb the loss of rent on two beds than to keep paying for repairs and medical bills. He is happy that you two get along so well, or Diego would have a single in a four-man room."

They thought about that in silence for a moment.

"Coffee, Jack?"

"You're not supposed to have that in here, but yes, thank you."

"Oops. I thought it was stoves and refrigerators."

"Check the label. If it's less than a hair dryer, no one will notice, and it won't trip any circuit breakers." He took the mug that Joe offered. "Just don't dry your hair while the coffee is brewing."

"But I don't have a hair dryer." Then he caught Diego's look. They laughed. "I'll get rid of it. We have a Moka coffee maker we can use on the hotplate, and we prefer that coffee, anyway."

ଷଷଷ

That afternoon, the two friends walked to Cabell Hall for the welcoming address by the President of the University. Edgar Shannon looked like central casting's idea of a University President: handsome, confident, but modest and humble in his demeanor.

They paused at the edge of the auditorium. This was the first time that they had seen their whole class together. *They'll need the basketball arena for this in the future,* Joe thought.

What struck them both was that Diego was not the only dark complexion in the room. There were maybe a half dozen African faces and some men with Asian features in the sea of European types.

In his remarks, President Shannon told them that these were times of great change for the university. When he mentioned that he had written to President Nixon to protest the military involvement in Cambodia, most of the audience applauded. He noted that they would see women in their classes this year and that UVA would become fully coeducational soon. This caused no small amount of cheering. He cautioned them that the Administration and the Judiciary Committee expected them to be gentlemen and would not tolerate harassment of women or snubbing their Asian and colored classmates.

"I wonder how welcome Dixon and Ford feel now," Joe whispered to Diego. The Californian's face remained impassive as he admired the full-sized copy of Raphael's *School of Athens* behind the stage.

The Deans of the various schools and colleges spoke, as well as the Dean of Students and the Director of Residence Life. The announcements reinforced information that was in their orientation packets. It was news to those who had not checked in early. Joe's attention wandered. *What if Sandra were to transfer here?* He dismissed that thought. She only had another year to do at GW even with the extra time abroad. Nevertheless, thinking of her put him in a good place.

"Wake up, amigo." Diego jabbed him.

"Ouch, that's the wrong side."

"Sorry. You were daydreaming." Diego gave him a grin. "Sandra?"

"Yeah. She's easier to think about."

They made their way out to the aisle and up the narrow steps to the exit.

"Let's go to the Corner and price bikes."

"I hope they have something affordable."

"I wasn't expecting to be able to afford one, but we could ask for Christmas. Maybe you could convince your dad that having wheels would help you find a job."

"Okay. Let's go."

As they walked along the Lawn, the sun was halfway down over the Blue Ridge, shining almost directly into the rooms of the "lucky" fourth-years on the eastern side. There wasn't room for much besides the fireplace, a bed and a desk, but some of the occupants were already hosting friends, crowded in with their drinks.

At the edge of the Rotunda, they took the path that led to the crosswalk at Elliewood Avenue. The bicycle store occupied a plain, two-story building halfway down the street.

"Look, an Eddy Mercxx!" Joe pointed to a light-weight road racing machine in the window.

"Looks like a nice ten-speed, but not too practical."

"Just drooling, amigo. Let's see what else they have."

Inside, they immediately put the one-thousand-dollar Mercxx in the dream category. The shop had plenty of bikes equipped with racks, lights and fenders at a more affordable two hundred dollars or so. The salesclerk was a third-year working his way through.

They both liked the Nishiki Olympic, which was surprisingly light for a bike with fenders and a rack.

"These can go on layaway if you want."

"Gotta find a job first," said Diego. "But I'll be back."

"Wait a minute," said Joe. "I didn't think of layaway. How much?"

"Five bucks will hold it. Just drop something every month. Every week is better."

"Hey, I can handle that." Diego pulled out his wallet.

The two friends signed the layaway tickets. The clerk rolled "their" bicycles, blue for Joe and red for Diego, into the back.

Walking from the bike shop, they stopped where Elliewood Street met University Avenue, taking in the sunshine and the crowds filling the eating and drinking establishments.

"Wanna burger or something? I thought we'd eat after the president's speech, and now I'm starved."

"Sure." They turned left and downhill. The buildings in the little business district called "the Corner" mimicked much of the construction around the university: brick facades with white trim. They passed a dress shop, a men's clothier, and a bookstore before reaching the White Spot.

"Doesn't look like much," said Joe, "but I was told the burgers are good."

As they opened the door, a large man with a grease-stained apron came out from the back of the establishment.

"You can't come in here," he said, staring at Diego. "The *White* Spot – get it?"

"What do you mean?" said Joe.

"No darkies, even partials."

"That's ridiculous!" Joe raised his voice.

"Let's go." Diego tugged on Joe's sleeve. "This isn't worth it."

"What was that all about?" he asked as they walked back up University Avenue. "How can they refuse to let you buy one of their greasy burgers? And what's a darky, anyway?"

Diego stopped and looked at him in amazement. "You really don't know?"

"No."

"What country have you been living in, man?"

"Italy. Where else?"

"But you sound American, like an Anglo, y'know."

"Well, I *am* American, but I grew up in Rome. I only arrived a few days before we checked in. I told you that."

"I thought you meant Rome, New York, or Rome, Georgia. You mean you never lived in the States?"

"Not since I was seven years old."

Diego shook his head and whistled softly. "Man, you got a rough road ahead. You're gonna need protection."

"Huh?"

"You know what naïve means?"

"Yeah."

"Amigo, you are going to be like a lamb at the wolves' family reunion. Remember what that guy Dixon called me?"

"But your family is Spanish originally, isn't it?"

"Doesn't mean anything to whites who see all dark skin the same. Just hanging around with dark-skinned guys could piss off the bigots."

"You're kidding! Everyone can't be that way. And I can hang out with anyone I like. It's a free country."

"Wait till you've been here a while before you decide how free it is. And take a piece of advice from your amigo."

"What's that?"

"Keep your head down and your mouth shut when you hear whites talking trash about the rest of us. They really hate what they call nigger-lovers."

"My two best friends back home are a Negro from the Virgin Islands and a Chinese."

"Well, don't volunteer that to anyone else."

They had supper in the cafeteria near McCormick Hall.

5. CAPTAIN'S MAST

SUNDAY MORNING, Diego and Joe walked through the cemetery to Alderman Road and attended Mass at Saint Thomas Aquinas Church. Joe was not comfortable with the guitars and the camp songs, and he thought the translations used for the English-language Mass were terrible.

They should use modern English or something sacred-sounding, like the King James or Douay-Rheims Bible, he thought. Diego had put on his impassive face again, so Joe could not guess what his friend was thinking.

As they walked to the cafeteria for breakfast, he asked Diego what he thought of the Mass.

"Not impressed." Diego pushed the door open and held it. "Back home, we kept using Latin until the Diocese cracked down last year."

"I read that everyone here in the States liked the shift to the vernacular."

"Yeah, but in our parish, that would be Spanish."

"You have to use English?"

"That was a different battle. When we dropped Latin, Santa Rosaria offered Spanish and English Masses. Six months ago, we moved the English Mass to eight in the morning because no one was coming to it at ten."

"I still mumble the Latin to myself."

"Me too."

"And we know what it means too."

"*Claro.*" Of course.

Back at the room, they found a note taped to the door. "P.S.M. – Jack." They walked to the RA's room at the end of the hall.

"One of the sailors at the NROTC unit delivered this an hour ago." He handed them an envelope.

"Do you know what it is?"

"Yes, but you might as well read it yourselves. Lucky for you, classes don't begin until Wednesday, or you'd be doing that at night, on top of everything else."

As they returned, Joe opened the envelope.

"Report to the CO's office at zero-nine-hundred to-morrow. Tropical Khaki Long."

He held the door for Diego.

"Helluva way to start our naval careers, isn't it?" Diego took the letter and read it for himself.

"This will go in our service records, won't it?"

"No idea, but maybe we should ease over to the library and read up on Articles 15 and 133 of the UCMJ."

The librarian at the main desk in Alderman smiled when they asked where they could look up the Uniform Code of Military Justice.

"Army, Air Force, or Navy?"

"Navy," they said together.

"Captain's Mast." She reached under the counter and pulled out a pamphlet, which she handed to Diego. "The Code itself is on the next floor down. Northwest corner of stacks. You'll see the sign "UCMJ" in addition to the Section numbering."

"Thank you."

The Department of Defense pamphlet, *Your Rights and Duties under the UCMJ,* contained an explanation in lay language of the unique law that governed uniformed personnel.

Article 15 described a procedure called NJP, which stood for "non-judicial punishment." Article 133 defined "Conduct unbecoming an officer and gentleman" as punishable by court-martial.

"That's pretty vague," said Joe.

"Look at 134 under it. 'General article.' That covers anything they forgot to mention."

"This doesn't look good."

They walked down to the stacks to see the wording in the UCMJ itself, but it read just like the pamphlet without any explanation.

Back in the room, they discussed what to do with the rest of the day. Neither felt like going out, so they ate at the cafeteria again and spent the evening checking their khaki uniforms and shining their shoes. After that, they both chose to read in bed.

"Diego?"

"*Sí, amigo.*"

"How bad could this be?"

Diego did not answer immediately. "What do you think the worst could be?"

"Explaining to my grandfather why my naval career lasted only two weeks."

"And sweating your lottery number."

"Huh?"

"You *did* register for the draft, didn't you?"

"Of course, but I got a letter saying I was 1-Y because I had – oh shit!"

"Uh-huh. That's the worst."

"Could I be drafted out of college?"

"You asked for the worst. That's it. Unlikely, but if you suddenly become a civilian, you better file for a college deferment *muy pronto.*"

"What about you?"

"I'll swab decks for two years, but I probably won't go to Vietnam."

"Facing my grandfather is still the worst."

They read in silence for a while.

"Joe?"

"Yeah?"

"You're really worried, aren't you?"

"Yeah."

"I just thought of something Papa would say."

"I thought he didn't talk much."

"He doesn't. Makes it easy to remember what he did say."

Joe looked over and arched his eyebrows.

"I got suspended and sent home for fighting at school my junior year. The principal called him. I didn't hear them talking, but when he hung up, Papa said I could go back the next day.

"He asked me what I learned. I shrugged because I still could not figure out why I was the one sent home when the other kid was bullying a freshman. Papa asked me, 'what are you going to do next time?' I was still mad, so I said, 'drag his sorry ass behind the bushes so there wouldn't be witnesses.'

"He asked me, 'You sure you did the right thing?' I said yes. 'Do it smart next time – drag his sorry ass out of sight.'"

Joe laughed so hard he dropped his book on the floor. He got out of bed to retrieve it.

"How would that help us tomorrow?"

"It won't, but Papa's point was not to worry about it if you're doing the right thing. That freshman is president of the junior class now and a varsity athlete. I think Norwood must call us in because we got in a fight, but I also think he is a very fair man."

"Even if you're wrong about him, I'd do it the same."

"You didn't have to piss off Dixon, you know."

"*Insulti costui insulti me.*" Insult him, you insult me. Joe scowled at Diego.

"Gracias, amigo."

"De nada."

They turned out the lights at ten, but sleep was a long time coming.

ଧଧଧ

After breakfast, they changed into the short-sleeved khaki uniform mentioned in the summons. They smiled and returned greetings from the few students they recognized from early check-in, but mostly they walked with somber expressions.

At eight forty-five, they entered Maury Hall. Captain Norwood's secretary, Mrs. Blankenship, pointed to the chairs against the wall near her desk.

"He's in. Neither of you has been to Mast, right?"

They shook their heads.

"The others will arrive about five minutes before nine. Sarge will call you in when the Captain is ready to begin. The Executive Officer will point to where you should stand. Captain's Mast is not like court. There is almost no set procedure, so he can ask for whatever evidence he wants and conduct the proceedings as he sees fit. Usually, he has the XO present the case, but he follows the conversation until he understands what happened. Then he passes out whatever punishment is called for."

Joe swallowed the lump in his throat.

"Anything else we should know?"

"Yes. Don't speak unless spoken to. Many young men have dug their own graves by volunteering information that tied the Captain's hands. You get my drift?"

They both said, "Yes. Thank you, ma'am."

When Sergeant Henry walked in, they rose, but he simply nodded and went into the CO's office. They were still standing when Major Jackson, the Executive Officer, also went in, without acknowledging them.

At nine, Sarge opened the door and motioned for them to enter.

They walked in and stood where the major pointed. He stood on their right, the sergeant to their left. Captain Norwood, also in Tropical Khaki, stood at a lectern near his desk. His hands rested on the edge of the lectern, his face impassive.

Major Jackson read from the sheet, "Midshipman de la Torre and Midshipman Lockhart, charged with violation of Article 133 of the Uniform Code of Military Justice."

"Do you recommend we handle them together or separately, Major?"

"It appears to be a single incident, though Mister de la Torre was standing, and Mister Lockhart was on the ground at the end."

"We'll hear them together, then. I understand the general circumstances. Do we have any witnesses?"

"Cadet Schlesinger is outside, sir."

"Call him in."

The XO nodded to Sergeant Henry, who left the room.

The Captain looked at them and let the silence hang for a while. "It appears you two have set a record for the earliest Captain's Mast in any academic year. We've never had an incident on Move-in Day."

Joe started to apologize but caught himself.

"Since you attracted the most attention, Mister Lockhart, let's hear your story first."

Joe recounted the event as accurately as he could from the time Diego wedged the door open until the two assailants left with the resident assistant.

"Do you have the names of the two civilians?" the CO asked the XO.

"Steven Dixon and Matthew Ford, sir."

"Mister Lockhart, tell me again what you and Mister Dixon said to each other."

"Yes, sir.

"He said, 'This room 214?'

"I said, 'Right address. The upper bunks are free. The right side gets the afternoon sun. I'm Joe,' and I put out my hand. He ignored me and looked at Die – Mister de la Torre. Then he said, 'What's he doing here?'

"I said, 'Our roommate, Diego.'

"He said, 'That's bullshit. Ain't rooming with no nigger!'

"I said, 'He isn't a Negro, and you owe him an apology.'

"Then Mister de la Torre —"

"Just what you and Mister Dixon said."

"Yes, sir. After I explained the insult, he said, 'And I don't care. He can get out and find another room.'

"I said, 'Doesn't work that way, Steve. We've been here for two weeks, and we're staying.'

"Then Mister Dixon turned to Mister – uh – Ford and said, 'what do you think, Matt? Do we take this shit from a nigger-lover?' Mister Ford said 'nope,' and they rushed us.

"We exchanged no words after that, sir."

There was a single knock on the door, and Sergeant Henry escorted Ed Schlesinger into the room. The cadet was in his light blue, short-sleeved uniform. The sergeant pointed to the floor next to himself, and Ed stood at attention at the end of the row of men standing in front of Captain Norwood.

"Good morning, Cadet Schlesinger," the CO said. "Thank you for joining us. Are you familiar with Article 15 NJP?"

"Only what we covered in Military Science, sir."

"Enough. I've read the report from the Executive Officer, Major Jackson, and we've heard Mister Lockhart's account. Would you tell us what you saw?"

Ed recounted what he saw, almost exactly as he had for Jack right after the fight.

"You did not see Mister de la Torre here?"

"I saw the one called Matt rush him. Mister de la Torre seemed to step aside, but not completely. Then my view was blocked by Mister Lockhart and the one who attacked him flying out the door."

"Mister de la Torre, what happened between you and Mister Ford."

"He rushed me as the others have said. I grabbed his wrist as he went by and used his momentum to put his back in front of me, whereupon I took his other wrist and immobilized him, sir."

The CO and the XO exchanged glances.

"Did you teach him these moves, Sergeant?"

"No, sir, but I might note that no one could ever bring him to the mat."

Captain Norwood let the silence linger for a while.

"Personally, I think I have the picture." He wrote on the pages before him. "Mister Lockhart."

"Yes, sir."

"What have you learned from this?"

"That I need to learn to do what Mister de la Torre did. He used just enough force to control the situation."

"You wouldn't do anything differently with Misters Dixon and Ford?"

"I've thought about it, sir, and I can't say that I would. I think my response was appropriate."

"Very well. Cadet Schlesinger, thank you for your help. It isn't often we get decent testimony of what happened from third parties. You may go."

"Yes, sir." Ed saluted. Captain Norwood nodded (the Navy doesn't salute bareheaded or indoors). Ed did a sharp about-face and left.

"Sergeant, please take Midshipmen Lockhart and de la Torre out to wait. I want to confer with the XO."

Standing in front of Mrs. Blankenship's desk, Joe noticed that no one invited them to sit. He felt a trickle of sweat run along his backbone. Sarge stood in silence by the door. Diego smiled but said nothing. *Don't speak unless spoken to,* Joe remembered. It wasn't over.

After about five minutes, Major Jackson opened the door and beckoned to them. Henry held the door while they marched back in and took their positions.

When everybody was in their places, the Captain said, "Midshipman Lockhart, I find you in violation of Article 133, and you are hereby warned. Mister de la Torre, you are not in violation of anything, and your name will be deleted from these proceedings.

"Dismissed."

As he spun around in the sharpest about-face that he could execute, Joe felt confused and shocked. He followed Diego into the anteroom.

"Don't go anywhere yet, boys." Mrs. Blankenship pointed at the XO, who had just come out.

"So much for the formal part." Major Jackson held the door. "The CO wants to talk with you privately now."

They went back in. The lectern had disappeared into a closet, and the skipper sat at his desk. He waved at the two chairs in front of him. With an uneasy look around, they sat.

"Relax, gentlemen. If this experience is to do anyone any good, we need to follow it up with a debrief. Everything is off the record now because I want to hear your questions."

They looked at each other and back at their commanding officer.

"What just happened?" asked Joe.

"Why did I get off?" asked Diego.

"Same answer to both questions. Mister De la Torre, your response was spot-on, and it was possible only because you could immobilize your opponent and defuse the situation with minimum force. Thus, your conduct was not only not unbecoming, it was exemplary. Yours, Mister Lockhart, could have been, but I can tell by the way you leapt at Dixon that you don't know how to fight, not really. So, you get a warning because there was a fight, a civilian was injured, and it was in public. You understand?"

"Yes, sir. I'm sorry."

"You shouldn't be. Frankly, in your place, I might have behaved the same. I'm still grinding my teeth about those two.

"But you do need to learn a few things, like fighting smarter, restraint under pressure, and staying aware of your surroundings – all valuable traits that an officer needs."

"What happens now, sir?"

"Nothing as far as the unit is concerned. Upon graduation, we will shred all records of this. You don't carry non-judicial punishments into the Fleet with you. Feel better?"

"Yes, sir, but I don't know what to do about the way people treat Diego."

"This whole race thing has you confused, doesn't it?"

"Yes, it does, sir."

"Well, even though Mister de la Torre here is not a Negro, I can tell that he has more street-savvy than you. You are friends, aren't you?"

They both nodded.

"Then follow his lead, Mister Lockhart, and talk about it when he tells you something that doesn't feel right."

"Isn't that just accommodating them, sir? I want them to see Diego for what he is, a proud Californian."

"Save your energy. You have a bigger problem than defending your friend's honor."

"Sir?"

"What did Dixon call you?"

"Nigger-lover, sir."

"That will get around Grounds like wildfire. You are now a target for anyone with a grudge against Negroes, Affirmative Action, equal rights or who-knows-what else. I'm afraid that you are likely to be assaulted again, maybe more than once."

"You mean I must stop being seen with Diego?"

"No point in doing that because you're already marked. Might as well be yourself and stand up for what you believe. But I would take some self-defense training beyond what we offer here in the unit."

"I'll look into it. Thank you, sir."

"Can you help?" he asked Diego.

"I'll try, but I learned by getting beaten up repeatedly. I don't think you had that in mind, sir."

"No. Check with Sergeant Henry, Mister Lockhart. He may have some ideas or know where you can turn."

"Thank you, sir."

The Captain stood, a signal to end the talk. Joe and Diego rose. He wished them luck. They left.

Though it was only midmorning, they had a full plate of things to do. They spent the day filling out their course preference forms and checking out the places where they would need to be on Wednesday. They also applied to take language exams: Joe for Italian and French; Diego for Spanish and French.

Being first-years (as UVA calls its freshmen), their initial semester was limited to basic courses in the liberal arts and sciences: Intro to Physics, chemistry, or biology; sociology; pre-calculus; English; and choices of language, writing, and engineering.

Tuesday morning, they walked to Cabell Hall. After a two-hour exam, they went to lunch at Newcomb Hall nearby. In the afternoon, they sat for a similar exam in French.

"How did that feel?" Joe asked on their way to the tennis courts in the Dell below Alderman Library.

"Well, I'm glad the Spanish will validate the language requirement because the French won't. How about you?"

"Italian will validate for sure, but I want to major in it, so I hope they let me have some credit. French was okay."

The junior varsity tennis coach welcomed the five dozen men who showed up for tryouts with a short briefing of the routine. The new students rotated through sets against each other and against varsity players tapped to help.

"Results will be posted by Friday on the bulletin board in the gym. If you're on the list, be at the first practice Saturday morning at eight."

Diego and Joe approached the JV coach after dismissal. "We're NROTC, sir. Will there be a conflict?"

"De la Torre and Lockhart, right?" They nodded. "NROTC comes first, but the ROTC units let us have you in lieu of the physical courses when there is overlap in the schedule. Trust me, you'll wish you were crawling through the mud with them when you see what we have planned for your conditioning. Good luck."

He shook their hands, then turned to catch up with the Varsity coach.

"I don't think I'll make the cut," said Diego as they walked back.

"Me neither. You were varsity, weren't you?"

"Yeah, but so was everyone else out there today. Tough competition."

"I have no way to tell since we didn't have a tennis team. But you looked good, I thought."

"Thanks, amigo. We'll see."

The other first-years left together in a happy, jostling crowd.

"They seem to know each other," said Joe.

"They do, from school matches. Most are from the East Coast. I played three of those guys last year."

"Where was that?"

"Baltimore."

"Diego! I didn't know you were a state champion. They didn't act like they recognized you."

"Just as well. I probably won't make the cut, because they won't want to be reminded."

They did not feel like going out that night. The memory of the White Spot was too fresh.

ଶଶଶ

Wednesday morning, the routine began, not much different from high school, with classes all day, tennis in the afternoons, evenings studying in their room or the library.

Friday, they checked the boards in Cabell Hall. Joe validated two semesters of both Italian and French, so he signed up for Italian 201. He also enrolled in Spanish and German 101.

Diego received credit for two semesters of Spanish. Better than he hoped, the French validated the language requirement.

At the gym, they found that they both made the cut for the junior varsity.

Sunday, they went to Saint Thomas Aquinas again, which impressed neither of them.

By the end of the second week, Joe had been bumped up to a majors course in Italian Literature, which he preferred. It was in translation, meaning the assignments were in English. He had read the assigned texts in Italian, so he entertained himself by revising the translations in pencil in his textbook.

ରୟର

On Thursday of the third week of school, Joe walked down Rugby Road, feeling good. The shadows were lengthening as he neared the Corner, where University Avenue (US Highway 250) ran east-west past the University of Virginia and toward downtown Charlottesville. The golden light spilled over the mountains to cut through the magnolias in front of the Rotunda. Looking west, he marveled once again just how blue the Blue Ridge appeared near sunset.

After visiting a half dozen fraternities on Rugby Road, he was glad to be walking back to his room in McCormick Hall on the other side of the Grounds. He had stayed only a few minutes at each "rush" event.

As he paused for the red light, he spotted Diego coming up behind him with an easy grace and confidence.

"Hey, roomie," Joe said. "After that game outside the DKE house, I lost track of you."

Diego moved up next to him. "What do you think?"

"Not my sort of thing. I don't think I want to pledge any of them."

"Me neither. Waste of my time. Two of them wouldn't let me in the door, and at another, I got called a spic. Would never happen back home."

"You're not a spic. You're from California!"

"Yeah. My family's been farming this country since before the *Mayflower*. We don't have any spics there."

"Says more about them than you. Heading back to the dorm?"

"Residence hall, amigo, residence hall."

"Right. I forgot. It's like learning a foreign language with all these different names for everything."

"We can handle three languages, so how hard can it be?"

6. SHUFFLE
THE LANGUAGE CLASSES

"*SIGNOR LOCKHART, POTRESTI RIMANERE?*" Could you stay behind? Joe whirled around. His classmates, all third-years (juniors, at other schools), also stopped.

"*Certo, professore.*" Certainly.

The teacher waved for the others to leave, which they did, softly murmuring among themselves.

The conversation continued in Italian.

"Where did you learn Italian so well?"

"I grew up in Rome."

"I could tell immediately that this course is well below your level. You shouldn't be taking this in translation."

"I agree, Professor, but this is where I was assigned."

"I will talk to Professor Gonzalez."

"Thank you, sir."

"Have you read the assignments in Italian?"

"Yes, sir."

"I suspected as much. What do you think of the translation?"

"Honestly?"

"Certainly."

Reaching into his book bag, Joe took out his textbook and handed it to the instructor. "We studied the first three cantos of the *Inferno,* so I revised the translations as an exercise." Revising is the checking of a translation by another translator. "It's a wonderful read, but I found three mistranslations. The question marks are where I wondered if he missed the point or needed to maintain the poetry."

Giraldi scanned the marked-up cantos quickly. "Amazing. You learned this in high school?"

"Yes, sir. Of course, we weren't translating it but learning what the words meant during the Renaissance. Like studying Shakespeare or Donne in English."

"May I borrow this? I'd like to show it to Professor Gonzalez when I see him."

"Certainly, sir." Joe smiled. "I've read the rest of the book." Giraldi smiled back.

"Do you have a phone number?"

"There's a pay phone in the hall." He dictated the number.

"We'll be in touch."

Giraldi shook hands, and Joe trotted to his physics class.

ଝଝଝ

"Hey, Lockhart! Telephone!"

Joe picked up the handset dangling from the phone across from his room.

"Joe Lockhart."

"Ah, Mister Lockhart. This is Professor Gonzalez."

"*Sí, señor, dígame.*" Yes, sir, I'm listening.

65

"You have finished your midterm examinations, have you not?"

"Yes, sir."

"When will you leave town?"

"Tomorrow, sir. My grandfather is coming for us."

"Would you please come to my office at one thirty? I am convening a meeting with you, Professor Giraldi and Professor Schultz, to consider rearranging your studies."

"Is there something wrong?"

"Not at all, but we want to discuss our ideas with you."

"I'll be there, sir."

The chairman thanked him and hung up. Puzzled, Joe went back to his room and finished putting away his books.

After lunch, Joe and Diego walked to Cabell Hall. Diego went to his last exam while Joe walked to the department office on the ground floor. The chairman's secretary smiled broadly and motioned to a seat. Then she called on the intercom.

"He said to go in," she said, waving at the door.

Inside, the sun beamed powerfully into the room, lighting up the walls with a red glow from the Moorish carpet. Gonzalez appeared to be in his fifties, about five-foot-ten or less, and not quite as slim as he once was. Except that he was from Texas, Joe did not know much about him. He stood and pointed to a chair at the conference table in the middle of the room.

"Sit, please. Coffee?"

"Yes, thank you, sir."

At the sideboard, the professor turned on the hot-plate under a Moka-style coffee maker.

"The others will be here soon." As if on cue, there was a knock on the door, and Joe's other two language teachers walked in.

Nunzio Giraldi was new this year, having just earned his PhD from Columbia University. About six-foot-two, with a marathon runner's frame and shining black skin, he always raised eyebrows when he opened his mouth in Roman-accented Italian. His parents had emigrated from Eritrea when it was still an Italian colony and settled in the Trionfale section of Rome. Young Nunzio had gone to international schools, so his English was as American as Joe's.

Dietrich Schulz was a heavy-set man with a florid complexion, red hair and icy blue eyes. His Celtic ancestors had probably given Caesar's legions a run for their money.

Both professors gave Joe a warm smile, then beamed in the direction of the coffee maker.

"We are brewing African Sidamo today, Nunzio. This is as close to home as I can get you."

"That little Moka will get you reelected department chair every time," said Schultz. To Joe he said, "Professor Gonzalez discovered the secret to ensuring attendance at his meetings: exotic coffees."

"It does smell nice, sir."

The coffee maker sputtered as they sat. Gonzalez went to the sideboard and poured out four demitasses of the rich brew and passed them out. He gestured for Joe to fetch the sugar bowl and start it around. When he sat, he looked across his desk.

"So, which language shall we use for this meeting, gentlemen?"

"Anything but German," said Dietrich. "I'm behind the enemy lines here." They shared a laugh. Joe looked nervously at the three men.

"Don't look so worried, Mister Lockhart," said the Chair. "If you were in trouble, you'd know it. We are the ones with a problem. You are the first student ever to turn in completely error-free midterm examinations in his first year." He looked at Giraldi.

"Our difficulty, Joe, is that we don't know where to put you. One thing is for sure. We can't teach you Italian. In fact, your Italian is better than that of our graduate assistants."

"It is clear that you are still hiding your Spanish under a bushel," said Gonzalez, "even after I moved you to my second-semester class."

"We are considering booting you up a semester in German too. Your accent is impeccable."

"*Claro.* How do you explain this?"

"I don't know what to say, sir. At school, we used French, Spanish, and Italian amongst ourselves, but I never studied Spanish formally. My mother is fluent in Italian, German, and French. Between hearing her talk to others and our travels in Germany and Switzerland, I must have picked up more than I realized. We always had books and magazines in the house, and we both read them."

"Sometimes, I have the impression that you are trying to hide, to play down your skill with languages. How does it feel in our three classes?"

Joe paused. "Honestly?"

"That's why we're here."

"Professor Giraldi knows about my Italian. I expected it to be easier than my other subjects, but I would be going nuts if he had not allowed me to revise the translations in the textbooks. That has been a good drill for me as a translator, but it is not exposing me to literature I haven't seen.

"My Spanish is all pick-up, but it comes easily. Most of the words that are different from Italian are common ones that I was using with my friends. And the grammars are very similar, so conjugating verbs or guessing the genders of nouns is not that hard.

"German is teaching me new things because my listening and reading was a matter of getting the gist. But when I see the material in the textbook, I know where it is going. German class is gathering things together that I wasn't using every day the way I was in Italian and Spanish."

He stopped. They sipped their coffee in silence. Schulz spoke first.

"Would you like to try German 102 for the rest of this semester?"

"I would need the texts and the syllabus first, to study what I missed."

"*¿Y el español?*" Gonzalez continued in Spanish. "If you understand this much, I would think that you could skip the second half. I am inclined to have you take Spanish 201, skipping 102. Otherwise, you might never get the kind of challenge you need to grow."

"*Puedo solo intentar, señor.*" I can only try, sir.

"That is two-thirds of our proposal: German 102 and Spanish 201, starting next week. What do we do about Italian?"

Giraldi took a moment to speak. "I am thinking of two things. One, an independent study project for next semester. We assemble a reading list of literature that we would teach in Italian if we had more of this kind of student. Then turn him loose to submit a draft report by midterms and a final journal article for the end of the year. If that works, I would have him take graduate courses for his major."

"What about this semester?" asked the Chair.

"He's spoken little and successfully hid his knowledge from the others until I spoke to him directly. But when queried, he offered perspectives that were helpful and not showy. In my opinion, he should continue to revise the readings. Then he should prepare a lecture – maybe two – on what it is like to translate the texts we've been reading, with examples of good and bad translations in the texts we've been studying."

"Should he continue to come to class?"

"I hope so. He's a resource."

"What do you think, Mister Lockhart?"

"I'm the only first-year." He looked at the Italian instructor. "I've already had upperclassmen give me a hard time."

"You won't be the only A on the bulletin board next week," said his teacher. "It was my mistake to expose your Italian. I will watch closely, and maybe they'll forget it. We'll be shifting to Montale and Manzoni for the second half."

"Any questions?" Gonzalez looked around the room.

"One question, if I may," said Schultz. "Did I understand that you are revising John Ciardi's translation of Dante's *Inferno*?"

"Just for practice, sir."

"How are his revisions, Nunzio?"

"Very solid, I would say. His grasp of metaphor and meaning transfer is among the best and, from what I've seen this semester, better than Ciardi's."

"That's saying a lot."

"What I mean, Dietrich, is that Ciardi did not grow up in Italy. His translation is engaging, strong, thoroughly modern, and American. The students enjoy reading him, which you know is most of the battle in a literature class. But Joe here catches those Italian nuances and meanings that Ciardi misses or that he sacrifices for his beautiful poetry. I think it enriches the class, and from what I see, the others like it too."

"How do you make comments without exposing your Italian?"

"If I can't think of a way to say something using the English in front of us, I don't say anything, sir. It worked so far, with cognates and archaic English dictionary definitions – that sort of thing."

Schultz nodded admiringly. Giraldi beamed.

"Well, Mister Lockhart," said Professor Gonzales, standing, "I'm afraid we're sending you off on fall break with a load of homework, but we want you to enjoy the challenge here."

"I'll do my best, sir." He shook their hands and left them gathering around the coffee maker for seconds.

7. FALL BREAK

THE NEXT MORNING, Joe and Diego tossed their sports bags and tennis rackets into the trunk of the Ardwoods' car. As they merged into the east-bound lanes of Interstate 64, Joe explained his "homework" assignment for the week.

"Poor dear," said his grandmother, "you won't have much of a holiday."

"I'll be fine. Otherwise, I would not have brought my tennis racket."

"I understand studying the past midterm for the new classes," said his grandfather, "but don't they build on what you will miss by not staying in the old classes?"

"They do, but I didn't tell them that I read ahead in German and Spanish, so I know what they will study between now and final exams. It was very repetitious, nothing new."

Driving to the west end of Richmond, they talked about their other courses, what the level of tennis play was like, and their impression of the fraternities. General Ardwood cocked an eyebrow at them in the rearview mirror.

"I'm not surprised that you weren't impressed by the Greeks. Did you try Alpha Pi Omega? It's just for Eagle Scouts."

"We liked it because it is a service fraternity," said Joe, "but all the activities conflicted with tennis practice."

"We went for tennis," said Diego.

"I understand. Here's our exit."

The next week was everything that a break should mean for the two friends. They spent mornings on the tennis court, playing mixed doubles and singles and rotating partners. Joe gained a new appreciation of his mother's athleticism as he worked to keep up with his grandparents.

In the afternoons, the Ardwoods attended to chores or went out to meetings at the various charities or associations they supported. Diego took a nap or studied physics while Joe read the books and syllabi that his language professors had given him. He had that finished by Wednesday. The two students found the bus stop near the house and went downtown to walk around Shockoe Bottom and the Fan District.

Evenings, the four gathered in the living room for a glass of wine before dinner. Tuesday night, the general spoke to Diego.

"I called your father. He was very troubled, but after a while, he admitted being sorry to have bottled his war years inside him. I'm not too proud to say we both shed some tears by the time we hung up."

"Why was that, sir?"

"I hope you never find out, but either of you may someday. Combat scars a man. Can you imagine seeing men blown apart by artillery or pushing your way to the beach past the bleeding bodies floating in the surf?" He stopped, took a sip, then a long breath. "Your father was twenty when I met him, and he was already a sergeant.

He had seen it all. I watched him working with his men as we sailed to the Solomon Islands.

"His company was almost wiped out at Guadalcanal. Only his platoon and parts of two others survived. His officers were all dead. He didn't lose a man, but his squads attacked the gun emplacement that had decimated the others and silenced it. I saw him restrain his soldiers when they were about to go berserk. He did it by grabbing two of them and hugging them until they stopped and fell sobbing against him. Then he stood back and barked the rest into file, and they advanced into the palm trees.

"When I got back around to his unit after we had secured the beachhead, it was even worse than I thought. Your father was the ranking NCO [non-commissioned officer] left. He had his platoon, plus half of another. He put a private first class in charge of the half-platoon and set up a treatment area for the wounded. He had runners going to the hospital tent, bringing supplies back to his medic, and carrying the injured out one by one."

"Why didn't they just carry them out all at once?"

"There were more wounded than survivors, and he wanted to maintain a security perimeter. Good thing because that night, the Japanese came out of the woods to attack several of our positions. Again, your father's preparations paid off. They repelled two attacks without losing anyone. I lost two hundred men that night in other units."

They sat silently for a while. Joe noticed tears welling in his grandmother's eyes.

"You've heard this, Grandmaman, haven't you?"

Annabelle Ardwood shook her head slowly and dabbed her eyes. "I knew he was on Guadalcanal from the newspapers, but he has never spoken a word about it since he came back from the Philippines at the end."

"Why not, Grandpa?"

The general tipped his glass toward Diego. "I needed that phone call with your father as much as he did."

ଊଊଊ

On Friday morning, they gathered in the study to call Nancy in Rome. With the time difference, they knew that Joe's mother would be home from work. They had scheduled the call by mail weeks before.

They took turns talking to the busy executive. First, Joe talking to his mother, then Matthew to his daughter. He passed the phone to Annabelle with a quizzical arch to his eyebrows. He looked concerned.

"*Allo, ma fille, quel plaisir t'écouter.*" Hello, daughter, what a pleasure to hear you. They continued in French.

"Oh *maman*, I miss you all so much. It doesn't feel like home here since Joe left."

"I can imagine. You are still coming for Christmas, I hope."

"Of course. I would not miss it for anything."

They listened to the silence. Annabelle spoke first.

"What's wrong, my darling?"

"Have you heard about the posters and hate mail over there?"

"No. You know the papers here don't cover Italian news very well."

75

"Just as well. Last month, the usual posters about American imperialists and such changed tone. Now they are focusing on specific American companies. Smithson is getting more publicity than the others, and my picture is starting to appear on phone poles and walls all over the country."

"That's terrible. Why?"

"We don't really know. According to our analysts and the people at the Embassy, the slant seems out of character for the left-wing parties. For their part, they deny having anything to do with the publicity.

"I tell myself that it will blow over, but it seems so personal, it gets me down sometimes."

"Maybe it is time to come home."

"I agree. Sandro and I are working on that. We'd like to find someone inside the company to come to Rome for the promotion." Sandro Moretti was the president of the Smithson Italiana SpA.

"Maybe you should take some extra time when you come. You might find someone here." Smithson's world headquarters was in Richmond, Virginia.

"That's an idea. I'll think about it."

"And call us if you just want to talk. Collect."

"Maman, you know I can afford the call."

"Then talk to your mother when you need someone to talk to."

"I'll do that. Promise. I love you, maman."

"I love you too, dear. See you next month."

They hung up. Annabelle looked at the three serious faces waiting for her.

"Things are not good…"

ଔଔଔ

The following Saturday, they all piled into the car for the return to Charlottesville. They enjoyed a tour of the room, a walk down the Lawn, and lunch at a café on Elliewood Avenue.

"Never thought to ask, Joe. Are you still translating?"

"It's a little hard with my clients in Europe, but I did a brochure about a new drug for Smithson in August."

"Would you like some business if I come across someone?"

"Yes, sir, but I have to be honest. The school workload is heavier here than at Notre Dame." His high school in Rome.

"If anyone asks, I'll give them that caveat. Just Italian?"

"Or French. I wouldn't want to tackle anything else."

Annabelle put down her ice cream spoon. "Matthew, his check!"

"Thank you, *chérie*." He reached into his coat and pulled out his wallet. He handed Joe the dollar-sized piece of paper.

"Omigosh! What is this?"

"Your savings account in Rome. Your mother finally got past the bureaucracy and had it sent to my bank. Can you deposit it?"

"Yes. There's a branch of the UVA Credit Union just down the street."

"Good. That should keep you in chewing gum and tennis balls for a while."

Joe looked past his grandfather at the bike store. "Diego, we can free our bikes."

"What bikes?" Matthew Ardwood turned around and saw the shop.

"We have a pair of bicycles on layaway."

"I have a better idea." He read the bill and left enough money to cover it and a tip. "Let's go liberate them now."

"But, sir," said Diego. "One of them is mine. You can't do that."

"Says who? It will make an excellent Christmas gift. Oh, you'll both get something under the tree, but you probably need wheels now as much as later." He rose, and they followed him. Thirty minutes later, Diego and Joe wheeled their new bicycles out the door. Diego still appeared upset and embarrassed.

"Sir, you should not do this for me. I don't need you to."

The general stopped and spun around. He leaned toward the young man. "No. I don't need to. I want to. I also said you should consider us your East Coast home. Family does things for one another, doesn't it?"

"I am in your debt, sir."

"No, you're not. Does Joe owe me anything for buying him a bike for Christmas? Neither do you."

"*Gracias, señor general.*"

"*Mi placer.*" My pleasure. He reached over the bicycle and hugged Joe's roommate.

8. Tony Madison

MONDAY MORNING, Joe and Diego walked to Cabell Hall.

"Not that one, amigo." Diego tapped his friend before he entered the room for Spanish 102.

"Oh yeah. What am I thinking?"

"You're not. I think you're more worried about this than you let on."

"There weren't any surprises in the material I studied last week, but still, everyone knows everyone else. I hate coming in midsemester like this."

"You'll be fine."

At the door to Spanish 201, he scanned the room, then chose a seat in the back row. Professor Gonzalez arrived exactly on the hour. He noticed Joe but mercifully did not acknowledge him.

There were only twelve students, half as many as in the introductory course. With the graduation requirement out of the way, few opted for additional language training. From the general level of attentiveness and the questions, Joe could tell that they were engaged and enjoying the subject. It made him feel at home, even though he wasn't interacting with anyone.

Once, the teacher called on him. Joe gave the right answer, but his accent made most of his classmates turn around. They were still struggling with the vowels and the rolled "r."

In the hallway afterward, a sturdy Black student, clearly older than the others, accosted Joe. He walked with confidence, and the scar from his eye to his ear gave him a fearsome appearance.

"You're Lockhart, aren't you?"

"That's right. Joe."

"Tony Madison." They shook hands as they approached the stairs. "I'm local, so you haven't seen me much."

"You don't have to put up with the residence halls."

"No, thank goodness."

"How'd you get around the first-year residence requirement?"

"GI Bill. I did my freshman year at San Diego State while on active duty and transferred in."

"Have you had lunch? I don't have a class until two."

"Anywhere but the White Spot. Mister Saunier hasn't cracked that one yet."

"Who's he?"

"With your history, I'm surprised you have not met him. Special Assistant to the President, trying to pull the university out of the Jim Crow era."

"That's a tall order."

"I wish him luck. To his credit, he has managed to integrate the businesses on the Corner – except the Spot, of course."

"What about the students?"

"They're more problematic. We're supposed to be student-run: Judicial Committee for discipline, Honor Code and all that. The administration can't just expel students for being assholes or threatening people."

They walked toward the Corner.

"Doesn't it bother you to walk with me? I'm still trying to figure out this color thing."

"So I've heard. No, I outgrew the need to fight every cracker that wanted to beat me up. After 'Nam, they don't scare me."

"You do make a scary first impression."

Tony touched his scar. "I guess. That was a VC with a machete." Viet Cong. "Jumped out of the bushes at me. I was lucky to duck. My buddy took him out."

As they walked under the railroad tracks, Tony pointed up the road. "Let's try that diner. Friend of mine runs it."

"Chuck's Canteen? Sounds like a mess hall."

"Chuck was an Army cook. Almost every guy in our high school was either drafted or enlisted, so it's a hangout for veterans and their friends now."

Over their food, they exchanged backgrounds. After graduation from Jackson P. Burley, the Black high school, Tony enlisted and served two tours in Vietnam in Force Reconnaissance.

His family had lived in the Fifeville neighborhood since the Civil War, first as laborers at the university, then as shopkeepers on Vinegar Hill. When he came back, he found the area that had been his family's livelihood demolished. His father operated out of the ground floor of their house now. His mother was a midwife, but that did not bring in as much as they had made with the full shop. Fortunately, Tony and his siblings had grown up and were not a burden.

After Joe described life in Italy, they ate silently for a while.

"Now that I know about Rome, I understand why your Spanish seems so natural." Tony speared a French fry. "You got a girlfriend?"

"Kind of. She's at George Washington in DC."

"Don't see her much, do you?"

"Not as much as I'd like. But we're both busy. Sandra's trying to fast-track an accounting major in two years."

"That's my major."

"Why'd you pick it?"

"Couple of reasons. I may want to open a business here, either take over from my father or open my own doing something else. Then I found out that the FBI is trying to integrate, and they need accountants."

"Are you going to be an FBI agent?"

"Not sure. But it gives me another reason to take accounting besides the business angle."

"Sandra interned at the FBI office in Rome last year. From what I see, it's a lily-white outfit."

"I know, but if I can get through this place, I can deal with that too. At least there, I should meet more veterans."

"That's a thought."

They finished and paid their checks. Tony turned east toward home, Joe west. As he walked under the bridge, he saw the owner of the White Spot scowling at him from the door. Crossing the street, he avoided the Corner by cutting across the hospital grounds and past Maury Hall. Back in his room, he changed out his books and went to physics in the Jesse Beams Lab next door.

9. A NOT-SO-GENTLE REMINDER

ONE THURSDAY, Tony, Diego and Joe walked to Chuck's Canteen for lunch. Diego ordered soup because he wanted to go to office hours before the next class. Just as Chuck put their meals on the counter in front of them, they heard a familiar voice behind them.

"Hiring two bodyguards is not what the skipper meant, Mister Lockhart."

Diego and Joe both jumped off their stools and stood at attention. "Jesus, you two! Don't do that out here. Sit down. Hey, Madison." He shook hands with Tony.

"Hey, Sarge. What brings you here?"

"I can only eat in the cafeteria for so long. I come here for my regular dose of GI food poisoning." Sergeant Henry waved at Chuck. "Hi, Cookie. I'll take my usual – over in the corner."

Tony explained. "He was my first platoon sergeant in 'Nam. Same unit as your XO, Major Jackson."

"I guess you marines stay tight," said Joe.

"Once a marine, always a marine."

"Speaking of which, Madison. Did you get your invitation?"

"Yes, Sarge. I already RSVP'd."

"Good. These two will be there, too, if one of them isn't beaten up first." Slapping Tony on the shoulder, he went to the booth for his lunch.

Joe realized what Tony meant. "The Marine Corps Ball. You'd be there, too, wouldn't you?"

"Every marine in town will be there," said Tony.

"What was that crack about bodyguards?" asked Joe.

Diego said, "Didn't Captain Norwood say something about self-defense training?"

"Yeah. I completely forgot."

Tony took his arm. "Joe, your commanding officer told you to take self-defense classes, and you *forgot?*"

Joe looked down. "Not at first. I meant to, but after the semester got going, I kept forgetting to ask Sarge about it."

"Mm. No reminders like the one that got you sent to Captain's Mast?"

"You know about that too?"

"Of course. We were expecting something from Dixon and Ford. Their fathers were worse."

Shaking his head in amazement, Joe thought for a while. "I guess I'll have to apologize and ask for recommendations."

"I'd do that," said Tony. "He's a good sort under all the bluster. Besides, you've been reminded now, so no excuses."

"You're right." He got up. Tony grabbed his arm.

"Not now, man! He's off duty. First thing tomorrow at the unit. That's the way to do it."

"Oh right. Thanks."

"No problem. You will need those lessons if you keep hanging out with me and Diego here."

"But except for some wisecracks and muttering, nothing has happened since Move-In day."

"Because you had bodyguards."

"You two?"

"Not on purpose. Still, no one is going to mess with Diego or me."

"But eventually," said Diego, "someone will catch you alone." He put his money on top of his tab and got up. "See you back at the room."

Joe ate his collard greens quietly. Tony took a bite of his hamburger and chewed.

"Tell me more about accounting."

"Think of it as the language of business." Tony sipped his beer. "By being able to convert everything to expressions of financial performance, people from different businesses can communicate."

"The language of business. I like the sound of that."

"For example, what's the value of your translating?"

"I charge two dollars and fifty cents per page generally. Depends on the source documents."

"That's your price. What's the value? What's it worth?"

Joe thought. "I have no idea. What do you mean?"

"Say translation is your business. With accounting, you could use financial terms to describe how well it's doing and even forecast whether it will keep doing well. All that to someone who knows nothing about translating."

"But I'm making money. Isn't that enough?"

"How do you know? What are your costs? Are they more or less than your revenues?"

"I have money in the bank."

"Yeah, but did you pay for your rent, clothes, food and tuition with it? Who buys your paper, ink, postage stamps, dictionaries?"

"Uh, I think I understand. I buy the paper and everything I need here, but you're right. My mother pays for the heavy stuff: college, meal plan, clothing, housing, and so forth."

"From what I can see, you have a heavily subsidized business. You can't be making a living on it."

"I agree." While he chewed his steak, he thought about what Tony had said.

"And if you want to make a career as a translator, you need to figure out if what you are charging is really enough to live on and grow your business."

"Good point. Mom won't be paying forever."

Tony winked and pointed a French fry at Joe.

They finished talking about the JV tennis meet on Saturday. Tony was planning to come, though he had stayed away from most athletic events on Grounds so far. After they settled their checks, they went out to the street.

"See you tomorrow."

Tony gave him a thumbs-up and turned east to walk home. Joe walked up to the Corner. As he passed the alley just above the White Spot, an unfamiliar voice called out.

"Hey, nigger-lover, don't like your own kind?" Laughter from three or four male voices. He pretended to ignore them and kept walking.

"Hey, asshole, I'm talking to you." A hand on his right shoulder turned him around. He recognized Dixon behind two strangers. The one who pulled him around stood about six feet, but outweighed Joe by thirty pounds. The other one was about three inches shorter.

Both wore ball caps, leather jackets and jeans, not the typical university attire.

"I still haven't heard anyone call me," said Joe.

The big one drilled a roundhouse punch into Joe's stomach. As he gasped and bent over, something cracked the back of his head. A blinding flash collapsed into darkness.

❧❧❧

Light bled through his eyelids. Carefully, Joe peeked but shut his eyes immediately when the pain of the bright overhead light hit him.

"Welcome back, Mister Lockhart. You had us worried there for a while." Turning his head to avoid the light, Joe opened his eyes. A doctor by the bed reached forward and checked his eyes, then his pulse. Behind him, Diego stood against the wall. Next to him was a UVA police officer. A nurse opposite the doctor was adjusting the IV bag.

"Where am I?"

"UVA Hospital. They brought you in about four hours ago."

"What happened?"

"We were hoping you could tell us," said the policeman. "A passerby called us from the pay phone at the Virginia Diner. You were lying in Minor Court Lane off University Avenue."

Joe tried to sit up. The doctor held him down. "Don't move just yet." He scowled at the two visitors. "You and his friend please wait in the hall while we finish examining him." He turned back to Joe. "I'm Doctor Wallenborn. This is Nurse Addams."

"I want to answer them. I was attacked."

"We could tell that much. You took a blow to the back of the head, maybe from a baseball bat. Let me continue checking for injuries. There are some things I can't check with you unconscious."

"Oh."

The doctor probed different parts of his body and had Joe move his limbs deliberately and answer questions. Then he let Joe sit more upright.

"How do you feel now?"

"Okay, I guess. My head feels tight in the back, but I don't have a headache."

"Good. The stiffness is from a contusion back there." The doctor nodded at the nurse. She went out to motion Diego and the policeman into the room.

"Nurse Addams will stay here," he said. "Go ahead, Officer Sprouse." He walked out the door and turned right.

A half hour later, Sprouse left with Joe's statement. Joe reached out for his friend's hand. "Gracias, amigo. Have you been here long?"

"Only an hour. Jack put a note on our door, so I didn't find out until after class."

"What about JV practice?"

"I told the coach. He said to come here and to let him know how you're doing." He looked at the nurse.

"We'll keep him overnight in case signs of a concussion develop. The doctor won't want him playing tennis or trying anything strenuous until he comes back for a follow-up exam."

"She's absolutely right." Wallenborn came through the door. "Mister de la Torre can bring you anything you need, but I recommend that you mostly rest. You won't be going to school tomorrow. Stay in your room this weekend."

An angry but controlled voice came in from the hall. "I have every right to be here. Now, which room is Lockhart in?"

Joe looked at Diego.

"Better stop him before the hospital loses staff." Diego disappeared and came back with Tony Madison. A scowl from Doctor Wallenborn made the two orderlies following him back up and leave. Tony glared at the physician. His scar glowed almost red.

"Are you still running whites-only wards here?"

"No, but we only integrated last year. Word is slow getting out."

The veteran took a deep breath. "Sorry about that. Joe, how are you?"

"Better, thanks to Doctor Wallenborn and Nurse Addams here. This is my friend, Tony Madison." Tony shook hands with the two healthcare professionals. "How did you find out?"

"Cousin works janitorial in ER. He overheard the people booking you in and called me at home."

"Have you got a whole spy network watching me?"

"Not really, but I told you that you made an impression on Move-In Day."

"Now I won't be able to ask Sarge first thing in the morning."

"That may still happen," said Diego. "I stopped by the unit on my way here. They know."

"It seems that you're going to have a crowd of visitors," said Doctor Wallenborn. He said to the nurse, "we can overlook the rules for visiting hours, but keep them down to a half hour each and no one after ten p.m.”

“Yes, Doctor.” She squeezed Joe's hand. “Use the button to call us, even if only to kick this bunch out!” She smiled at Tony as she left.

“I like her,” said Tony. “And if you don't learn to take care of yourself, I'm going to see more of her than I planned.”

They discussed what books and things Joe would want, then left as an aide wheeled in a supper tray.

While Joe was eating the ubiquitous red Jell-O, he heard a knock on the door. Sergeant Henry's slim frame stepped into the room.

“Sorry, Sarge, I was going to see you first thing in the morning.”

“I figured that. So, you won't forget now.”

“No, sir. Thank you for coming.”

“Not entirely a friendly visit. I swung by the police station and found out that Dixon was there.”

“Yes. I saw him.”

“If it's any consolation, we won't let this slide into the usual swamp where racial violence disappears.”

“Huh?”

“Oh, I forget how clueless you are.” The Marine took a seat by the bed. “Interracial beatings often don't get the priority they should. Your case might attract some attention because you're not a Negro. But at the unit, we're pissed. Dixon knew that you were NROTC, so it makes it an attack on a military officer. Stupid of him: we'll keep an eye on this case.”

“I'm not trying to cause trouble.”

“Another problem you have. You're too nice. You didn't cause the trouble; they did.”

"About the self-defense training."

"I gave that some thought because there isn't a martial arts studio here. They have them in big cities like
Norfolk and Washington. But I have an idea." Joe
reached for a pad of paper on the table. "No need to write
it down. Talk to Tony Madison."

"Tony? Why him?"

"He never told you what he did on active duty, did
he?"

"No, but I'm getting used to that, now that I understand that veterans often don't like to talk."

"Well, this was after 'Nam. He was a drill instructor
at San Diego, then taught hand-to-hand combat at
Camp Pendleton. If anyone can teach your hopeless ass,
he can." He smiled as he said it. Joe grinned too.

"I'll ask him. I wonder why he didn't mention it
before."

"We didn't expect you to get beat up before you
could see me." He stood and moved to the door. "See
you on Monday."

"Thanks again, Sarge."

Sergeant Henry peeled a sharp right turn outside the
door.

10. THE TRAINING BEGINS

JOE WINCED and put his hands to his head. "Ouch!"

"Stop cheering so hard," said Tony. "Diego can wipe this bunch without your help."

"Yeah, but he took some grief from some of our teammates at the High School Nationals. I want him at the top of the ratings."

"I knew he had to be good, but not this good."

"Most of these guys were state champions."

"What about you?"

"We didn't have a tennis team, so I can't tell."

"We'll find out next week against Tech."

"Maybe. Anyway, if the varsity is doing this well, we won't see NC State again this year."

After the last set, Diego came off the courts and joined his friends. The other players headed off on the other side together.

After chatting about Diego's standings, Tony got up to walk home.

"Remember, dinner at my house after you beat Tech next week."

Joe and Diego walked back to their room.

ໝໝໝ

The next day, Joe let Diego convince him to skip Mass at Saint Thomas. He was surprised to feel no guilt about it. Diego rode his bicycle to the church downtown and returned before lunch with a scowl.

"So, how was it?" Joe looked up from his physics text.

"Worse. They're running one of those white academies in the education wing, and I could tell from the stares that they didn't want me there."

"Do they have any idea that you look more like Jesus than I do?"

"Of course not. How are you feeling now?"

"Fine. I enjoyed staying in, but now I want to ride somewhere."

"Not yet, amigo. Let's go eat and take it easy today."

A knock on the door. "Hey, Lockhart. Telephone!"

Joe got up and walked out to the pay phone.

"Joe Lockhart."

"*Ciao amore, che fai?*" Hi, darling, what are you doing?

"Wishing I were there with you. The doc has me confined to quarters."

"I take it you're recovering."

"Yes, but Diego's being a nursemaid. He doesn't want me riding my bike until tomorrow."

"He's a true friend, Joe."

"I know. I'm not complaining."

"Listen, I know you can't stay on the line long —"

"There's no one here now."

"I got a letter from your grandmother inviting me to Thanksgiving."

93

"I hope you'll say yes."

"Of course, silly, but won't it be crowded? Didn't you say Diego will be there too?"

"Yes, and my great-aunt. A classic family feast."

"Is there a hotel or guesthouse nearby?"

"Don't even think of it. You would hurt their feelings. They've got extra empty bedrooms upstairs."

"Oh okay. If I catch the train Wednesday, could someone pick me up?"

"They're getting Diego and me at lunchtime, so I'm sure we can pick you up if you arrive after three."

"Great. I can't believe I'll see you twice in one month."

"Me, either. Oh-oh, I've got company. Gotta go." Joe waved at the guy from Room 218 standing by the phone.

"Love ya. Bye." They hung up.

ଔଔଔ

Monday afternoon, Joe caught up with Tony leaving Spanish class.

"Sarge said to talk to you."

"I wondered when you were finally going to."

"I didn't know you were a martial arts instructor."

"I'm not now, but I was." He squeezed Joe's biceps. "Maybe we can do something with that."

"When can we start?"

"You needed to start last year, but I'm still trying to arrange a place. I may have an answer this afternoon. Meanwhile, let's meet at Mem Gym tonight. I want to see how much you forgot from last summer."

Joe's gaze fell. "I haven't been practicing anything."

"You're the one person in the unit who should have been." Tony slapped his back gently. "Relax. I don't want to show off to any other students who may be there."

"What time?"

"How about eight? We'll be done by eight thirty, so you can get back to the room to study."

"Okay. Do I need to bring anything?"

"An attitude would be good. Besides that, anything more casual than what you're wearing."

That evening. Joe ran across Emmet Street and into Memorial Gymnasium. He had spent enough hours there, between the NROTC physical training and the tennis conditioning on rainy days. He found Tony stretching and limbering up in the weight room. Two football players were taking turns doing bench presses in the corner. They carefully ignored the skinny first-year and the muscular veteran with the ugly scar.

"Did you remember to warm up?"

"A few stretches – and I jogged here."

"That'll do." Tony smacked him on the right arm so hard that Joe fell to his left on the mat. Tony reached out to pull him up.

"What was that all about?" Joe rubbed his arm.

"Just checking whether you keep your guard up. You knew you were coming to an unarmed combat lesson, right?"

"Yes."

"So why are you standing around like you don't expect anyone to take a swing at you?"

"Oh. But you're my friend."

"So, friends don't ever get pissed off or drunk?"

"You mean, just like that?"

"Sure. You seem to be a nice clean kid. When was the last time you got wasted with your buddies?"

"Uh – never."

"I thought so." Tony twirled around and stopped in front of Joe, who sucked in a breath and raised his arms.

"What are you looking at?"

"I don't know. Anything. That was so sudden."

"At least you weren't surprised this time." He fired a lightning-fast jab into Joe's stomach. Joe bowled over but kept his balance. His vision spun. "But not that time, eh?"

"What's the idea here?"

"Do I need to call you names? Fight back, stupid!"

"Oh." Joe assumed a boxing stance and threw a punch at Tony's chest. Tony grasped his arm before he could retract it, pulled him forward off his feet, then tugged, making him spin to fall on his back.

"Are you going to teach me that?"

"No. Sarge already did. Let's review what else you should remember."

For the next fifteen minutes, they deconstructed different punches and blows. Joe began to recall what he learned last summer.

"Did you watch Diego during those drills?" Joe nodded. "What was he looking at?"

"It looked like he wasn't watching anything. I mean, his gaze didn't shift from some point." He shrugged.

"He was looking, believe me. Stand here." With Joe in front of him, Tony pointed to his own chest. "Look here. Don't move your eyes." Tony flicked his hand up and down. "See that? Don't move your eyes!"

After ten minutes of drilling Joe to use his peripheral vision, Tony repeated the jab at Joe's gut. Joe grabbed Tony's wrist with both hands, letting the force push him back, and snapping his head forward to head-butt Tony with a loud crack.

"That's better! Now you're thinking."

"You've got a hard head."

"Yeah, noses give more easily. Let's quit." They shook hands. "Can you do this every other day?"

"At night?"

"No. We can use the basement in my church every other afternoon. How about Monday, Wednesday, and Friday right after tennis? You'll be warmed up then."

"I guess I can do that. How much?"

"Let me think about that. I have to practice what I preach, but you might qualify for a military discount, a student discount and a GPI discount."

"GPI?"

"General-Purpose Idiot: you need the help."

They stepped into the night. Joe felt almost disappointed that no one accosted him as he walked through the trees by the Dell and climbed the hill to his residence hall.

As he entered the room, Diego looked up from his desk.

"So, how was it?"

"Surprising, but it should not have been. If this was just to check me out, I'm going to be sore all the time."

"Got what you need here." Diego got up, pulled his toilet kit from the closet and tossed his roommate a small glass jar.

"Tiger Balm! Mom and I swear by this stuff, but I can't find it anywhere."

"That's 'cause you're not from California. You can buy this in Chinatown or any grocery store in the Bay Area or the Central Valley."

"Could your folks send me some? I'll pay you for it."

"Already thought of that. I wrote for an extra-large jar for each of us."

"Gracias, amigo."

"De nada."

Joe showered and finished the studying he had saved for the last minute. By eleven, the room was dark and quiet.

11. MARINE CORPS BALL

TWO WEEKS LATER, Joe stood by the tracks at the train station in Charlottesville when the *Southern Crescent* pulled in on its way to New Orleans. He craned his neck to get a glimpse of each passenger coming out the car door.

He need not have worried. Sandra's blond ponytail stood out against the Southern Railroad car as she emerged. In his haste to join her, Joe almost knocked down a man next to him.

She swung her small suitcase out of the way and stepped behind the crowd just as he arrived. Their embrace and kiss lasted long enough for people to stop around them. He saw an elderly couple smiling sweetly at them as he opened his eyes.

"I think we have an audience."

"Let's take this show somewhere else, shall we?" she said. He took her suitcase and waved toward Main Street.

"Up that way."

Twenty minutes later, they climbed the steep stairs to a rooming house on the corner of University Avenue. A four-story, brick and wood home, it had seen better days. Joe introduced Sandra to Mrs. Page, who rented rooms to upperclassmen.

"Delighted to have you here, Miss Billingsley." She indicated a door past the foyer. "I have a small room for female guests. Women are not allowed above this floor." She eyeballed him. "And no gentlemen in these rooms."

"I understand, ma'am. I'm grateful that you could let Sandra stay."

"Matt and Annabelle are old friends. I was their guest in Paris and Berlin before the war."

"Thank you," said Sandra. "We have a full weekend. I won't be underfoot much."

"Annabelle told me that you are musical. Feel free to use the piano."

"Thank you."

He moved Sandra's suitcase to the door of her room. "I should get back while you change. First-years set up the ball. I'll be back about six." He nodded to the land-lady and let himself out.

Back in the room, he and Diego changed into Full Dress Blue, which was simply the Navy-blue suit (Service Dress Blue) with white gloves and the National Defense Medal instead of a ribbon. They walked to Maury Hall, where the first-years and a few upperclassmen were hanging streamers and posters. About five thirty, Dining Services delivered the cake. After excusing himself, Joe walked along the East Range to the boarding house.

As he reached the front porch, he heard *Für Anneliese*. He slipped in without knocking. Sandra sat at the grand piano in the parlor. Mrs. Page had her back to the door. He waited until the end of the piece.

"That is beautiful."

"Joe!" Sandra stood as her hostess turned around. "Just something I could play from memory. Your piano has a wonderful sound, Mrs. Page." She eased around the instrument. She wore a full-length black evening gown and had her hair up in an elegant style of curls. While he stood speechless, she walked over to take his hand.

"Thank you." Mrs. Page beamed. "Now, run along, you two, and have a good time."

Helping Sandra into her coat, he whispered, "You always look beautiful, but you are stunning tonight." She blushed and smiled.

They walked through the chilly evening air toward Maury Hall.

"You've made a quick hit with her," he said. "Two of the guys in the unit board there. They say she's a bear."

"I don't know what they're talking about. She's a dear. Did you know she was an operatic soprano? She spent several years on the European circuit. That's how she knows your grandparents. I didn't know your grandfather was the military attaché in Berlin and Paris."

"Only in Berlin; he was the assistant attaché in Paris. He met my grandmother there."

"That's romantic."

"Like the Villa Medici at sunset?"

Taking his arm, she hugged it tightly. "I miss Rome. Do you?"

"Terribly. Fortunately, this place keeps me too busy to dwell on it."

ଌଌଌ

Dining, dancing, and watching the time-honored ceremonies, Sandra let herself be swept up in a different romantic mood. Her father had played for many balls as an Army musician. She had not witnessed those occasions, but she did know the words and music to *The Halls of Montezuma.* That gained her approving side glances from both Sergeant Henry and Major Jackson.

As they mounted the steps to the porch after midnight, they yawned at the same time.

"It's been a long day, but wonderful. Thank you so much, Joe."

"Thank you. I wish I had a place for us to spend the night, but just having you here is a dream for me."

"You still have the tennis matches tomorrow."

"We can sleep in. Is eleven too early for me to come back?"

"I'll be here."

They kissed quickly, and she went into the quiet house. Joe floated back to McCormick Hall.

He entered quietly, but Diego was reading in his bed. He looked up and grinned.

"Hola, amigo. I can see why you're in love with her. I could lose my heart too."

"She's quite something, isn't she?"

"Yes." While Joe undressed, Diego turned out his light. Ten minutes later, the room was dark and silent.

ღღღ

"Game, set, and match!" Whoops and cheers erupted from the bleachers. Diego and Joe walked to the net to shake hands with their opponents. Returning to their bags, Joe saw Sandra jumping excitedly next to Tony Madison. He waved and smiled.

He had been concerned about having her watch him, but on the court, he found an ability to concentrate. Diego lost one game, but Joe was undefeated that day. It felt good, so good.

"You two are awesome," said Tony. "Are you ready to put some of those calories back?"

"Sure, where shall we meet you?"

"If you trust me with this dazzling lady, why not Chuck's Canteen?"

"I'm not worried," said Joe, winking at her, "but you should be." Tony laughed.

"See you soon." While Tony and Sandra walked toward the Canteen, Diego and Joe trotted back to their room.

જ્ઞજ્ઞજ્ઞ

As the late afternoon shadows reached across West Main Street, Tony pointed to the woods growing between the hospital and the train station.

"This is the most likely place for an ambush on the way to or from my house."

"Is it that dangerous?" asked Joe.

"Not for me, but I'm not the one who got beat up in broad daylight on the Corner."

Joe hung his head. "Oh yeah." Tony nudged his arm.

"Always in training, right?"

With a weak smile, Joe nodded.

"He told me about his problem," said Sandra, "but I can understand it better now." She squeezed Joe's arm. "Tony says you're getting quicker instincts. How does it feel?"

"There are some days I almost wish for someone to give me a hard time, but then I find myself on the mat looking up at this smug bastard." He reached out and tapped Tony on the back of the shoulder. "And my confidence drains out."

From his position on Tony's other side, Diego said, "You have three bodyguards tonight. Easy, eh?"

Sandra squeezed Joe's arm. "Yeah, easy."

The Madisons lived in a three-story brick house with a wraparound porch off Fifth Street. Tony's father and mother met them outside. With only the slightest touch of gray in their hair and perfectly smooth skin, it would be hard to believe that Tony was their son.

"I heard a lot about Tony's new friends. Welcome!" Alvin Madison held the door for them.

Thelma Madison accepted Sandra's offer to help, and the two women disappeared into the back of the house. Tony went with them and came back with four beers.

"Tony tells me you have a shop here, sir," Joe said. "This is a lovely house; it doesn't look very commercial."

"Down in the basement. My customers know to come around to the side." He tilted his head toward where they had seen the steps earlier.

"What do you sell?"

"Everything a Negro family needs that most supermarkets and drugstores don't carry, from pomade and pig's feet to hair bands and canning salt."

"There's no sign."

"Nope. Everyone who needs us knows where we are."

Conversation moved to the tennis match with Tech and the Marine Corps Ball. Alvin had fought in World War II in North Africa and Italy. It was clear that he was immensely proud of his son, "the jarhead," as he called him. Sandra came in after the beer bottles were empty.

"Dinner is served."

"I didn't mean to put you to work, miss." Alvin seemed embarrassed.

"Not to worry, sir. Mrs. Madison and I were having a ball." She looked at Joe. "She's really cool. You wouldn't believe what a midwife has to do around here."

They adjourned to the dining room. Alvin recited a long grace, after which the food, drink and talk ran long and pleasantly.

Just before midnight, Diego, Joe, and Sandra excused themselves and started back to the university. After the meal, they were glad for the long walk.

"Now that I've decided to take accounting next semester," said Joe as they crossed the street, "I find myself thinking about the cost of everything. That meal must have set them back."

"Not really," said Sandra. "Thelma said that although the shop made more money, they actually have more available now with the children out of the house. No mortgage, no tuition. She said they do very well now."

"Good, I —" Diego slapped him on the arm. About fifty yards ahead, a half dozen young men were walking toward them, very deliberately. They had on the same jackets and ball caps that Joe's assailants had worn. "Oh hell, Diego, what do —"

"Shut up and focus, amigo." He said to Sandra, "¿Señorita?" She moved to put Joe between them.

"Give me the two street-side. You two argue about the other four."

She had picked the two largest men. One held a baseball bat. The other wore gloves with something shiny on the outside, probably brass knuckles.

Diego nudged his friend. "Go for the third or fourth one in or whoever moves first. I'll cover the others."

Joe nodded. His heart was pounding. He tried to remember the mnemonics that Tony had taught him, but fear was freezing his brain.

Something clicked when he recognized three of them as the ones who attacked him. As he stared between the third and fourth man, a deep rage enveloped him. His focus returned as it had on the tennis court that afternoon.

"Hey, nigger-lover, we see that you don't listen." This from the third one. The outer man swung the bat back.

"Yeah, here —" He brought the bat over and down toward Joe, only to find himself flying forward behind it. Sandra lifted her leg over his back and slammed him facedown as she grabbed the arm of the next one. A head-butt and an elbow to the temple left him on top of the batter.

The one to Joe's right lunged. Grabbing his right arm, Joe stepped back and pulled him through, chopping his temple as he went by. He snapped the man's wrist, yanking back on his arm so that the shoulder popped as he went down on his left side. Joe looked to the third man, but he was bent over, puking, after Sandra had lowered her right elbow into the back of his neck. He went down on the other three.

Joe looked to his right. Both men were unconscious. Diego was dusting his hands.

Sandra stood back. "We should report this."

"Of course," said Diego. "It is our civic duty to call in the fight we saw walking home. Maybe someone was hurt."

"We can call from Mrs. Page's," said Joe. "I think it's the closest place at this hour."

"If the police come, they should be gone. They don't seem to be the type who want to explain things to the cops."

"Three of them are wanted."

"That settles it," said Sandra, stepping between them. She took their arms. "Let's have a nice walk to that telephone."

12. THANKSGIVING

SUNDAY MORNING, Joe's alarm went off just before dawn.

"Good grief, Joe, I'm the early riser. What are you doing?"

"Sorry, Diego. The northbound *Southern Crescent* comes through at eight o'clock. I want to see Sandra off."

"Of course. Give her my love." Flipping over, he pulled the pillow over his head.

As the sun rose above the sleepy town, Joe knocked gently at Mrs. Page's door. Sandra opened it and stepped out with her small suitcase. She looked as fresh as if she had slept eight hours after a perfumed bubble bath. Putting down the luggage, she embraced him. They kissed long and hard.

"Maybe I should rent my own place next year." He picked up her suitcase and took her arm.

"That would be expensive, don't you think?" They set a brisk pace along University Avenue.

"Just dreaming; I sure would like not to have to turn you over to Mrs. Page at night."

"If we're going to fight our way back each night, being forced to get some sleep might be better."

"How much sleep did we get? Maybe four hours?"

"No more than that. I plan to catch up on the train."

"I'm trying to figure out which church pews are softest for dozing or whether to go back to the room." They walked under the C&O railway bridge.

"I was talking to Mrs. Page about Saint Paul's next door to her house. She's very proud that they did not go along with Massive Resistance."

"What's that?"

"It happened before you got here. Virginia ordered all the public schools to close rather than integrate. Most of the white churches in town offered rooms for private academies, so the white kids could still go to school. Saint Paul's and three other churches refused to participate."

"It all seems so crazy."

"I know," she said, squeezing his arm. "If you want to keep going to church, you might find some like-minded people there."

"I saw the sign as we walked past. I'll check it out on the way back."

The train arrived fifteen minutes late. Another long embrace and a kiss, and Sandra stepped back.

"See you in Richmond."

"Can't wait. Love ya."

"Love ya too." She turned to climb into the carriage.

ଛଛଛ

"Diego, you are in here." Madame Ardwood opened the door to a room on the corner. "And Joe, you are next to Sandra's room. We will be down on the end, with Mary on the other side. Will that be good for you?"

"Omigosh, it's amazing,"

"Grandmaman, did you know that you put Sandra in my room?" Annabelle smiled and stroked Joe's face with the backs of her fingers.

"Yes, I did. I'm happy that you remember it. It *is* the nicest room on the floor, *non?* That is why I thought you would want it for her."

He shrugged. "Mom and I were gone so long, I guess none of the rooms are anyone's anymore."

"A good way to think of it, young man," Matthew Ardwood said from the landing. "If and when your mother ever leaves that bomb-weary country, there'll be more moving around."

"Oh right. You're in her old room."

Tousling Joe's hair, the elder man said, "Do you want to go meet your lady friend?"

Joe looked at his watch. "Sure! Should we go now?"

His grandfather pulled the car keys from his pocket. "I don't need to look at a couple of lovebirds." He hugged his wife. "I have my own."

Joe's face darkened. "I don't have a license, sir."

The general swung to Diego. "*¿Quieres ser el chofer?*"

"*Con mucho gusto, señor general.*" Diego took the keys and rapped his friend on the arm. "When we get back, you're going to the DMV." The Department of Motor Vehicles. He hoisted his duffel and went to his room, shaking his head. "We'll make a gringo out of you yet, amigo."

"Diego's right. You file the application, and we'll work on the practice and testing during the Christmas break. You'll be driving us back to school in January."

Still embarrassed, Joe put his things in his room. The two friends walked outside together.

"Just tell me where to go." Diego handled the big sedan with confidence.

"Take a right on Broad Street. It's less than two miles, on the left."

Most drivers were going the other way, city commuters escaping for the long weekend. At the station, Diego eased into a drop-off space that had just opened.

"This is too good to let go," he said. "You go find Sandra; I'll stay with the car."

"Okay, amigo. Thanks!"

The platform inside the Broad Street Station seemed more crowded than the siding in Charlottesville, but that might have been partly because of the enclosed feeling from the vast glass-and-steel roof. This time, Joe knew what to look for, and he moved to the correct car when Sandra appeared at the door. They stepped out of the crush of people going home and embraced by the wall.

"Has it been only ten days? Feels like forever."

She punched his chest lightly. "Forever was last year. I can handle being on the same side of the Atlantic as you."

They joined what remained of the crowd and headed for the main entrance. Outside, Joe stopped suddenly. She followed his gaze.

"What the heck?"

Diego leaned against the car, facing the station. He was spread-eagled as two Richmond policemen frisked him. Joe hurried down the steps, stopping just in time to catch Diego's wink.

"Officers, what is going on here?"

"Is this your car, sir?"

"No. It's my grandfather's. I mean, what are you doing with Mister de la Torre here?"

"He was loitering here. If this car is in your family, may I see your license?"

"I don't have one. And *that,* Officer Payne, is why Mister de la Torre is here." He leaned in to read the badge of the other policeman. "Officer – Tomkins – would you please unhand him, so we can be on our way?"

Reaching for the rear door, he held it for Sandra. He walked around to the trunk and put her suitcase in it. Then he let himself into the seat behind the driver.

"Come along, Diego. We need to return the car to the general in time to collect his sister."

"*Sí, señor* Lockhart." Diego stood back, brushed his hands off, and swiftly slid into the driver's seat.

Joe saw the two policemen in the rearview mirror. Payne was scratching his head. Tomkins seemed to be saying, *what was that?*

When they were out of sight, Joe mimicked a British public-school accent. "I say, Diego, if you are going to stay in my employ, you simply must do better at staying out of trouble."

Sandra and Diego both laughed loudly. Diego pulled over for a moment.

"I was so afraid you would be your usual clueless self. Thanks."

"That was brilliant, Joe," said Sandra. "You two had that act down beautifully."

"What act?" Joe slapped Diego on the back of the head. "I don't think I'm the problem. It must be hanging around with you two."

Diego put the car in gear and eased into traffic.

"You really don't have a license?" asked Sandra.

"No. I didn't need one for the Vespa, and I've only been in the US for what, maybe four months?"

She thought a moment. "Never occurred to me. I had my Ohio license when I went to Rome."

"On the other hand, I could get used to this." He turned and kissed her. "Eyes in the boat, de la Torre!" Diego chuckled, but he took his gaze off the mirror and looked ahead.

ଓଓଓ

Just before sunset, a British racing green MG turned into the driveway and parked behind the sedan. The family was in the parlor, enjoying an aperitif before supper. The Ardwoods almost ran to the front door to embrace the new arrival.

She was a trim, hardy-looking woman with graying hair pulled back and eyes that sparkled when she smiled. Sensible shoes and a tweed suit marked her as a professor even without introductions.

"Hi, Aunt Mary." Joe stepped forward.

"My goodness, you are quite the man now. I haven't seen you for what, twelve years now?"

"I think. You're the math prof." They hugged. "This is Sandra Billingsley, my best friend, and Diego de la Torre, my roommate and next-best friend." Handshakes all around.

While Joe took her coat, Matthew poured a glass of white wine for his sister. Annabelle asked about Mary's classes and the drive to Richmond.

"The drive was simple enough: just take US 60 to your house. But it took all day to get out of there. I've been working with two young women who were struggling with calculus. Some tutoring in my office. Today, I gave them a pretest this morning, which I graded over lunch and explained to them this afternoon."

"Why so much trouble?"

"Because they're both worth it." Mary's eyes flashed with some anger. "They're each the first in their families to go to college, and I know that they can master the material. But they've never learned to study effectively."

"Affirmative action scholarships?" her brother asked.

"Yes. The other women at Sweetbriar grew up in the white private school environment. They internalized study methods and the European canon years ago. These two are smart and determined, but they're playing catch-up all the way."

"Are you tilting at windmills again, Mary?" The general smiled kindly as he said it.

"Maybe. Some of the faculty probably expect them to wash out after the school takes credit for letting them in. But that won't happen if I can help it. When they graduate, their daughters and granddaughters will be back, I'm sure. And that would be the idea of the program, wouldn't it?"

"Too bad you're not the president of the college."

"Not necessary, Matthew. It takes more than one person, even the president, to bring about the kind of change we need. If their other teachers get on board, the next generation should benefit." She took a hefty swallow of her wine. "That's off my chest now. Sorry." She looked at the two UVA players. "Did I hear that you two beat both Tech *and* NC State this year?"

Joe and Diego glanced to the floor and grinned. "First time for everything, Aunt Mary."

Conversation moved around the room. Mary was interested in the different reasons that Sandra and Joe had for taking accounting and Diego's ambition to make a naval career.

A ding from the kitchen alerted Annabelle that the coq au vin was ready to come out. Diego and Joe went to Mary's car to bring her luggage upstairs.

"She is one cool lady." Diego admired the gleaming finish on the sports car. "She's not married?"

"No, but don't call her a spinster. She has no shortage of suitors, even at her age. But she is happy and does not need a man to feel complete."

"Kind of like Sandra?"

He paused lifting his aunt's suitcase from the back seat. "I think so. Sandra's independence is part of what I like about her. And she knows that I like it."

"You two are perfect for each other. The Navy and the FBI are tough on relationships." Diego held the front door.

"Aunt Mary told my mother that she became a teacher because she loves children – when she can send them home at the end of the day."

Dinner ran until midnight, but there were no commitments that weekend. Thursday, they walked to the University of Richmond to use the abandoned tennis courts. Mary showed that skill on the court was a family trait. She spent some time working with Sandra while the other four blasted away in a high-energy doubles match.

As they walked back, Sandra took Joe's arm. "That was so much fun. Joe, we have to play more."

"My pleasure, signorina. Anywhere we find a court, you're on!"

Back at the house, they showered and had a light snack before settling in to fix the Thanksgiving dinner.

It was a traditional feast in almost every sense, except that the herbs in the turkey and the richness of the gravy told them that Annabelle had dropped some of her family's traditions into the mix.

☙☙☙

On Friday, the general gave Diego the keys again, and he took Mary, Sandra and Joe into the Historic District. They spent several hours at the Virginia Museum of Fine Art, then walked up Boulevard Street to Monument Avenue and Broad Street. The trees were bare, but they framed the many statues and gave perspective to the stately homes in the neighborhood.

"Diego, are you nervous about something?" Mary asked as they ate a late lunch across from the train station.

"This is Payne and Tomkins' beat, you know." He winked at Joe and Sandra, who laughed.

"I would almost like to see them catch us now." They told her about the encounter with the pair of Richmond's Finest.

"It will take a long time to wrap up the Civil War, I'm afraid."

"It keeps us darkies nimble, though, doesn't it?" Diego reached for the check. "Let me buy this."

He went to the cash register to pay. The cashier, a middle-aged white man with thinning gray hair looked sourly at him. Diego pointed to the ball cap on the wall behind the register. "Tropic Lightning. Were you in the Twenty-fifth Division, sir?"

"Yeah. Why?"

"My father fought in the Twenty-fifth at Guadalcanal. Twenty-seventh Regiment."

The man raised his eyebrows in surprise. "Me too."

"You were a lucky man from what I heard. I'm glad you came back." He took his change and shook the man's hand. "Have a nice day, sir."

As they turned down the street, Diego glanced back through the window. The man was motioning one of the women to take over the register. He grabbed his ball cap and walked to the back.

"A class act, Diego," said Sandra, patting him on the arm. Mary smiled at him and nodded her agreement.

Diego sighed. "Every once in a while, I do something right."

Saturday, it rained, so the family played board games, read, and chatted easily about their pasts and their dreams. In midafternoon, the rain stopped while Sandra and Mary were sitting on the back porch, watching some ducks in the pond behind the house swim in a vee-formation.

"Miss Ardwood —"

"Mary, please. I'm neither your teacher nor your boss."

"Sorry. I keep forgetting." She waved her glass of iced tea. "You're the kind of person who commands respect just walking into the room, you know that?"

"Thank you. I have heard that before, but not often. Usually it's something like 'here's that pushy bitch again.'" She chuckled.

"I get that, too, sometimes, but probably not as much as your generation." Sandra paused. "May I ask you something? If it's too personal, just say so."

Mary put her hands on her abdomen. "Oh dear. Does it show already?" Sandra laughed so hard she almost tipped over the rattan table. "I doubt you can ask anything so shocking that Joe's mother hasn't already asked."

"I forgot about that. You Ardwood women are amazing."

"What's on your mind?"

"Well. You never married, and from what I understand, it doesn't matter. You sure don't look or act like a spinster, whatever that's supposed to be. What's the story from your point of view?"

"You're looking at it." Mary refreshed both their glasses. "When I was your age, I wanted nothing more than to be what I have become. It was hard as hell to explain to everyone that I really didn't need a man around the house, and, no, I wasn't a lesbian. We were well off, so I could go to Sweetbriar and take my doctorate at MIT before Pearl Harbor. Having the men gone allowed me to do interesting work at the War Department in Washington. After that, NASA hired me as what they called a computer in those days.

"By then, I knew that I wanted to stay with mathematics. I also met some of the most courageous women I have ever known. Many never married, but they all accomplished incredible things that the men could not match."

"At NASA?"

"Yes. They were computers too, but in their own building, because they were Negroes. Most had graduated from Hampton Institute or similar colleges. They could run calculations faster and more accurately than anyone else. I was amazed. You know about the Gemini and Apollo missions, don't you?"

"I watched the moonwalk on TV."

"We calculated those trajectories at Langley, using hand-cranked calculators and procedures developed by

Katherine Johnson. She and others – I'm thinking of Dot Vaughn, Mary Jackson and Christine Darden – showed up for work every day in their segregated building and ran the calculations. They reared their children, supported their families, put men on the moon, and took shit as Negro women in Virginia. I was humbled: I had found my heroes. Not one of them ever wondered or cared that I did not want a husband or children."

"I've never heard of them."

"And you may never. Anyway, Sweetbriar exists to educate women for leadership, so when one of my classmates called me about teaching mathematics, I was ready to say yes. I figured it was a good place to launch more women like those hidden computers. At least, I could help the ones who wanted to be independent not feel weird or alone."

"Now I understand your passion for those two scholarship students."

"Are you thinking about Joe?"

"Yes, but I'm more concerned about my family, in particular my mother. What did you do when your parents or your friends asked you when you were going to find a man and 'settle down'?" Mary sipped her tea, then set it down.

"I was incredibly fortunate, Sandra. I went into the workforce as the war was opening these so-called men's jobs, then I moved to NASA where my sex and my colleagues' skin color did not prevent us from continuing in those jobs. But before I met Katherine Johnson and Dot Vaughn, I think it was my brother Matthew who helped me most."

"How so?"

"He invited me to come to Paris while he was stationed there. I encountered a whole class of strong-willed women who moved successfully through French society like invisible power sources."

Sandra smiled at that and thought of Mary's niece: Nancy Ardwood Lockhart. Before she had ever met Joe, Sandra knew that the Vice-President for Operations at Smithson Italia was one of only two female executives in the country.

"So many of our assumptions seem just silly to me. Did you meet Annabelle then?"

"She was my friend first. I introduced her to Matthew. See how that turned out?"

"Let me guess, she was one of those strong-willed women your brother wanted, but he couldn't marry his sister, could he?"

"You're sharp for a pretty coed, you know?" Mary grinned.

"Oh God, I get that so much."

"I figured you did."

"What about your parents?"

"Well, look at what they raised. They only wanted us to be able to make our way and be happy. If Mother ever wondered about my nubile status or deliberate barrenness, she never breathed a word."

"My mother asks me every time if I have met any nice boys. She worries to death that I don't have a man to protect me, living alone in DC."

"Has that been a problem for you?"

"No. Having a man at home would have done me no good at all when I was attacked in Dupont Circle."

"Sorry, I can't answer your question. The people whose opinion I valued never contradicted mine. But I can think of something that might help." Sandra arched her eyebrows. "You're studying to be an investigator and an accountant. I'm a mathematician. What is important to us in making choices?"

"Analyzing the facts."

"Exactly. You can still love your mother and father and take in all they have to say. Then act only on the facts. Somewhere in their emotional appeal to a traditional life will be gems of wisdom or good reasons to do something you would have missed if they had not mentioned them. It might even have nothing to do with what the conversation was at the time." She sat silently while Sandra considered this advice.

"My mother was critiquing one of my landscapes one day – I had asked her opinion. She had me tell her the story about how the painting came to be. She listened carefully, all the while looking closely at it. Then she said, 'sometimes, I think you like the stories better than the pictures' and walked downstairs to start supper."

"Did that hurt?"

"Strangely, no, it felt right. When I got back to school, I switched from Art to Art History, and it was the best decision I ever made. Is that sort of what you're suggesting?"

"Yes. Look for those pearls. Sometimes, they'll be buried in the emotional detritus of an argument or something else. I hope that helps."

"I think it will. Thank you."

"Speaking of women's liberation, shall we go see if they have reduced Annabelle to the status of a galley slave."

"Pun intended?"

Mary smirked and picked up the pitcher. They carried the crystal to the kitchen. To their surprise, they found Joe preparing a sauce, Diego chopping vegetables and Matthew whipping a meringue.

"Where's Annabelle?"

"Change of plans. When the rain stopped, she decided that she wanted steak, so she took the car to the butcher shop. We have the grill started."

"I take it you don't need any help?"

"No, but if you would make sure the wine is chilled and check on the grill, I won't have to leave this meringue."

Mary arched an eyebrow at Sandra, who smiled at Joe and followed his great-aunt to the backyard.

13. Christmas

"*GRAZIE, SANDRO.*" Nancy Lockhart stood after thanking the president of Smithson Italia SpA and continued in Italian. "Do you think it will make a difference?"

"Put it this way, Nancy. No American executive – damn it! no executive of any nationality – has been targeted like you have: posters, flyers and ads in the newspapers."

"But why?"

"Beats me. Regardless, if they want to amplify their impact, something during the holidays would be perfect."

"Good thing that I planned to return to Richmond for Christmas."

"Give Joe our love, Nancy. He's family around here, and we miss him."

"Thanks. I will."

"Call me after the *Befana*, before you return." The Italian holiday on the Feast of the Epiphany was almost two weeks after Christmas.

"Are you putting me out, Sandro? No need to sugarcoat it for me. You know that."

"Oh goodness, no, please! Just give me an update. Americans think Christmas is all over on the twenty-sixth of December. Take time to shake a few hands and renew some acquaintances around Richmond. Face it: you *are* years overdue for a promotion and a transfer. Maybe you can find someone there who would like to come to Italy. I promise to pay for Italian lessons, though no one alive could fill your shoes."

"A half dozen invitations to office parties have already arrived. Let's see what shapes up."

Sandro came around his desk, and they exchanged kisses on both cheeks.

"Have a wonderful vacation, Nancy. Merry Christmas."

"*Buona Befana.* Give my best to Cornelia. *Arrivederci.*"

Pedaling Joe's bicycle back home, she tried to quell her unsettled stomach. The exercise helped, but her fears came back as she locked the bike in the garage and walked up to her apartment. Almost five months, and she was still not used to the empty feeling of the place. No smells of supper. No Italian love songs in the kitchen. No voice from Joe's bedroom, asking how her day was.

In the silence, she sensed only dread.

She dreaded the nightmares of the employees dying in the blast at the Aprilia plant the day after she cut the ribbon to open it. She dreaded walking past dozens of light poles with her picture, calling for death to Yankee imperialists. She dreaded the sensation that this was not the usual anti-American activity by the Communists.

This was too personal. *Why me?*

On a practical level, she dreaded the flight home.

Motion sickness was the price she paid for her adventurous life as a top executive in a multinational pharmaceutical company. Last year, Luke Arland had helped her overcome it on flights in Europe, teaching her to focus during takeoff and landing. He had transferred back to New York. This would be the longest flight she had ever made.

When Maria Grazia, her secretary, had made her reservations, Nancy had called Luke's office. He was in Argentina and might be stopping in Panama on the way back. His assistant promised to get word to him. Since then, the silence had been deafening.

ଧଧଧ

Sandra poured the last pail of milk into the trough that led to the automated churn and separator. Arnie was already drawing off fresh cream and putting cans of milk on the cart to take them to the refrigerator. After breakfast, they would come back for the butter.

"Takes most of the work out of it, eh?" she asked her brother as she did some of her morning stretches. Back in Washington, she would do those in her room after getting up, but the sun was still below the eastern horizon.

"Can you imagine trying to handle all these cows without it?"

"Looks like we've been replaced by machines."

"I hope so. I keep bugging Jim to automate as much as possible. Mom and Dad can't keep this up forever, and Jim isn't knocking himself out to get a wife. Without machinery, he can't work the farm alone."

"But he doesn't want a wife. He wants a husband. Maybe someone bigger than he is."

"Sshh, Sandy! Mom might hear you."

"She doesn't know?" Stopping her squats, she gaped at her baby brother.

"Let's just say she's in denial. Besides, Jim can't meet anyone openly in a town like London, Ohio."

"Guess not. What about Dad?"

"As far as I can tell, he's okay with it. If they've had words, they kept it to themselves. After all, Dad loves them both, but he's married to Mom."

"And you?"

"Doesn't bother me. He's always been my brother and always will be. How long have you known?"

"Since the summer before I went to Italy. Some of my classmates at GW are queer. Not a big deal there."

"Well, let it be our family secret unless someday Jim can come out. Maybe he'll meet someone at OSU."

As they pushed the cart to the refrigerator, they chatted about Arnie's studies at Ohio State University, then went in for breakfast.

The smell of bacon, home-fried potatoes, and pancakes filled the big house. The two elder Billingsleys were putting out dishes, dancing their morning ballet as they put out a meal for seven people without crashing into each other.

"Are you two ever going to need help with breakfast?" asked Sandra as she came from washing her hands in the little washroom off the hall.

"Just take notes," her father said. "When it's your turn, you'll have to work out your own orchestration."

Her other brothers, Martin Jr., Walter, and Jim, came in from feeding the chickens and pigs, collecting eggs, and turning the cows out to pasture.

Jim caught Arnie's eye. "I'll get the butter after breakfast."

"Let's do it together," Arnie said. "I've got an idea for the hay conveyor I want to show you."

Surrounded by her full family for the first time in years, Sandra basked in the happiness of seeing her brothers and her parents catching up. She enjoyed the repartee between the three eldest men: a retired Army musician, a Navy musician, and a Marine. Younger brothers Jim and Arnie were studying at Ohio State University: Jim in agriculture, Arnie in engineering.

"Where does the butter go today, Dad?" asked Jim as they were clearing the table.

"Caldwell's."

"Keys in the usual place?"

"Yup. Remember to bring back an empty vat."

"And leave a pound for us in the refrigerator," said Marcia.

"Okay, Mom."

The two younger brothers walked to the hallway, donned their coats and boots, and disappeared.

When the five left over began bumping into each other, Martin called everyone to stop.

"Why don't you ladies take the day off? We have all the experts we need here for KP. Remember that we're going to that holiday luncheon party at the VFW. The whole town wants to meet our two war heroes."

"Zeb will be there too." Mother turned to daughter. "Want to visit Samara and Karen?"

"Let's! I'll call them."

ଷଷଷ

Like the Billingsley family, the Monroes had settled in Ohio when Zebadiah retired from the Army. Before they ever met Zeb's wife, the renowned artist Samara Majib, Marcia and Sandra had admired her paintings. Karen was

Sandra's age and became a friend during the year that they were both at London High School. The phone call resulted in a lunch invitation.

An hour later, the two mothers and their daughters stood in front of a painting on the wall in the Monroes' living room.

"What do you think, Sandra?" asked Samara.

"Oh. My. God. This is amazing."

She stepped back and stared at the painting. The boy could not be more than twelve or thirteen. He lay on three of his friends, looking out at her. The blood from the wound in his chest ran up his neck and over his right cheek before falling into a pool by the foot protruding from the pile of bodies. It was still a bright red against his shining black skin.

The eyes of the dying boy looked straight into her soul. She shivered, and her throat closed.

Helpless. She felt so helpless. Whenever pain or joy had moved her, Sandra was at least in contact with another person. But she could not reach this boy, who called her name with his eyes.

A tear fell down her right cheek.

"Mrs. Monroe, you've outdone yourself."

"Not I. Please call me Samara now. I am not surprised that you missed the details to the side. Those eyes do that to everyone."

Sandra blinked and looked around the scene. In the corner, she saw it, painted the same color as the sand in the street, so only the texture of paint that dried later revealed the artist's initials, K. M.

"Karen!" Whirling around, Sandra gaped at her friend.

Marcia smiled. "You were gone, dear. This was her senior project in high school."

"I know you went to the Art Institute of Chicago, but looking at this, I can see that they can't teach you anything. How did you do this? Did you go to Africa?"

"No. This was a nightmare. It came to me every night for a week after that PBS program on the war in Biafra."

"This is from a picture?"

"Not quite. In the dream, I was with the squad that was killing these boy soldiers. Someone was holding me, forcing me to watch. Maybe I was someone's sister, I'm not sure. This is how vivid it was." She waved at the scene. "That was the week your mother told us to choose a project. For that, I owe her because painting this stopped the nightmares."

For the next few minutes, they stood in front of the picture in silence, each deep in the thoughts and feelings that the art evoked. Sandra forced herself away from the eyes to take in the sand and the sun, the huts, and the way the lines and colors drew the eye to the face of the dying boy.

"It seems fitting that the daughter of the creator of *Bride of the Chief* would do this." Sandra smiled at Samara. "Where is it now?"

"In the dining room. Come."

As they walked through the house, Sandra was amazed and delighted by the new art everywhere. Before Sandra had gone to college, pictures by Samara had covered the walls. Karen's homework assignments had been in her room. Now there was an even mix of items from each of them.

Sandra's favorite, *Bride of the Chief,* occupied a prominent place over the sideboard. She had first seen it at Samara's exhibition at the Corcoran in Washington when she was eleven years old. Even then, she had associated it with the *Dama con Liocorno* by Raphael.

"You need a gallery for all these wonderful paintings."

"Working on it," said Karen.

"The house is full of best-sellers."

"We'll see. I don't want to sell any originals unless they pull my scholarship. Mom told me about some printmakers back East, and I'm taking business classes at the Institute in Chicago."

"Lucky you: you'll make a living doing what you love."

Lunch was a collaborative affair, assembled in the kitchen, then carried to the dining room. Although the two girls had been writing regularly, there was so much that would not fit into letters. Over four years of high school and into college, Karen had also become close to Marcia, the high school art teacher.

"Speaking of high school," asked Sandra, "whatever happened to the Westers?" The two Wester brothers had bullied Karen as a new freshman until Sandra had put a stop to it.

"They're still here. Jimmy works at the Esso station on Main Street. Jerry got drafted and just came back. I think he's still looking for a job."

"So, it's been quiet since I left?"

"Like I wrote you, I only had one more run-in with them, and the word got out pretty fast to leave me alone."

"Nobody bullies the class president, do they?" Samara squeezed Karen's hand.

"No, but I still think Dad's lessons are what gave me the confidence I needed."

"Did he teach you self-defense?" Sergeant-Major Monroe had been a Green Beret.

"More than that. Want to see our studio in the basement?"

"Isn't it upstairs in that room with the picture windows on three sides?"

"Different studio. Come on." Putting her napkin down, Karen said, "I'll get the dishes when we come back, Mom."

"Don't worry about it, dear. Marcia and I can chat while we do them."

Taking her hand, Sandra's friend pulled her downstairs. Half the room had a thick mat on the floor. There was a punching bag, racks of free weights, and a treadmill.

"This is quite a gym."

"Dad decided to outfit it so we could practice more than basic self-defense."

Sandra slid out of her shoes, took off her sweater and stepped to the mat.

"Want to show me some moves?"

❖❖❖

A half hour later, Samara called down the stairs.

"Are you two still down there? What's all that thumping?"

"Just playing around." Karen's voice. "Want us to come up?"

"If you want. Just wondering."

The two young women came upstairs, shining with sweat and catching their breath.

"What —?"

"She's awesome, Mom. "I'd love to watch her take on Dad."

"What?" Marcia gasped. "Sandra, what is she talking about?"

"Just rassling around. Don't worry about it." Taking the tall glass of water from Karen, she drank it in one move. "Thanks."

"I'm aware of what Zeb has taught her. How do you know such things?"

"A little martial arts studio in Georgetown, three times a week. Ever since I came back from Italy."

"Why?"

"Same reason as her. You're worried about my being alone in DC. Believe me, Washington is as safe as Chicago or Columbus now. What I can't handle, someone else probably can't do for me."

Her mother started to say something, then shut her mouth and stared out the window behind Sandra's shoulder.

♲♲♲

The seat belt sign came on, and the ding of the notification woke Nancy. The pilot announced their descent to JFK International Airport, which she still thought of as Idlewild. After checking her belt, she smoothed her suit as best she could.

Did I just sleep for eight hours?

Amazed, she considered the impact that leaving the danger and stress of her life in Italy had on her. Luke's advice to focus on pretending to fly the aircraft and to relax her arms and legs worked. It helped that the big

Boeing 707 rose more gently than the smaller jets that carried her from Rome to Cologne, Brussels, and London. For the descent, she repeated the drill.

While she stood at the baggage claim waiting for her luggage, she heard a familiar voice behind her.

"*Vuole un passaggio in città, signora?*" Would you like a lift into town, ma'am? She whirled around.

"Luke!" Without a care for who was watching, she hugged him, then slid her hand behind his head for a long, lingering kiss. He responded with no hesitation. At last, she stood back. "I tried to give you my itinerary, but nothing came back."

"They told me when I called from Buenos Aires. There was a conference in a remote hacienda on the Pampas. Totally isolated."

"Wait a minute. This is the international area."

"Just arrived myself. That's my bag." He pointed to the next carousel. "We can clear customs together. What about my offer?"

"Of course. I have a booking at the Mansfield."

"I live around the corner from there. Please be my guest for the rest of your stay."

With a mischievous smile, she reached for her luggage and walked with him to his claim area. "You could be my guest tonight."

"Sorry. Prior date. You must be exhausted, or I'd introduce you to Elly. She expects me to visit. Tomorrow, Bea is taking her to the in-laws for Christmas."

"I slept all the way across the Atlantic, and I would love to meet the niece I've heard so much about – and your sister. Do you think they'd mind my dropping in?"

"Not at all. Let's check you in, and I'll call them from the hotel." ….

☬☬☬

After a hug, Joe stood back on the platform as his roommate turned and boarded the train. It would take him four days to travel to Salinas, California, but Joe could sense how excited he was. For the first time in his life, Diego would be able to talk with his father about the war and what Don Carlos had gone through when he was Diego's age.

"Hey, amigo, don't crash the general's car! I need a lift when I get back."

"See you next year, roomie."

At the entrance to the station, his grandfather was leaning on his car, reading a newspaper.

"Ready for the test?"

"I think so. Once I got used to the response and not needing to lean into curves, it's been easy. Thanks for the tips about sighting over the hood ornament to the curb. That wasn't in any of the driver's ed literature."

"You're welcome." He tossed Joe the keys and got in on the passenger's side. "Your appointment at the DMV is at eleven, isn't it?"

"Yes, sir."

Two hours later, they came home for a late lunch, the ink still wet on Joe's paper temporary license. He would receive the laminated, permanent license in the mail after Christmas.

"*Notre fille nous ha appelés, mon cher.*" Our daughter called, dear. Annabelle kissed her husband on the porch and continued in French. "She plans to do the sights in New York for a couple of days."

"That's good," the general said. "What's it been, twelve years she's been in Europe? What hotel is she at?"

"She was at the Mansfield when she called but would be staying with a friend after. A colleague who was in Rome."

"*Ça doit être Luke*," said Joe, winking at his grandparents. That must be Luke.

ଷଷଷ

Christmas Eve, light flurries started in the late afternoon. The Billingsley men were out securing the animals and checking on things that might need cover if the storm became any worse than predicted.

For the first time since she arrived, Sandra found herself indoors with her mother. Supper was cooking. The Christmas Vigil service wasn't until eleven thirty, but the family sextet needed to be there early to rehearse with the choir.

Mother and daughter took mugs of coffee up to the art studio, which had the best views in the house. They also liked being surrounded by Marcia's works in progress, the pictures that Sandra had left, and the biting aromas of paints and powders.

"This has been a wonderful vacation, Mom. When was the last time we had everyone home?"

"Last year – no, Walter was still in Vietnam. I guess Marty's senior year."

"Six years, then." Sandra looked around and sighed.

They sat in amicable silence for a while, watching the snowflakes accumulate on the muntins of the windowpanes. Later, the wind would rise and blow the windows clear.

"How's your Joe?"

"He's hardly mine, but he's doing well. The faculty at UVA were bowled over by his language skills, so they

135

moved him to upper-class courses. He'll be taking graduate courses in Italian next semester."

"Is he in Rome for the holidays?"

"No. Richmond, their hometown before. His grandparents kept the house and retired there. His mother is flying in to be with them."

"Sounds wonderful. Are you two serious?"

"Mom, we're close, but no one is making wedding plans. I mean, this is his first year, and I still need to finish GW."

Marcia started to say something but stopped. They stared at each other for a while.

"Do you have someone in Washington?"

"Yes. I have some good friends and classmates."

"Anyone special?"

Sandra forced down the urge to snap but couldn't keep it completely out of her voice.

"No one as much as Joe, but if you're worrying about me, my friends are as close as a call – and don't need a man in my apartment for security."

"I just want you to be happy —"

"I *am* happy. I'm happier than I've ever been. I'm taking fantastic classes, seeing the best art in the world, meeting famous scholars and artists, and learning all sorts of things. I love Washington." She caught her mother's concerned look. "And I don't want to settle down. Mom, I'm only nineteen, same as Joe. Why are you pushing me?"

Marcia's eyes widened slightly.

"I'm sorry, dear. I keep forgetting how young you are." She looked away and stared at the snow for a moment, then sighed. "I wasn't ready for anything at nineteen, and I wasn't even sure I was ready at twenty-three when your father proposed." She sipped her coffee and smiled at Sandra. "But you were always like this, so much more mature than your years. Forgive me."

Having been prepared for a knock-down-drag-out fight with her mother on this subject, Sandra's first reaction was a sense of deflation, then weightlessness as a crushing burden lifted.

"Nothing to forgive. Worrying about me is in your job description as a mother, isn't it?" They sipped their coffee. "I know you love me."

"The martial arts is a surprise. Seeing how Karen handles herself, it makes me feel better that you have those skills."

"I can handle it, Mom." She reached over and squeezed her mother's arm.

A loud crash downstairs signaled the return of the five men. Laughing, slamming, and the general ruckus of removing and stowing boots and coats and jackets rattled the quiet house. The two women rose and joined them.

❖❖❖

Christmas Eve, a light drizzle started in the morning, just heavy enough to cancel tennis at the University of Richmond courts. Just before noon, Mary Ardwood arrived in her MG. Just after lunch, Joe drove to the Broad Street station.

His hands trembled on the wheel, and his heart was in his throat most of the three miles to the station. Every other car looked like a Sherman tank or a Roman war chariot with metal-gouging blades protruding from the wheels. Twice, impatient drivers honked behind him, but he was not about to risk a speeding ticket on his temporary license.

After a blessedly uneventful trip, he found three open parking places together in the lot, so he could pull into the middle one easily. Locking the car, he walked to the stairs out front. A pair of familiar faces were standing under the overhang at the main entrance.

"Good morning, Officer Payne, Officer Tomkins." He greeted them cheerfully. "Merry Christmas to you."

"Same to you. Where's your driver?"

"Gone home to California. I have my own license now. Have a nice day."

They tipped their hands to their hats as he passed into the hall.

He was twenty minutes early, and the train was a half hour behind schedule. Looking around, he considered the variety of people who gathered in railroad stations. Families rich and poor, little children running from exasperated parents, two unkempt men sleeping on the benches, businessmen lined up for coffee or a newspaper, and elegant ladies chatting nearby.

For no reason, Tony Madison's advice, *always in training,* went through his mind.

A man crashed into his left side, someone just a little shorter but heavier than he. Instinctively, Joe grabbed the arm on his chest and twisted to pull the man through, snapping his arm backward as he fell over Joe's foot.

A woman shrieked somewhere.

A police whistle blew.

Without taking his gaze from the face of the man, Joe held the arm up, pressing his foot on the man's groin. "Don't move!" he hissed.

"What's going on here?" It was Office Payne. Joe glanced at him then looked back at the thief. The man was in his thirties or forties, clean-shaven, wearing a wool overcoat, dark suit, white shirt and a tie.

"Just a pickpocket, Officer Payne." He wiggled the thief's arm, then put his hand on the wallet in the man's hand, removed it, and gave it to the policeman. "Unfortunate enough to try to pick mine."

The man on the floor started to move. Joe pushed down with his foot.

"Hold still, you," he said. "These gentlemen may have some questions."

The two policemen reached from either side and lifted the man, then handcuffed him.

"Geordie Harris. Got you at last." Officer Tomkins turned to Joe. "We've known about this one for a long time, but he's been too slick to catch. You'll need to file charges at the station, sir."

"I'm here to meet my mother. Could I take her home first?"

"We can hold him for a while. Your ID, please."

Joe got out his Navy ID card. "Will this do?"

"Something with your address would be better." He smiled. "That license you just got?"

While Tomkins wrote down the particulars from the license, Payne got identifying information and addresses from a few witnesses, including the woman who screamed.

"It's Christmas Eve, Officer. What happens to him?"

"Probably spend it in jail. The magistrate won't be back until after the holiday."

Joe looked at the man for a while. Harris stared at the floor.

"Do you have a family, Mister Harris?"

After a long silence, Harris nodded.

"Whose Christmas is going to be ruined when you don't show up?" Joe stepped a little closer. Harris smelled of Old Spice and fear. Tears welled in his eyes.

"My wife and daughters."

"Names and ages, please."

"Agnes, twenty-nine. Mary, five, Genevieve three."

"Do they know about this enterprise of yours?"

"No."

Joe thought as he looked from one policeman to the other then Harris.

"I have an idea: I take your address. You will go to the station and turn yourself in the day after Christmas. When I report the attempted theft, I'll make note that I did not lose my property and that you kept your promise."

"You can't do that, Mister –er, Lockhart."

"Sure, I can. You don't have a case unless I file charges. I want this man's family to have Christmas with him, but I also want him to show us that he can keep his word. What do you say, Mister Harris?"

Harris looked at the three of them, then scowled.

"Why should I do this?"

"Simple. You love them. Am I right?" The man nodded again. "Good. You saw how I brought you down. How often does a mark do that to you?"

Harris looked down and mumbled.

"Excuse me, could you repeat that?"

"First time."

"Told you he was slippery," said Tomkins.

"Guess what, Mister Harris." The pickpocket arched his eyebrows in question. "I have at least three friends who are faster and stronger than I am. One of them is a girl. If you don't show up on the twenty-sixth to turn yourself in, we'll come get you."

"Mister Lockhart, you can't threaten him."

"Not a threat. Just an offer of free transportation." Joe said to the pickpocket, "Of course, if you appear on your own, you get my character reference. If we must bring you to the station, you may be enjoying the hospitality of the City of Richmond for a while. Am I clear?"

The four men stood facing each other while Harris pondered the deal.

"I accept. Will these two let me go?"

"What do you say, officers? Shall we give the Harris family Christmas together?"

They gave Joe the address and phone number, then unlocked the handcuffs.

"Merry Christmas, Mister Harris."

"Thank you, Mister Lockhart. Merry Christmas to you too."

The loudspeaker announced the arrival of the train from Washington on Track Two.

"I hope you don't mind. My mother is coming in."

"Go ahead. I wonder if Geordie'll show up."

"If someone needs to remind him on the morning of the twenty-sixth, tell him it's better than trying to run from my friends: a street fighter, a federal investigator, and a Force Recon Marine. They *will* find him. Merry Christmas, again."

"Merry Christmas, Mister Lockhart." As the two policemen walked away, Joe overheard them expressing relief that they wouldn't be late to clock off their shift. He smiled to himself as he followed the signs for Track Two.

&&&

Nancy looked past the rain streaking the windows of the coach, taking in the familiar countryside. So much had changed in Washington and New York, but the rolling horse country south of Fairfax was exactly as she remembered it, traveling the other way twelve years earlier.

Then, her grieving heart was still broken. Jason had died of a wasting disease in only six months after returning from French Equatorial Africa. She had spent most of the trip northbound holding their young son in her lap, comforting his tears and anxiously listening to his long silences.

This time she was still basking in the warmth of a romantic interlude in Manhattan. They had not waited to make love the first afternoon as soon as she checked into the Mansfield Hotel. That night, she met Bea and Elly and had her suspicions confirmed about the precocious teenager and her strong mother. Luke's sister was an emergency room nurse and had seen it all.

Elly had to grow up quickly after her father died in a gangland crossfire on his way to pick up pizza. She was as much support for her mother as the other way around. And she adored her uncle Luke.

The second day, Bea and Elly drove to upstate New York to be with Elly's paternal grandparents until Luke would join them on Christmas Eve. Nancy and Luke had risen late each day, visited the newest exhibition at the Metropolitan Museum, and taken in both an opera and a Broadway show. Neither had enjoyed this much free time in many years.

With her book unread on her lap, she looked out at the scenery, recognizing the familiar places and day-dreaming about Luke.

As the train passed Ashland, her thoughts turned to her family. She could not imagine her father and mother much changed, but Dad *was* retired now. Aunt Mary could not have aged; she was a rock.

Joe must be different. She could hear it on the phone and read it in the writing style of his letters. More confidence, more maturity. He thought before speaking, and he had surprising things to say when he did. Knowing that he was still seeing Sandra, she wondered if that relationship was still flourishing as it had in Rome.

It made Nancy shake her head now and again that Sandra was the same age as Joe. *Was she graduating this year or next?*

The conductor walked down the aisle, calling out the stop for Richmond. Nancy stood and gathered her suitcase from the rack above her. She waited at the door as the train slowed.

She paused to scan for a familiar face but saw no one she knew. That left her a little uneasy as she descended to the platform and moved with the flow toward the doors to the hall.

"Hi, Mom!" A voice behind her. She whirled around.

"Joe! Where were you?"

"At the foot of the ladder, but you looked out over the crowd."

They hugged until it became clear that they were blocking traffic. He picked up her valise. She unfurled her umbrella before they stepped out.

"You want to drive?" he asked as he unlocked the passenger door. "This is my first time driving alone."

"This battlewagon? Are you kidding?"

"Oh yeah. Bigger than the Fiat, isn't it?"

"If you got here in one piece, I'll take my chances with you going back." She let herself into the passenger seat. He got in the other side and checked the dashboard and controls.

"Okay, but I'm a nervous wreck." He smiled weakly and started the car.

Another mercifully uneventful three miles. Joe sighed when he set the parking brake behind Mary's MG.

"Welcome home, Mom."

"Yes, it is. The flat in Rome hasn't felt like home since you left."

They got out in the drizzle. He reached into the back seat for her suitcase while Nancy went to the porch. Nancy paused to admire her parents and aunt, then ran into her mother's arms. Joe's throat tightened as he watched them take turns hugging her. Seeing tears in everyone's eyes, he let his go too.

"Come in, everyone. It's not getting any warmer out here." Matthew held the door for the ladies. As Joe walked past him, he tapped the suitcase. "Put it in your old room."

When Joe came back down, the women sat in the living room, and the general was filling glasses with Moselle. He looked inquiringly at Joe, who said, "Yes, please." His grandfather poured another glass.

"You are looking better than when you left, dear." He nodded at his grandson. "And you did a great job with this one. How do you feel?"

"Wonderful, now that I'm home." Nancy looked at the expectant faces. "What do you want to know first?"

"You don't write much about Luke," said Mary, "but it wasn't hard to read between the lines. Is he more than a satisfactory tennis partner?"

"Yes. We share a distaste for phonies, so we make a good match. Neither of us needs or wants anything from the other. It should be obvious that he and Joe helped me finally complete my grieving over Jason."

"For that, I will always be grateful to him, even if I haven't met him," said her father.

"Any chance of that?" asked Annabelle.

"He's with his sister and niece for Christmas. And who knows where I'll be next year?"

"Thinking of a transfer?" asked Mary.

"Probably. The hate campaign in Italy has gotten ugly, as you know, but what I was not expecting was how empty the flat is without Joe and Angela. Before I leave, I'll make the rounds at Smithson and other places."

"Don't you have friends in Rome?"

"Yes, but they are almost all associated with work. I would be involved with them even if I came back to the States."

"What about that tennis pro at the Cavalieri Hilton?" Joe grinned at her.

Nancy swatted his knee. "Stop it! He's only a couple of years older than you." She smiled. "He probably would love to pick up an American widow for the green card, wouldn't he?"

"I don't know what you are doing with my room, now that I'm not there!"

"Just because you're in the Navy, you don't have to talk like a sailor. The Red Brigades are already working overtime to ruin my reputation."

Mention of the left-wing group cut off the hilarity. They sat silently for a moment.

"Can you talk about that?" asked her father.

Nancy took a sip of her wine. "It's not easy, and we have time over the holiday to get into it."

"You're right. No rush."

"Are we going to the Christmas Vigil this year?" she asked.

"*Bien sûr, ma fille*," said Annabelle. "Some things have not changed."

"Still at eleven thirty, then?"

"*Oui*. And presents afterward."

"I forgot to ask about church," Joe said. "Where do we go?"

"Saint Stephen's. Only two blocks from here."

Nancy caught Joe's look of slight embarrassment. "Aren't you going to Saint Paul's in Charlottesville now?"

"Yes, but…"

"You never knew because it never came up." She put her hand on his knee. "Your father was the Catholic. I signed a promise to raise you Roman Catholic when we married."

"And you?"

"Episcopalian. And, no, I did not need to convert. I was baptized and confirmed in Saint Stephen's."

Joe let out a long breath. "You know, Mom, this is a relief. With the changes, Diego and I are more comfortable at Saint Paul's. Why did I think you were Catholic too?"

"I am, dear. Remember what Father Pat called the Episcopalians at Saint Paul's-within-the-Walls?"

"*Cattolici di rito inglese.*" Catholics of the English rite.

"Few Americans here understand that, but to the Church in Rome, we aren't a different Church."

"So many attitudes are different here. I'm still getting used to it."

"How is that going?"

Joe shrugged. "Most of my white classmates shun me, but I don't care. Guys like Tony and Diego see the whole picture, so I think I can learn more from them."

The oven timer rang. The family took their glasses to the kitchen. Putting out dinner was a team effort. They ate early, but still, they finished the dishes barely in time to change and go to church.

14. LADIES AND UNICORNS

ON A RARE SUNNY DAY in late January, Sandra rode her bicycle to the National Mall. As she turned away from the FBI Headquarters building on Pennsylvania Avenue to go down Ninth Street, she saw a familiar figure on the sidewalk by the Department of Justice. She came to a stop before him and jumped onto the sidewalk.

"Agent Redwood!"

Her former boss in Rome came over to shake her hand. "Sandra! What a pleasant surprise! I was going to look you up next week after we settle in."

"Thank you for the Christmas card, sir. The note didn't say that you were coming to DC."

"We didn't know. We were going to Austin, but at the last minute, they wanted me here for Special Projects. It was so sudden that we are renting downtown to let our tenants finish out the lease."

"How are Mrs. Redwood and Doug?"

"Doug's playing basketball at Villanova, and Arlene is delighted to be back with the NSO." National Symphony Orchestra.

"You are probably going somewhere just now, but may I stop by sometime?"

"Please do. Here." After writing his home number and address on the back of a business card, he handed it to her. They shook hands again, and he walked into the FBI building.

Checking carefully, Sandra fed into the traffic on Ninth Street and rode to the National Gallery of Art. Knowing that she would be there all day, she locked her bicycle to a parking sign behind the NGA before walking in.

For her term paper on the development of art criticism, she wanted to check out sixteenth-century paintings from central Italy in the regular collection. There were some pictures that the art historian Giorgio Vasari wrote about during the Renaissance.

Most of all, she was there for the first day of the exhibition on loan from the Borghese Museum. The magnificent building in Rome's vast central park had been almost a home away from home for her.

After taking notes in the Italian Medieval and Renaissance sections, she went out to the sidewalk for lunch at one of the food carts. In another two months, the Mall would teem with tourists and tour buses, but today, Sandra was alone with a glorious view of the Washington Monument and the Lincoln Memorial. Soaking in the sunshine, she swung on a heavy chain between two bollards, eating her hot dog.

The only thing to make the day more perfect would be a Vespa ride behind Joe. Or maybe his arms around her as she drove the scooter. She smiled to herself, thinking of him.

The National Gallery felt dark after the brilliant sunshine. As her eyes adjusted, she walked to the exhibition in the East Wing. Natural sunlight abounded, but the high windows prevented any wall from receiving damaging direct sun. Sandra paused at each room to take in the pleasure of seeing so many old friends. Paintings by Titian, Bernini, Caravaggio, Reubens, Correggio and Raffaello adorned the walls.

After the first room (Bernini, Titian and Caravaggio), she scribbled a few reminders in her notebook. She didn't need to take full notes with these pictures. She had done that in Rome.

Moving into the next room, she paused briefly at the *Deposition of Christ* by Pieter Paul Reubens, then at the *Danaë* of Correggio.

She saved the *Lady with a Unicorn* by Raffaello Sanzio for last. The gaze on this bride had always fascinated Sandra. In her mind, she pictured the girl maturing into a Florentine noblewoman, navigating her patriarchal world with the power of those same eyes. Taking a seat on the bench, she quietly enjoyed her daydream for a while.

The shadows lengthened on the wall. With a sigh, she rose and turned toward the exit. At the door to the first room, she stopped.

No! It can't be! Wheeling around, she walked back to the Raffaello in the second room. She looked from a distance, and she stood close. She sniffed, attracting the attention of the guard at the door.

"Please don't touch, miss."

"Of course not. Could you tell me just where the exhibition came from?"

"You'd have to ask the curator, but he will have gone home by now."

"Thank you. I can do that."

"I think it was in London before here, but Dr. Morgen will have that information for sure."

"Thanks." With a final glance, Sandra counted details, then walked to the lobby. She took some notes, lest she forget something. After unlocking her bicycle, she rode to her apartment near Dupont Circle.

It was dark by the time she got home. Once again, she was grateful not to be walking by the bushes in the circle. The traffic did not bother her, being so much lighter and more disciplined than in Rome.

She picked up the telephone to call Agent Redwood's house, then stopped. *I should let this percolate until tomorrow. The painting won't go anywhere, and this is something he'd rather hear about in the office.*

After taking fuller notes about what she had seen, she assembled a big salad and baked a filet of frozen fish for supper. She washed the dishes and made sure that she had done all the assignments for the next day (she had). Then she outlined the term paper connecting the sixteenth-century paintings at the NGA with Vasari's opinions of them.

ଷଷଷ

"FBI Special Projects Division. How may I direct your call?"

"Special Agent Redwood, please."

"Whom may I say is calling?"

"Sandra Billingsley." She expected a long wait, but her former boss came on the line almost immediately.

"What a pleasant surprise! You didn't have to call so soon."

"I wasn't going to, but something came up after I saw you."

"Are you alright?"

"Yes, sir, I'm fine, but I stumbled on something, and I need advice about where to turn."

"Uh-oh, isn't that what your boyfriend said last year when he first walked into our office?" She took in a slight gasp, but the pause told her he was smiling.

"I hope nothing that dangerous. May I show you my notes?"

"Sure. When would you like to come?"

"I have classes this morning, but I'm free this afternoon. What about after lunch?"

"What about lunch too? Now that you're not in my office, I could treat. I certainly owe you for your work in Rome."

"Well, okay."

"Are you on that bike I saw yesterday?"

"Yes, sir."

"Let's meet outside the Ninth Street entrance to the FBI Building. We can lock it in the courtyard. Would twelve thirty be convenient?"

"Perfect. See you then."

After they hung up, Sandra let out a long sigh. Grabbing her book bag, she locked the apartment and walked briskly to her art history class.

ଷଷଷ

Special Agent Redwood was waiting as promised. They walked to an Italian restaurant nearby.

"If you specify *al dente,* they won't overcook the pasta," he said.

They each ordered *bucatini all'amatriciana*. The only red wine was a Chianti, so Sandra had water, and her former boss had a Coca-Cola.

"Not a fan of Chianti?"

"Too acidic. I think it must not travel well because even as close as Florence was, I thought it was turning."

"Frascati does that too," he said. "You have a refined palate."

"Not really, sir. With the reasonable prices for everything in Rome, I could try different wines. I settled on what I like."

They caught up on the past year during lunch. He was pleased that she was still in contact with Joe. She was delighted that he was in DC.

"Having you two nearby makes up for having to work at Headquarters," he said.

"That bad? I always wondered what you were like in the field or in an office with more people."

"The agents are fine, and I've never served anywhere that Arlene and I did not enjoy. But the bureaucracy here would make the Roman Curia cringe." She laughed at that. "Politics and red tape everywhere. What a mix."

"You're not encouraging me to be an agent," she said, grinning.

"From what I learned about you, young lady, I don't think this old codger's whining is going to discourage you."

"Why check on me?"

"At first, to find out where you were and how you're doing. Moseley would be one depressed drill sergeant if he didn't go home laughing almost every Saturday after watching you beat up your classmates." Sandra blushed. "He said that you're having way too much fun in his class."

"Why depressed?"

"He's supposed to breaking you all, making it tough. Instead of crying, they critique each other on what happened sparring with you."

"What did they expect? Sergeant Mosely pointed me to the dojo in Georgetown, and his friend Sarge Robinson works with me three times a week."

"He didn't explain that. Now I understand. Are you happy?"

"Yes, I am. It doesn't matter what happens to me next summer. Stuff me in a typing pool here at Headquarters. I won't care. This training taught me more about myself than I ever knew."

"That you enjoy beating up guys?"

"No. I could do that back home with my brothers. This is different. I'll be ready. Just knowing that I could be called to put on a badge is very satisfying."

"Good attitude, especially since we can't promise you a billet – yet."

"The delay gives me time to finish school, and the Bureau may need me for something else in the meantime. Like Joe and his translating."

"Speaking of that, do you want to tell me about what came up yesterday?"

"Could we do that somewhere else?" She looked around. He waved for the bill.

In Rome, Redwood had enjoyed a beautiful office in a palazzo, and Sandra had reigned over a generous reception area. In DC, he worked in a cubicle. The outside corner was a concession to his seniority, giving him more room, two windows and no traffic past his space. On their way, they stopped by the break room for mugs of coffee.

"Have a seat," he said, waving to the chair as he went around the desk. He set out a coaster for her drink.

"What does Special Projects do, sir, if I may ask?"

"You may, and I'm not sure. It seems that we get any buck they can't pass to a division with less political pull, but I'm just letting my attitude show. We *are* a catchall. If it doesn't have its own line item in the budget, if no one wants it, or if the brass doesn't want to touch it, we get it."

"Like my program?"

He put his finger to his lips. "Not here. Not anywhere in this building."

"Sorry."

"You're lucky. I'm one of only three people at Headquarters who know." He sipped his coffee. "What do you have for me?"

"It might be another project for you. At least I can't guess who would handle it. You know I'm an art history major, right?" He nodded.

"And accounting and a couple of languages. You poured it on when you got back."

"Trying to catch up. Anyway, I spent a fair amount of time at the Borghese Gallery."

"That's where we took the IACP delegation when they came to the Interpol conference." International Association of Chiefs of Police.

"It was my favorite museum. A traveling exhibit called the Best of the Borghese just opened at the National Gallery. I was going there when we met yesterday."

"Something you saw troubles you."

"Yes, the *Lady with a Unicorn* by Raffaello. I don't have the credentials to criticize the art experts handling the tour, but either the painting hanging in Rome last year or the one in the National Gallery here may be a forgery."

They looked at each other for a while.

"Serious."

"Even if I'm wrong, I can't not report it. Where do I go with this information?"

"What makes you think it's a forgery?"

"I didn't say it was. I spent hours loving that painting. I studied every detail of it."

She took her notebook from her bag. "It seems to me that the lady here does not have as many loose, fine hairs as the one in Rome. The unicorn's head tilts ever so slightly to the right so that there is less daylight between the tip of the horn and her shoulder than the picture in Rome, and the left eye has more definition. The fur on the animal here is more articulated and detailed."

She stopped.

"Is there more?"

"I can't date a painting, and the original underwent two in-depth restorations in the twentieth century. I think two colors are off. The silk on her bodice is different, but I'm not sure how. The red of the sleeves is not quite the shade I remember. In Rome, I thought it had more of a burgundy tone. I wonder if one of the two paintings was not done in 1505."

"Impressive. I always admired your attention to detail, but I never appreciated how strong it is. A powerful gift for an investigator."

"Don't get my hopes up, sir." He nodded and returned her smile.

"You're right. This would be the place for something like this coming into Headquarters, and I can pass this to the right people." Sandra sat up straight. She took a pen out of her bag. "No need to write it down. Remember Bob Worthman?"

"The SAC in New York?" Special Agent in Charge.

"Yes. His office includes the Art Crimes Division, whose mission is investigating thefts and forgeries. This is right up their alley."

"What if I'm wrong?"

"They pay us to investigate. They don't dock our salaries if nothing comes of it. I'll call Bob." He opened a three-ring binder and found the organizational chart of the New York Field Office. "He should ring me back, but there are two agents in Art Crimes: Charley Spears and David Vasari."

"Vasari? You're kidding."

"No. And his family emigrated from Arezzo."

"Will they call me, or should I call them?"

"They'll contact you. I imagine one of them will come here to let you show him what you found. They may or may not call me first, so I can give you a heads-up."

"I'll be ready, then. I think I know how Joe felt last year, but I was on the inside then."

Agent Redwood smiled broadly. "By the way, Arlene was talking about having you to dinner soon. Would you prefer a weekend or a weekday?"

"I don't have classes Monday or Thursday mornings, so Sunday or Wednesday evening would work best if it's the same to you."

"I'll check with her and call you." He stood.

"Thank you, sir. Great to see you again."

"Likewise. Be safe out there."

At the exit, Sandra turned in her visitor's badge, waved to her old boss, and walked to her bike. Plenty of time to do her weekend homework and sleep before Quantico training tomorrow.

15. VASARI

ON A TUESDAY in late February, the phone rang as Sandra let herself into her apartment. She dropped her bag and picked up the handset.

"Miss Billingsley?" The man had a smooth baritone voice. Sandra imagined it singing an aria by Verdi or Handel.

"Yes?"

"This is Special Agent David Vasari from New York."

"Agent Redwood told me you might call. You were lucky to catch me at lunch between classes."

"I'm glad. I'd like to talk to you and look at the painting before we go any further with this."

"Of course. My last class today ends at two thirty. I can meet you at three almost anywhere."

"Headquarters is a short walk from the Gallery. Let's use one of the meeting rooms."

"Okay. I'll lock my bike by the south entrance."

"I'll be there."

Locking her bicycle to a heavy chain, Sandra had no trouble identifying the man waiting outside the door. Unlike most agents she had seen, Vasari did not have a crew cut or black-rimmed glasses. Aquiline nose, high cheekbones and forehead, and black, curly hair that was beginning to take a widow's peak shape.

There's proof old Giorgio had children, she thought. *I don't care what the official biographies say.*

"Miss Billingsley?" Vasari approached with his hand extended and a broad smile. Sandra smiled and shook hands. "I arranged to use the conference room next to Special Projects. Are you familiar with it?"

"Yes." After showing her driver's license to the security guard at the counter, she took the visitor's badge and clipped it to her belt.

On the next floor upstairs, the meeting room was empty. The FBI agent had left a vacuum carafe of coffee and a pair of mugs on a tray by his briefcase. He poured while Sandra took out her notebooks.

"I read Redwood's report on your meeting," he said. "He also shared some of your personnel file, so I understand why he was so quick to refer the case to us."

"I knew he'd know who to call."

"Who else knows about this?"

"No one. I meant to ask the curator about it today, but you called first."

"I'm glad you didn't. We will need to check out all the people involved if it appears one or the other is a forgery." Sandra nodded her understanding. "Why did you pick out the Raffaello?"

"Ever since I saw it in one of my mother's art history textbooks, it's been my favorite. I spent hours in the Borghese each week. On my way out, I would always walk up to the room with the *Dama con Liocorno* to spend some time with her. It was her gaze, mainly. I imagined entire worlds and lifetimes unfolding before her from the time she sat for the painting."

His expression during the silence told her that he understood deeply.

"Do you have a background in forgeries?"

"Only the copies we made for class, "she said. "Not very good ones, I'm afraid." He chuckled. "I subscribe to *Forensic Science*, which often runs an article on forgers' techniques."

"Criminal justice major?"

"No. Art history."

"Agent Redwood couldn't write down everything. Mind taking me through this again?"

Sandra repeated her story, adding that she looked up the painting in the encyclopedia, but the illustration was not of high enough quality.

"When did you last see the painting in Rome?"

"About eighteen months ago now, August before last."

"After all this time, you can still recall these details?"

"I'm not swearing to my recollection, but I did spend a lot of time with it. Think of seeing something different in the face of a parent or sibling. I could as easily tell you that my mother's stylist had changed the brand of hair color she was using."

"I get it." He reached into the briefcase. "Here are some professional photographs of the *Unicorn*. Some are copies." He laid them in a line. "Can you pick out the one from Rome?"

Without looking, Sandra asked, "Is the one at the National Gallery here?"

"No. One was taken two years ago in Rome, when you were there. One is the placeholder at the Borghese during the tour, enlarged so the prints would all be the same size. The other two are paintings confiscated from art collectors."

She moved to the end of the table to put the light from the window over her shoulder and slid the photos with her. With her hands behind her back, she bent over each one in turn.

"The second one is the original. The fourth one is the placeholder; the definition is fuzzier."

"Are you sure?"

"Yes. You did say two were confiscated from collectors, didn't you?"

"That's right. Why?"

"They look to me like they were done by the same forger."

Vasari took the photos and looked closely at them. "Sonofabitch – sorry." He flipped them over and wrote furiously in his notebook.

"Something wrong?"

"No – I mean, yes. Oversight. Two years and four thousand miles separated the two cases. One was in Munich; the other in New York."

"A lab analysis could clear it up one way or the other."

"At the time, each jurisdiction had their labs compare their confiscated painting with the original, not being aware of the other forgery."

"There's the one I saw in Rome," Sandra pointed to the second one. "For what it's worth, I recognized it before I noticed the similarities between one and three."

"Redwood said you were good, but this is amazing." Vasari's admiration glowed on his face.

She blushed. "I did spend a lot of time with the *Dama.* I'm not so special."

"Shall we walk over to the Gallery?" They packed up their respective papers and left.

In the exhibit room, Sandra indicated the *Lady with a Unicorn*, centered on its wall. "I went over and —" Vasari raised his hand.

"Let me get a first impression."

"Of course. Sorry." She stood in the center of the room while the FBI agent went through the same routine as she, attracting the same attention.

"Please don't touch, sir." The guard glanced at Sandra as he warned Vasari. The investigator stepped back.

"Thank you. It's encouraging to see someone care about their work so much." The guard shrugged. Vasari motioned her over. "She and I are in an art history class studying this very painting. We need to take a close look and compare it to some photos from catalogs about it. May we?"

"Just don't touch." He went back to his position on the opposite wall, where he could watch the entire room.

"Can you show me what you were explaining?" Vasari said in a low voice.

Pointing from far enough not to worry the guard, she showed him the hairs, the space behind the unicorn's ear and the arm of the lady's gown. When she finished, he took out the photographs.

"You've got something here."

"Are you confident about the quality of the photo?"

"Maybe the hue of the sleeve is off, but look at the definition of the hairs and the background of the unicorn. I'm convinced. Let's go."

Sandra took his arm. "Let's check the Rubens on the way out," she said, loud enough for the guard to hear. "I wrote my paper, but I want to see it in the afternoon lighting."

"Let's do that." They both smiled and thanked the guard. He returned the smile and wished them a good day.

Crossing Constitution Avenue, Vasari said, "Quick thinking, giving him something else to go on."

"Joe gave me the idea."

"Your boyfriend?"

Sandra nodded.

"I thought you didn't tell anyone about this."

"I didn't. While helping us in Rome, he made sure everyone around him, including his mother, thought he was working on a summer homework project in the library downstairs."

They stopped at the south entrance of the FBI headquarters building. "I think I have everything I need to open a case on this," said Vasari. "I'll be back, and I want to keep you in the loop."

"I'm only an undergraduate, hardly an art expert."

"With a sharper eye than most experts. We could use you on our team."

"Thanks. You have my number. I'd like to help."

They shook hands. She admired his broad shoulders as he walked away, then unlocked her bicycle and rode back to her apartment.

ଓଓଓ

The following Monday evening, the phone rang as Sandra was putting some penne in boiling water. It was Vasari.

"News already?"

"Yes. I'll be coming to DC to interview some people, and I'd like to see you again." The pause and the drop in his voice gave her an unexpected thrill.

"Headquarters again?"

"No. We'd rather not have you too close to the case publicly, not knowing where this will take us."

"I understand."

"Besides, Jim Redwood told me of an Italian place in Northwest I should try. Can we do this over dinner?" Sandra looked over at the stove.

"Too bad you didn't call yesterday. I'm making *penne all'arrabbiata* tonight." They chuckled. "Sure. I'll order something else. When and where?"

"I'll be there tomorrow, and I only have two meetings scheduled. Do you know the Scoglio restaurant near Dupont Circle?"

"Yes. It's two blocks from here."

"How about six thirty there? I can fill you in on the two interviews and what else we found out."

"This seems strange, like you're reporting to me."

"I told you I'd keep you in the loop, but I also would like your help."

"All right."

"Thanks. I'm looking forward to seeing you again."

"Me too. See you tomorrow."

The pasta was al dente. She turned off the flames under the water and the simmering sauce and assembled her feast for one. Pouring herself a red Aglianico, she placed a glass upside down across from her place at the kitchen table.

Once a week, she fixed a Roman meal to remember the dinners she had prepared with Joe in Rome before she had returned. She had enjoyed those nights at her apartment on the Via della Giuliana more than the dates to movies or clubs.

As she ate, she considered the dark-haired agent from New York. *Well, not New York,* she thought. *Arezzo.* It pleased her immensely to meet someone in the FBI who understood the kinds of things she found fascinating. That he might want her on the art crimes team was music she dared not listen for.

When she applied for the Quantico program, she expected a long apprenticeship in small field offices as the "token girl." It excited her to look forward to helping David on such a relevant project while she was still in training. His apparent interest in her didn't hurt, either.

As she was drying the dishes, the phone rang again.

"*Ciao, bella, come stai?*"

"*Benissimo. Ho tanto da raccontarti.*" Excellent. I have so much to tell you. They continued in Italian because they enjoyed it.

"I can't wait for spring break. What's happening?"

"I'm involved in a new project for the Bureau. I don't know how much I can tell you, but what I can, I'll share when you get here. Do you have midterms this week?"

"Next week."

"Me too. Are you still enjoying accounting?"

"Yes. Such a new way of looking at things. Is second-semester cost accounting better than business law?"

"Much better, thank you. You'll never guess what happened to White."

"Well?"

"We got a new dean: Marjorie Cummings. He retired over Christmas."

"No one misses him, I imagine – Gotta go. A line is forming."

"Thanks for calling. Love you."

"Love you too."

As she put the last pan away, the Moka Express coffee maker gurgled and spat. She turned off the flame and took her espresso into the living room, where her books were. She felt like a very lucky woman tonight.

ଷଷଷ

The next afternoon, Sandra ran to her apartment from her self-defense class. She could have suggested seven for the meeting with David (*was it a date too?*), but she knew she had time. The run counted as a cooldown after the drills.

An hour and a half later, she turned at O Street and crossed to the restaurant. David was standing outside. He wore a royal blue sport coat and a burgundy turtleneck. Sandra thought the outfit looked tailored. It certainly followed his physique nicely.

"Are you allowed to talk business without your gray suit?"

He laughed. "Only after six p.m. Are you hungry?"

"This would be the wrong place if I weren't. How about you?"

"Famished. The first meeting ran into the afternoon, so I missed lunch. Shall we?"

As he turned toward the door, she took his arm. David had asked for a table against the far wall from the door, where they could talk securely. They ordered a bottle of S. Pellegrino mineral water.

"Your file says you're from London, Ohio," he said as he opened his menu. "I was stationed in Columbus for a while. We used to toss coins with the Springfield office to see who would respond to cases in Madison County. Did you live in town?"

"Almost. A small farm off Highway 38 north."

"You don't fit the profile for an Ohio farm girl, I think."

"You haven't seen me milk the cows and slop the hogs." She smiled as he laughed. "Seriously, I'm the first one who can say she grew up on the farm. I was twelve when Dad retired from the Army and bought the place."

"Aha! Where were you before?"

"I vaguely remember Stuttgart when I was really small, but then we came here to DC."

The waiter came to take their orders. David ordered the *bucatini* and Sandra the *zuppa di pesce.*

"Do we order a bottle of white since you're having fish soup?" he asked, holding the wine list. She took it from him and glanced quickly at the list.

"No, thanks. I prefer red, which works well with your pasta. How about the Primitivo?"

"Fine."

The server collected their menus and the wine list and vanished.

"This is the first time no one made me pick the wine." He smiled. "Everyone thinks I should know all about wines, being Italian, but I don't have a clue."

"And because you're a man, right?"

"That too."

The waiter returned and showed the bottle to David, who nodded to Sandra. Surprise flashed on the waiter's face for only a second. He turned to the young woman, who let him pour the sample. She checked the color, sniffed and slurped the wine gently before rolling it around in her mouth.

"*Andrà bene, grazie.*" It will do well, thanks. She pointed to the middle of the table. He set the open bottle there to chamber and left.

"I'm impressed, but I think he was stunned."

Sandra shrugged. "Part of the ritual I learned in Rome at the better restaurants. At the trattorias, they plop the local *vino sfuso* in front of you." Bulk wine. She sipped her water. "How about you? How far removed from Arezzo are you?"

"My parents came over before the war. My mother taught art, and my father was a conservator. Being Jewish was not fashionable at the time." Sandra nodded. "After selling their house and things to Gentile families, they settled in Brooklyn."

"My mother teaches art at London High School."

"So, this runs in the family for both of us."

"Why the FBI?"

"I was training to follow my father. He worked for the Metropolitan Museum. I was fascinated by the forgeries we discovered and how the agents would quiz us and rely on us to help them chase down the forgers. I was Security Battalion in the marines – the military police – so when my enlistment was up, I applied to the FBI, and here I am."

Sandra held up her glass. David poured for them and took a sip. "It tastes good to me. Is it really?"

"Yes. It's fine, what I expected."

"I am going to enjoy getting to know you. I like the way you take charge."

"Shrinking violets get stomped on in a house with five boys."

"Five?"

"Dad got more eye rolls from Mom than we did."

The soup and the pasta came in reasonable portions, so they ordered a *secondo.* Over the roast lamb and greens, they chatted some more. David became animated as he described working in the conservation lab both as a teenager and later as a special agent. They discussed their favorite artists, which, no surprise, were mostly Italian Renaissance.

Sandra quizzed him on the techniques she had read about and about the official story of Vasari having no children.

"David, you are living proof Giorgio had offspring somewhere. You have seen his self-portrait, haven't you?"

"Yes. It feels weird."

"Does your family have any explanation?"

"We can trace it, but you won't find it in your textbooks."

"Tell me." She put her glass down and stared straight into his eyes. He blushed slightly.

"I've never met anyone who was so interested in my family tree."

"You are art history on the hoof. I'm fascinated. Please go on."

"Well, it turns out Giorgio did have several illegitimate children. We know about three boys and two girls; there may well have been more. He walked away from the other affairs, but he was particularly smitten with Ester, the daughter of a Jewish merchant. He recognized her son, Beniamino. The records were lost in a fire in the synagogue in 1634, but the surname stuck and continued through Beniamino Vasari's family."

"So, there is this whole branch of Jewish Vasari?"

"Not a rare name around Arezzo."

"Any more artists I should be looking into?"

He laughed. "Several of my ancestors worked in studios of well-known artists, but the clerical and lay patrons tended to commission Christian themes, and Jewish artists were somewhat suspect. Besides, there was a comfortable living to be had in finance and retail, as you can guess."

"Of course."

"When the paintings started needing maintenance and repair, we were there."

"Conservators."

"Yes, and copyists, and forgers." He smiled. "My father is a third-generation conservator, but I can't swear that his forebears didn't do a little freelancing."

"Ever uncover any?"

"Not yet, but wouldn't it be a hoot?"

"Imagine having to recuse yourself from the case of an eighteenth-century forger."

They waited until the fruit and cheese before turning to business.

"You called this meeting, David. Is there something I should know?"

He finished chewing a piece of apple with gorgonzola on it. "This is bigger than we expected, though we should not be surprised, considering the stakes."

"More than the *Unicorn*?"

"We think so, although it is the only one we are sure was stolen at this point."

"So, the one here is the forgery?"

"Yes. You were spot-on to notice it."

"What now?"

"We conduct very discrete interviews while pretending to investigate something else. Scotland Yard and Interpol are working with us because we think the switch took place on the way to or from London. Would you be willing to help us?"

"Sure. How?"

"The insurance companies naturally have detailed photographs taken of the paintings at every stop. We are assembling those prints now. Could you look at them?"

"Don't you have experts?"

"Sure, but I've never seen anyone with as keen an eye as yours, and, besides, asking them would tip our hand. Whoever is behind this isn't aware of you – I hope."

"I'm flattered. How do we do this?"

"We'd like you to come to New York, ostensibly to examine something at the Met or the Frick. Can you create a cover, for example, an assignment for one of your courses?"

"We have to propose a topic for a term paper due after spring break. I was going to pick something at the NGA, but I can choose something in New York or even the Brooklyn Museum. Would that do?"

"Perfect. The less I'm seen running around interviewing museum directors and curators outside New York, the better. I think Dr. Morgen and his boss were nervous wrecks today. Maybe they were overreacting to me, or they could be involved in this or something else."

"Ouch. How do you calm down someone who is terrified because the FBI is asking questions?" *I could have this problem someday.*

"It happens. I'll call them from the office and drop them a thank-you note for their help."

"I guess I can take a few days off from school, but we have midterms. I can't miss those. Also, I work weekends."

"This is important, but not urgent. You tell us when you can spare the time, and we'll set it up."

"Will someone reimburse me for the train and a place to stay?"

"Yes. I talked to Jim Redwood. Special Projects has a budget line for this. Give him the dates, and we'll make the arrangements."

"That's a relief. Thanks. That class meets tomorrow. I'll pick something and let him know."

David signaled for the check.

"May I walk you home? My hotel is on Dupont Circle."

"Yes, thank you." She excused herself to use the restroom while he paid the bill.

At the door to her building, he said, "I enjoyed this. I could take you out in New York, too, if you'd like."

"I would." She smiled. "Good night, David."

He waited until she walked up the stairs inside before turning toward his hotel. She sighed happily as she let herself into her apartment. *This is going to be so exciting.*

ହହହ

The next afternoon, Sandra called Special Projects from a pay phone outside her art history class.

"Thanks for calling." Jim Redwood's voice had a warm quality to it. She imagined he charmed the bad guys more than he terrified them during interrogations. "Arlene and I were wondering if Sunday evening would be convenient."

"Yes —"

"About the other thing, I'll be at the coffee shop on Dupont Circle later. Can you meet me there?"

Sandra took the hint. "Sure. About four? I'll be in sweats."

"See you there." He hung up.

After class, she changed into the sweat suit she wore in the winter at the dojo. Donning her insulated rain jacket, she walked to the corner.

"Hi, Darlene, just coffee."

"Are you sure you don't want some steak for the exercise?" Darlene slid the mug toward her.

"Maybe on the way back. I'm meeting someone now." Sandra carried her hot drink to a table against the back wall. Jim Redwood pushed through the door. She waved as he shook the rain off his coat and hung it up. He looked at Darlene, pointed to the table and Sandra's mug. She brought it while he sat.

"You probably guessed why I cut you off on the phone."

"Of course. I was using a pay phone. I guess the case has taken a turn."

"Not quite, but we are tightening security on several of our special projects because of the stakes involved. We can't exclude wiretaps and other surveillance from the kind of people we may be up against." He took a sip of the coffee. "Vasari said you would have some dates."

"With midterms, I either have to do it the coming week or after spring break."

"How about going up Monday and coming back Wednesday?"

"Those days would work. Should I make the reservations?"

"We'll do that. Nine o'clock out of Union Station and back on the midafternoon train Wednesday. The Bureau has a contract with the Watson Hotel next to the Federal Building. Vasari will give you the key."

"No one will ever know I was there."

"That's the idea. Can you find an excuse for skipping classes?"

"Cramming for exams. Not unusual, and I can do the actual studying on the train."

"About security, have you told anyone about your training on weekends?"

"Only Joe's family and Diego."

"Not Vasari?"

"I assumed you told him, but no. It didn't come up."

"I've told him you work for me, so you're a talented civilian as far as he and anyone outside your cohort is concerned."

"I understand. Joe is coming up after exams. How much can I tell him?"

"Nothing about this case, please."

"He's very observant, but I'll do my best."

"It's all any of us can do. If you need to talk, use a pay phone and call this number. It patches through a secure system instead of the regular telephone network."

"Like that phone in Rome?"

"Same kind of gear, but we operate it rather than the Army Signal Corps."

"I get it. I don't have to call Vasari, do I?"

"Nope. Unless something unexpected comes up, you won't be seeing him outside New York from now on. Don't call him."

"I have another crush, sir, and he's on a pay phone too." They chuckled.

Redwood picked up the tab and walked her out. She turned west on P Street; he went east toward Logan Circle.

16. Spring Break

PAUSING AT THE STEPS, Joe scanned the crowd on the platform. No Sandra.

"Move it, kid," groused the big man behind him.

"Sorry, sir. Looking for my party."

As he stepped down to the platform, a strong hand pulled him to the right. Sandra wrapped her arms around him and kissed him ferociously. Letting his duffel fall, he kissed her back and lifted her off the floor.

"I didn't see you."

"That's the idea." Her eyes twinkled. "Practicing my shadow skills. Besides, this gets us out of the crowd." She pointed to his bag. "Come on."

Forty-five minutes later, she let them into her home.

"Sorry, I don't have a guest room," she said coyly as she turned around. He put his bag on the ground. A long, lingering kiss prevented any reply, but neither of them needed to talk.

When they separated, he took in the one-bedroom apartment. The entrance fed directly to the living-dining room. There was a small kitchen to the right. The bedroom and bathroom were opposite the door. The main room held an upright piano, with her viola case on it, a small dining table, a music stand, and a sofa. A dresser served as a sideboard and held a small TV.

"Isn't this fantastic? Spring break all week, and I don't have to go to work until Saturday."

"Would you like lunch or something?" he asked as she took his coat and hung it in the closet.

"How about something first, then lunch." She grinned and untied his tie....

That afternoon, they went shopping for an Italian supper.

"Nothing like the Trionfale market here," Sandra said, "but if you don't mind walking a lot, we can find authentic ingredients at various small shops."

"I'd walk anywhere to be with you. Lead on." Arm-in-arm, they turned into the wind on Connecticut Avenue.

&&&

Joe stabbed a shell and held it to let the excess sauce fall off.

"You said that you are working for Agent Redwood at Special Projects." She nodded. "Tell me about it." She finished chewing and took a sip of the Montepulciano d'Abruzzo before answering.

"After I talked to you, security on the case went up. Agent Redwood ordered me not to tell you or anyone about it. In fact, if he needs to talk to me, I'll have to go to a pay phone to call him back. I hope that doesn't come up."

"I have a Secret clearance now."

"So do I, but I asked him about you, and he told me no. Sorry."

"I can deal with that. It will all come out someday."

"Probably." She tickled his shin with her toe. "I don't want to discuss work. I have to leave you all alone in the big city on Saturday as it is."

He smiled at her. When they finished the pasta, he served up the greens from the stove while she divided the roast pork and potatoes.

"I never eat this well or this much when you're not here," she said.

"Me, neither."

After supper, they did the dishes and took a walk to the end of New Hampshire Avenue. The trees along the sidewalks were trying to bud, but it was still cold at night. The wind had abated, so they were reasonably comfortable leaning on the railing at the Kennedy Center, looking at the Potomac River reflecting lights from both shores. Joe put his arm around her as she snuggled against his chest.

"Not as dramatic as the Tiber," she said, "but I have missed watching the river with you."

"Now I wish I had applied to GW instead."

"Virginia's a good school, and we don't have NROTC."

He sighed. "True, but I miss you so much."

"I miss you, too, but I'm terribly busy."

"Me too." He squeezed her. "Maybe these long separations are what deployments will be like."

"One way to look at it." As they turned away from the Potomac, she took his arm. "Between the Navy and the FBI, I think we'd better get used to this."

"I guess so. Let's make the times together count."

"Yes. Let's." She hugged him tighter as they quickened their pace back to the apartment....

The next day, Monday, they slept in late. The telephone got them out of bed.

"Hello... yes, sir... He is." With her hand over the microphone, she called out. "It's Agent Redwood. He'd like to see you."

"I was wondering if we would have a chance to do that."

Sandra put the handset back to her ear. "Yes, sir… I'll tell him." She hung up.

"Is he coming in a *pantera* police car to whisk me away without breakfast again?" Joe asked as he made the bed. She laughed.

"Not this time. He saw his notes on his desk calendar this morning that you would be here for spring break. He wants to call Arlene about having us over for supper, but for sure we can stop by his office today or tomorrow in the afternoon."

"Let's do it."

After breakfast, they walked to the shop where Sandra had bought her bicycle. Joe rented a ten-speed, so they would not have to depend on the erratic bus system or expensive taxis.

They rode to the exhibit at the National Gallery of Art. The pictures were familiar and nostalgic for him because he had used the Borghese for homework and class reports. Although the cherry blossoms were not out yet, there were enough tourists and sunny days for the food carts to patrol Constitution Avenue.

Fortified with a hot dog and soda, they visited the Smithsonian and the National Archives, which had been too crowded when he had passed through Washington the summer before. At three thirty, they locked their bikes outside FBI headquarters and checked in. Special Agent Redwood came down the hall while they were clipping on their visitor badges.

"Wonderful to see you two together," he said. "Arlene is excited too. Can you come over tomorrow night?"

Sandra and Joe exchanged glances. "Sure," she said. "Neither of us has classes the next day."

"I can pick you up."

"That won't be necessary, sir," she said. "We're almost neighbors." The Redwoods had rented a townhouse in Georgetown.

"Fine. Come upstairs now."

With mugs of coffee from the mess, they settled into Redwood's corner cubicle. They passed a pleasant half-hour catching up on their respective adventures since Joe had left Rome last August.

The FBI agent seemed interested in Joe's freelance translation business and that he was taking accounting.

"Are you thinking of the Bureau, finally?"

"No, sir. My friend Tony is, though. He also made me realize that I needed to put my translating on a more businesslike basis. I was basically giving it away."

"Smart. How do you like the Navy unit?"

"They're my best friends on Grounds. I could say my only friends, except for Tony. I made myself something of a pariah with my peers."

"How's that?"

"I'm worse than color-blind; I'm clueless. The whole race thing confuses and annoys me. I've been assaulted three times already, and I catch as many insults and epithets as my Negro classmates."

"Sorry about that."

Joe shrugged. "After the second attack, I finally took my CO's advice and started training in self-defense."

"According to his roommate, he's not bad now," said Sandra, with a sly smile. "I don't have to defend both sides of him."

They laughed. "I can imagine," said Redwood. "Pity any idiot that tries to cross you two tomorrow night." His expression darkened, and he gazed out the window for a while.

"Joe, we have been following the problems your mother and Smithson are having in Rome." Joe's surprise made him smile. "I still have my old contacts, and it happens that what's behind the attacks and the hate campaign comes under Special Projects." He winked at Sandra. "Like I said, if no one else wants it."

"Do you know who is behind this?"

"We do. That is why I wanted to talk to you while you were here."

"Mom told me it's the Communists and showed me one of the posters at Christmas. The explosive at the Aprilia plant was from a batch used in a car bomb at Camp Darby in Livorno."

"Yes, it was, but the campaign against Smithson is more personal than that. This is not coming from the Communists or the left-wing parties." He paused. "They're being played. Plenty of American businesspeople receive threats and worse, but no one receives the sustained stream of abuse that Nancy Lockhart has."

"But she's not at Aprilia."

"That bomb was placed the week after she made international headlines breaking ground on the new plant. The news was a total surprise to the business community and made her a star with the Chamber of Commerce and the Christian Democrats."

"Did you say this is personal?"

He paused for a sip of his coffee. "Did she mention anyone else getting threats or poster publicity like this?"

After thinking a moment, Joe said, "No. Just her."

"Because she's the only one. At the other companies, one person is never picked out."

"Why my mother?"

"We wondered the same thing."

"And?"

"Whose mother is she?"

"Mine. Why?"

"Who do we know in Italy has the resources and the smarts to organize something this big and let his enemies take the fall for it?" He sat back with his hands behind his head.

Sandra opened her mouth, but her old boss shook his head and pursed his lips.

"It can't be." Joe stared in disbelief. "General Arcibaldo?" The agent nodded.

"General Ettore Arcibaldo, retired Carabiniere, Member of Parliament, and leader of the MSI party. It's a neofascist campaign, not a Communist one."

"You foiled his coup d'état attempt more than a year ago, Joe," said Sandra.

"He's been trying to get back at you ever since the *Polizia* arrested him," added Redwood.

"Mom had nothing to do with it."

"It doesn't matter. This is as close as he can come for revenge, and he wants to hurt you."

"Why are you telling me this, sir?"

Redwood glanced at Sandra and back. "You worked for us before, Joe. Would you do it again?"

"You need translations?"

"We might, but this is different. We're trying to come up with something that will either expose the general or make him call off the hate campaign against your mother – before it gets worse."

"How could it be worse?"

"What if a currently uninvolved party starts believing the general's misinformation and makes their own attempt on her life. Say, an anarchist group or a far-left Communist cell."

"The Red Brigades?"

"Among others. The general knows more about them than they do about themselves. Triggering them is child's play for him."

"The situation would spiral out of control. What can I do?"

"Not sure, but let me ask you this. What would you do to protect your mother from Arcibaldo?"

"Anything —"

"Stop, Joe. Think, then answer. Be realistic." In the silence, he stood. "More coffee?"

Sandra gave him their mugs. While he was gone, Joe's gaze oscillated between the flag flying on the building across the street and the agent's desk chair. Redwood came back and placed fresh coffee in front of them.

Joe sat back. The investigator arched his eyebrows.

"I said anything, and I meant it. But you wouldn't mind if I thought of something more concrete than that." The agent nodded. "I wondered why he hasn't ordered a hit on me here."

"Why not?" Redwood took a sip of his coffee.

"No publicity. No satisfaction. No one in his political circle in Italy would get the message about what happens to his enemies."

"He'd still have his revenge," said Sandra.

"I think our friend here is on the right track. Arcibaldo wants revenge, but he is too sophisticated simply to kill off the offender. He needs to make it count for his cause." He rolled his hand at Joe. "Continue your thought."

"What if I were back in Italy, where I could draw his attention off my mother?"

"Are you volunteering for a decoy mission?"

"Yes. I can't take him on myself, but I may be the only one who would make an adequate decoy if you want to mount a proper operation against him."

"That may be the only decent idea anyone has had yet. This would be dangerous, very dangerous. We can't use civilians like that."

"I'm not a civilian, sir."

"I guess part way through your first year at NROTC is something." With anyone else, Redwood's comment might have been sarcastic and insulting, but the agent smiled as he said it. Joe saw a light flash in his eyes. "Actually, Joe, we might be able to make something of that."

"You asked me what I would do, and that's the best I can come up with."

"Another thing, sir," said Sandra. "Remember that the general tried to catch him twice already. He was pretty slippery even without training." Redwood laughed.

"Good point. I can't use that in an operational plan, but it makes me feel better."

Looking at Joe, he said, "Your mother is a popular figure, and the United States does not want her to become either a casualty or involved in the troubles between the right and the left over there. The Polizia and the intelligence agencies hope to put something together to use on Arcibaldo before this turns into all-out warfare."

"Will you be letting me or Sandra know anything else on this?"

"Not right away. It takes months to set up an operation like this. What we did last time was miraculous, but look who was involved."

"Yeah, the President, the Cabinet and the Joint Chiefs all in the same sealed-off command center. That was pretty high-powered."

"Thanks to you, Joe, I'm sure they will support anything we need to do."

"Will anybody tell my mother? It might help her at least to understand who is really behind the trouble."

"I'll talk to the people in Rome."

"Thank you, sir."

"If the Italians can neutralize him on their own, you may not hear anything more." The FBI agent stood. "I'm looking forward to tomorrow night very much. Sandra, would you bring your viola?"

"I'd be delighted. Last week, we discussed Brahms' third piano quartet in c-minor. Do you still want to play that?"

"Yes." He walked them downstairs, where they unlocked the bikes and rode back to the apartment. The bicycles had burned off their hot dogs, so they ate in a pizzeria off Connecticut Avenue for supper.

❞❞❞

"Could I at least tag along?" said Joe, trying to curb a whine. The calls from FBI Headquarters had started at nine, and each time, Sandra had to find a different pay phone to return the call.

"I don't know."

"I won't listen. I'll take something to read." He picked up a paperback copy of *The Sun Also Rises* and put it in his jacket pocket.

"Oh, come on." Grabbing her coat and keys, she headed for the door. "This is getting ridiculous. Let's get lunch. I think Darlene is on."

"That could be fun. She's cool."

At the coffee shop cash register, Joe picked up the *Washington Post* because he had almost finished the Hemingway novel. He took a seat in a booth against the wall away from the door, where he could see the room and the pay phones.

Bent over to discourage eavesdropping, Sandra was giving her full attention to the other person on the phone.

"May I join you?" Joe looked up from the paper to see Special Agent Redwood standing over him.

"Certainly, sir." Joe tried to stand, but the agent motioned for him to sit. "Sandra is on the phone. I thought it was with you."

"No. I only told her to call someone else. While we wait for her, I can confirm that the Italian government is preparing an operation. Two operations, actually. One involves using you along the lines you suggested; the other doesn't."

"Meanwhile, he still picks at Mom?"

"They're working on that. Spreading counter-rumors is something the Italians haven't had to do since World War II, and, back then, the experts were the Fascists."

"Wrong team."

"You got it. We have some PSYOPS people from the Army, Voice of America, and the CIA meeting in my old office soon to map out a plan to help the Ministries of Interior and Defense."

"PSYOPS?"

"Psychological operations."

"Leaflets out of bombers and radio propaganda."

"Obviously, it can be more sophisticated than that. I want you to know we're working on it."

"Thank you, sir." He looked over Redwood's shoulder. "Here comes Sandra."

Darlene also appeared at the table with the coffee carafe. "Are we eating or drinking today?" Jim Redwood ordered a burger and fries. Sandra asked for the chicken salad sandwich; Joe waved to double it. Darlene filled their mugs and left.

With a quick glance around to make sure that no one was in earshot, the agent said, "Joe, I gave some thought to the operation Sandra's involved in. We need to brief you in, at least so you'll understand how important it is. Your relationship is more than casual, I would say."

"I hope so, sir," he said. She dropped her gaze. "Do you think the Bureau could spring for one of those radios in a backpack? I'd be willing to carry it around, so she doesn't have to keep looking for pay phones."

The FBI agent laughed, then asked her, "What have you told him so far?"

"Nothing, except that I couldn't tell him." They could hear the frustration in her tone.

"Good." He glanced around again. "Joe, you know that Sandra is an art expert."

"She has forgotten more than I will ever know."

"Nice way of putting it, but wrong. She forgets nothing, and her attention to detail is phenomenal, better than the experts in the Art Crimes Division in New York City."

"Please, Mister Redwood." Sandra blushed. He smiled and gave her hand a short squeeze.

"Did you two go to the National Gallery?" They nodded. He asked her, "Did you show him?"

"Show me what?" asked Joe.

"Right answer. Do you remember the *Dama con Liocorno* by Raphael?"

"Of course. I saw it with her in Rome. It was her favorite. Like seeing an old friend here in DC."

"Don't act surprised." He paused. "It's a fake."

Joe forced himself to breathe slowly to prevent a gasp. "Let me guess. Sandra spotted it."

"New York sent one of their experts, and she showed him. She also uncovered a forgery ring by looking at photographs of different artwork."

"Why does this not surprise me?"

"Joe, agents in New York and Interpol are working hard on this, but we are talking about well-connected people on three continents. People who make it their business to keep an eye on what the Art Crimes Division is doing. Can you see where I am going with this?"

"Not entirely, but I can understand the intense secrecy."

"Sandra is helping the New York office. The affair has spread beyond the original painting, and she has been invaluable. The hardest thing about this case is keeping her participation a secret. The agents can't be seen here, and we don't want anyone to suspect that she is in any way connected with them. The lead investigator is a Special Agent David Vasari."

"Not Giorgio?"

"A descendant," said Sandra, " and looks just like him."

Redwood continued. "I'm sharing that because all this secrecy can be stressful on the uninvolved partner."

"Thank you, sir. It does help. Sandra, are you consulting or something?"

She looked at the agent, who answered, "Exactly. She is not an active agent, although we pay her at her paygrade as an FBI trainee, which is also confidential."

"I get it. Is there anything I can do to help?"

"Yes. Be patient. Treat it as you would a secret military program, and you don't have a need to know."

"I can handle that. And if someone called Vasari leaves a note, she needs to see it right away."

"Yes. That sort of thing. He comes to headquarters when he accumulates several pictures for Sandra to examine. How many trips so far?"

"Only two here," she said, "and I went to New York that once."

"By the way, how did your cover work out for that?"

"Fine. I got an A. I may have been the only student who went all the way to the Brooklyn Museum to photograph and write a report for that class."

When their food arrived, they switched to lighter topics. Agent Redwood told Darlene to give him the check.

"But —" Sandra and Joe blurted out together.

"Save it for when you are highly paid officers. Today, I treat the two starving students."

"Thank you, sir."

"See you two tonight. I'm looking forward to it."

He gave Darlene a twenty-dollar bill on the way out and told her to keep the change.

⊗⊗⊗

The next three days moved like a dream. Tuesday night, Joe relaxed with the Redwoods, and tales of the house-keeper Vittoria kept everyone laughing. After dinner, their next-door neighbor came with his violin. With Jim on piano, Arlene on cello, and Sandra on viola, they warmed up with a couple of short favorites, then played the Brahms' piano quartet.

Wednesday and Thursday featured only one pair of phone calls, which felt like a relief after Tuesday. The two lovers slept in late each day and enjoyed riding and walking around the capital when they were not enjoying each other's company in Sandra's little apartment.

Friday morning, Joe made the coffee while Sandra whipped up omelets for them. As she cooked, she shared how she had identified the fake *Dama* and how lucky she was that she told Redwood before going to the curator. She told him about Vasari's interesting lineage and how he joked about having to recuse himself if they find any forgeries by his ancestors.

As she sat with a fresh mug of coffee, she noticed Joe's empty look.

"Tomorrow and Sunday, I have the training at Quantico. Will you go home to Richmond?"

"I hadn't decided. You want me to leave?"

"Of course not! Why would you say that?"

He stared down at his mug.

"Why, Joe, I think you're jealous!" She chuckled. He scowled. "Darling, I work with Vasari. This case is enormous, and I am very excited about it."

"About it or about him?"

Sandra put her mug down. Her face turned red, and her eyes flashed. She felt insulted, and a rage came over her. This was a new feeling for her.

"What the hell are you implying?"

"Heck, we hardly ever see each other. What am I supposed to think when you keep bringing him up?"

"So what? Do you want me to mope around like you when I'm alone? I had a life and my studies and my job before there was you, buster."

"What about us?"

"What *about* us? If you think that I owe you something, we need to figure out what that is."

"I thought you were mine."

"So, I'm property now? Go back to the Middle Ages, Joe. When you're ready to come back to the twentieth century, I'll be here."

"Fine! I'll do that." He threw his napkin down and stormed to the bedroom. Sandra could hear him packing. She sat in stunned silence as he crossed the living room and slammed the door on his way out.

She did not move as she heard his footsteps pound down the hall and become softer on the stairs. Then she put her head on her arms and cried.

Joe hailed a cab and went to Union Station. There was a train for Richmond at four o'clock, but the departures board showed that the *Southern Crescent* to New

Orleans would pull out in thirty minutes. He changed his ticket at the window and ran to the platform.

Riding south, Joe stared out the window in an angry funk. He wasn't even sure why. By the time the train reached Culpeper, the last stop before Charlottesville, his anger had dissipated, leaving him with the confused feeling of having made a big mistake without understanding why. He stared blankly at the farmland and woods until the conductor called for his stop.

Back in his room, he dropped his duffel by the desk, took off his coat and jacket and fell on the bed. Images of Sandra's face crowded his mind. He missed her laughter and the smile in her eyes. He turned on his side and cried.

❧❧❧

"You seem down, Sandra." Roy passed a Volkswagen minibus and pulled back into the right lane. "Is everything okay?"

"Not really. Joe and I had a fight."

"He left?"

"Not just left. He went away mad."

"I never would have figured. If you want to talk about it, call me. I'm sure Millie and Annie can help take your mind off it."

"Thanks. I'm looking forward to tomorrow night already."

After Roy dropped her off in Arlington, Sandra rode home. Dragging her heart up the stairs felt heavier than carrying her loaded bag. Once inside, she saw the shelf with pictures of Joe across the living room. Dropping her duffel, she fell into the armchair and cried.

At last, the tears stopped. She had to do something. She had no appetite but also no desire to sit in her apartment moping.

She walked to the piano and picked up the viola case leaning against the wall. She tuned the instrument and found the new revision of Elliott Carter's *Elegy,* which she had heard in Rome and purchased when she returned to the US last year.

She ran through it twice. Ten minutes of soul-haunting notes did much to restore her emotional balance. Packing the viola carefully, she put it near the door. Chamber music after dinner on Sunday nights had become a high point of her week – and little Annie's, she knew.

ଛଛଛ

As the door to the room opened, Joe saw Diego come in with his small suitcase.

"You're back early."

"Yeah. Myrtle Beach ain't what it's cracked up to be. After four days, I got tired of being the only one sober enough to hold down his supper."

"That bad, huh? Meet any girls?"

"Yes, I did – wait a minute. What are *you* doing back?"

Joe closed his book and stared at the wall behind Diego. "Sandra and I broke up – at least, I think, maybe we did. Kind of."

"What? Make sense, man."

"We had an argument, and I left in a huff."

"When was this?"

"Two days ago. I came straight here."

"Your grandparents don't know?"

"No. Only you – and Sandra, of course."

Diego put his suitcase next to his bed. "Must have been a hell of a fight. Want to talk about it? Let's take a walk."

Joe stood. "That might be good. I can't get my head around this."

"Your heart has the problem, amigo, not your head."

As they walked along McCormick Road toward the Lawn, Joe recounted the argument, stopping several times to rephrase himself. He had to remember not to mention just what Sandra and Vasari were working on.

"She says she works with Vasari, but her eyes shine when she talks about him and the work they're doing."

Diego was silent until he was sure that Joe had finished.

"Did you meet him?"

"No. He lives in New York and only comes to DC on the case."

"So, she likes him. She likes me, too, I think, and Tony. What's wrong with that?"

"Nothing. I think I'm jealous."

"No shit, Sherlock. Seems that you're the problem here, not Sandra."

"But —" Joe ground his teeth and thrust his head forward slightly.

"But nothing. She likes men, dummy, but she loves you. There's a difference."

Joe shifted from pouting to a sad expression.

"I think I ruined everything."

"Get over yourself, will you? Have you considered what this is doing to her?"

"She's got Vasari."

"Unfair, man. She does not *have* Vasari. She *works* with him. Not all that much, from what you tell me. She's going to school and the Academy, and he only comes by once in a while."

"But he sees her more than I do."

"So what? Are you afraid of that?"

"Yes."

"Why?"

"I dunno."

"You've never broken up with anyone, have you? Never been dumped?"

Joe shook his head.

"Well, I have. More than once. You never answered my question: what is this doing to her?"

Joe stared at him in a daze. "Huh?"

"Who slammed the door and stormed out?"

"I did."

"So, you have no idea what you did to Sandra, who loves you. Any idiot can see that."

"But Vasari —"

Diego slapped him on the back of the head. Hard.

"Fuck Vasari! Are you in love with him or Sandra?"

"Sandra, but —"

"Shut up and listen to yourself." As they walked in silence, Joe tried to digest what they had said to each other. Feelings of anger, confusion, sadness, loss, and jealousy swirled in him. He felt dizzy, almost nauseous. He stopped at University Avenue and sat on the low wall across from Saint Paul's.

"What the hell have I done?"

"You tell me."

"I just ditched the woman I love."

"Now you're making sense. I ask you again: what is this doing to her?"

"I don't know."

"Seems you have a research assignment, ace. You need to find out, don't you?"

Joe nodded, then looked down at his feet. "How can she like Vasari if she loves me?"

"You need to find out, my friend. I'll give you a hint if you want it."

"What?"

"Aunt Mary. And Nancy. That is your mother's name, right?"

"What about them?"

"Can you picture either one of them taking the shit you just dished out to Sandra?"

Joe thought only for a moment. "No. Not for a millisecond."

"So, Sandra is *not* the first woman you have met who makes her own way, likes men, but doesn't depend on them. She works with men, and she enjoys it."

"She doesn't need me."

"She never did. You told me you liked that."

"Let's go back. I think this will take more than a phone call. I need to write to her."

"Now you're working the problem. Let's go."

Joe shook his head, then started walking. "You said you met someone at Myrtle Beach. Tell me."

"Well, I can't say if she's a Sandra, but she seemed to share my opinion of the general debauchery, so we retreated to the trees to be alone. She lives near Annapolis and was staying with a cousin in South Carolina for spring break."

"Does she have a name?"

"Serena. Serena Alquilar."

"Don't tell me she's Californian too."

"Yeah. Originally from San Luis Obispo. Her father retired from the Air Force and works at NASA. I'd like to see her again, so you might meet her someday."

இஇஇ

Millie Yu and Sandra were silent as they walked back from Annie's room. The excited little prodigy had played long and hard. She had fallen asleep on Sandra's shoulder before they had reached her room.

In the living room, Ron poured a cordials glass of port for each of them.

"Have you talked to Joe since the fight?" Millie asked.

Sandra sighed. "No. I don't know what to say. I tried to write, but what can I tell him? He's the one who was jealous. I was just doing my job."

Roy and Millie considered their friend with kind eyes and a slight smile.

"Have you told him that at least?" she asked.

"Yes. Quite clearly."

Roy cocked an eyebrow.

"You mean you shouted it at him?" Raising both eyebrows, he spread his hands, palms up.

Sandra caught herself and considered what he had implied. "He probably didn't hear me." She stared into her port. "What can I do now?"

In a gentle voice, Roy said, "I remember being his age once."

"Last week, right?" said Millie. She put her hand on his knee.

"I don't think I heard half of what anybody told me when I was angry: parents, teachers, girlfriends – none of them."

"You mean, tell him again?"

"Not again. It'll be the first time he hears it."

"Especially if you remind him that you love him," said Millie. "He's not stupid. He understands not to be jealous of you and your colleagues."

That night, Sandra considered the conversation as she undressed in the guest room. Calling on the pay phone in the residence hall wasn't private. *I'll write tomorrow night.*

ଧଧଧ

Two weeks later, she was opening the door to her apartment when the tenant from below ran up the stairs. Mid-thirties, slender, with black curly hair and wire-rimmed glasses; jeans and a nondescript cardigan, unbuttoned, over a tie-dyed tee shirt.

"Miss Sandra Billingsley?"

"Yes?"

"This letter was in my mailbox. It might be yours."

"Oh, thank you." Her heart skipped a beat: it was from Joe. "People sometimes mistake his sevens for fours."

"No problem."

Sandra watched him return to the stairs, then let herself into her apartment. She put down her book bag and took the letter to the kitchen. She poured herself a glass of wine before sitting at the table to open the envelope. Fearing the worst, she realized that their letters must have crossed.

Charlottesville
20 April
Carissima,

It has taken me two weeks to write this letter. Please forgive me, both for my childish behavior and for taking so long to understand it. I must give credit to Diego for making me step outside my self-centered shell and realize what I had done.

You don't need me; I don't need you. Instead, I love you. I hope that you still love me. You delight in the company of the people around you, and you make their world better. I am not the only person in the world who has the good sense to appreciate that. I need not be jealous.

My infantile conduct deserves no consideration. But if you can take heart from the fact that we won't be teenagers forever, maybe you can let me learn from this, and we can move on together.

Now and always,
I love you,
Joe.

Whether from relief or joy, Sandra did not care, but she cried until the ink had run the letter into illegibility.

17. Orders

SWEAT FELL in his eyes as Joe served. He blinked, then drove the ball hairline close to the net straight down to the far corner. The Army cadet was in position and fired the ball low and straight. Diego parried it close to the net for another point.

"Game, set and match!"

Wiping his brow, Joe exchanged a hug with Diego then walked to the net to shake hands with the two players from West Point. Ending the year beating Army felt good, very good.

The tennis meet had been as close as possible. The varsity and the JV had each won by only one game. The US Military Academy had a strong lead coming in, so both schools were still in contention for the National Championship. The varsity teams would decide that later.

Diego and Joe made their way to McCormick Hall to shower and change. This would be the last Naval Science class before final exams.

"Good evening, gentlemen." Major Jackson addressed the first-years in Maury Hall. "Tonight, we will be going over ship assignments and procedures for summer training."

A knock on the door interrupted him. The commanding officer's secretary stuck her head in and motioned to the officer. He went outside but came right back.

"Mister Lockhart, go with Mrs. Blankenship. Take your things."

Followed by the quizzical stares of his classmates, Joe gathered his bag and stepped into the hall.

"Captain Norwood wants to see you."

"Is someone hurt?"

"No. Let him explain it."

He entered the CO's office and stood at attention. The captain was in Tropical White Long, the summer uniform that had been the Uniform of the Day since May Day.

"At ease, Mister Lockhart. Have a seat." Joe sat across the desk from his skipper. "Have you applied for next year yet?" Contract midshipmen needed to reapply each year. Regulars like Diego were in the program until expelled or commissioned. Joe breathed a silent sigh of relief.

"No, sir. I understood that we had until June. I was going to submit mine after exams."

"Points for prioritizing, but the Navy has a proposition for you."

"Sir?"

"Would you like to be a regular midshipman?"

"Like Diego – Mister de la Torre?"

"Exactly."

"Well, I was hoping to consider all that when I assembled my application. I'd like to go regular. Even after a year, there isn't anything I'd rather do after graduation than to be a naval officer. If I could major in naval science, I would. It's much more interesting than my other courses."

"Glad to hear it because the Navy wants to offer you a regular appointment. No need to apply."

"Sir?"

"I have orders to make the offer and to report your acceptance or not."

Joe sat in stunned silence.

"Do you want more time?"

"Er – no, sir. I accept!"

The officer pulled some pages out of a folder and turned them around. "We were hoping for that answer. Now we won't have to shred Mrs. Blankenship's typing." He shoved the package of forms toward Joe. "Read and sign. Ask me anything."

He recognized the familiar Oath of Office, but with his name typed in with "Midshipman, U.S. Navy" instead of "U.S. Naval Reserve." There was a boilerplate briefing for an Interim Secret clearance and a long Form 86, used to start the Special Background Investigation (SBI) that would lead to a final Top-Secret clearance.

Everything from his service record had been typed in. There were only a few blanks for the addresses he had lived at and the names of his extended family.

Lastly, there was a seriously worded document committing him to active duty for five years: as an officer following commissioning or as an enlisted man if he failed to graduate.

"Do you want me to fill these out now?"

"Normally, you'd do this in your room and bring it back, but I need to return the forms as soon as possible. We will make your change of status known to only a few people until you receive your first set of orders.

"Orders?"

"Your summer cruise is not a holiday. You'll be on assignment, and that requires orders. Major Jackson is giving the others their orders as we speak."

"I take it mine will be different." Joe continued to fill in his addresses in Rome and in Richmond before that.

"Maybe. Getting you on board is the extent of the mission for tonight." He smiled. "Your orders were not in the package we received." He paused. "Feeling safer now? I've heard impressive reports since you started training with Sergeant Madison."

"Yes, sir. Just one scrape this semester, and no one was hurt."

"Good."

Handing him the stack of papers, Joe asked, "Anything else, sir?"

"Yes. Mrs. Blankenship!" The CO stood. So did Joe.

"Here, Captain." She must have been right at the door.

"Midshipman Lockhart, raise your right hand." Standing at attention himself, Captain Norwood swore Joe in as a Midshipman, United States Navy.

"Don't tell anyone except Mister de la Torre in private, in case your orders require secrecy. We'll know more in a week or so."

"Aye, aye, sir."

"Dismissed." Joe did an about-face and left the office. The black oxfords floated like thick-soled tennis shoes as he returned to his room.

"What was that all about?" Diego looked up from his textbook as his roommate walked in.

"I'm still processing it, but I'm a regular now."

"How's that?"

Closing the door, Joe sat on his bed. "I'm not supposed to tell anyone but you for now. The Navy offered me a regular appointment, and the skipper swore me in right there. My orders were not in the pack tonight. Should arrive next week."

For a while, neither spoke. Finally, Diego put his finger in his place and closed the book.

"Someone's got plans for you, amigo."

"Who? Why me?"

"Heck, I don't know, but this didn't come from Norwood. You haven't even applied yet, have you?"

"No."

"Someone in Washington needs to lock you in. A contract can walk anytime. As a regular, you go where they send you. You're stuck for five years now."

"Yeah, but —"

"No buts. Someone needs you for something."

"Me? I'm just a college kid."

"So's your ass-kicking girlfriend, but look at her."

"She's not my girlfriend —"

"Yes, she is. You had a spat. You'll both come around."

"You have more faith than I do, Diego."

"Of course. I'm not the one with a broken heart. I can look at this from the side, as a friend."

"Still, what do they want with me?"

"Who cares? You said you wanted to go regular. Don't be complaining if the Navy does something right occasionally."

"What about you?"

"The day after graduation, we board a bus for Norfolk. Five pairs of us, one regular and one contract to each ship. They're all cruisers or destroyers."

"Any idea where you'll be going?"

"None. He said not the Mediterranean and not Vietnam, if that's any consolation. Second Fleet ships usually go to training locations near Puerto Rico or Newport."

"Sounds like fun to me. I've never been to either one."

"Me neither, but I could have a fantastic time in San Juan if they let me loose."

"*¡Claro!*" No doubt! Joe pulled out his chemistry notebook. "Gotta write up my notes from our last lab."

இஇஇ

As he pushed the door to Room 214, Joe's hands were trembling. All the way from the student post office in Newcomb Hall, he had resisted tearing open the envelope, so he could be alone to read it. He sat on his bed. The postmark was the sixteenth of April, so the letter had taken three weeks to reach Charlottesville from Washington.

Washington, D.C.
April 15th
Mio caro Joe,
This has been one of the most difficult letters I have ever written. Since the weekend after you left, I have cried every time that I have tried to work on it.

I am afraid that I shouted at you so loud that you could not hear me. Let me repeat myself here, so you can reread it if you need to.

I love you. I still love you. I don't plan to swoon for you or to stop my life for you. I don't need you. I choose to love you, first and only.

You know that I am not the dependent type, and I bristle at those who would try to force a role on me because of my sex. You said you liked that about me.

It is exciting and enjoyable for me to feel the attention and admiration of handsome men. That one is a musician or another an art investigator only increases the pleasure of sharing professional or artistic interests that we have in common.

I am well aware that sexual attraction may be there for me or for them, but that is natural, too. I think that I can maintain the boundaries with confidence, so I can let myself enjoy the relationship without infatuation.

On the other hand, I care deeply for you. Only with you could my emotions make me lose control when you got angry. That was childish on my part, and I apologize. I have calmed down, and I see my mistake. I hope that you can forgive me.

Now and always,
I love you,
Sandra

When Diego pushed through the door, Joe had re-read the letter seven times. Each time he felt a different emotion: relief, hurt, joy, arousal, appreciation, surprise, and, finally, a deep, satisfying sense of understanding.

While he put away his books, Diego watched his roommate quietly. Joe looked up. Diego arched his eyebrows.

"She loves me."

"Told ya. Let's get some supper."

❧❧❧

Final examinations claimed their full attention for the next ten days. Joe tried calling Sandra several times each day but was not surprised to get no answer. He knew that she had finals and then some kind of summer exercise with the FBI.

In the week between finals and commencement ceremonies on the Lawn, the two roommates boxed everything that they would not need at sea.

Diego was going to ship his home, but the Ardwoods insisted that he only send what he would need in California and leave the rest with Joe's things in Richmond. The resulting package was much cheaper to mail.

They were waiting on the sidewalk for Joe's grandparents on Wednesday when their resident assistant, Jack, came out and approached them.

"Hey, Joe. You got a phone call from the unit. They said to report ASAP."

"What about your grandparents?" asked Diego.

"Could you wait here, then drive over to Maury Hall? This might be my missing orders."

"All right, but if you go off on a secret mission before we get there, I'll eat your supper!"

Joe gave him a thumbs-up without looking back as he jogged toward Maury Hall.

His shirt was soaked when he hit the steps outside the NROTC Unit two at a time. Sergeant Henry grinned to see him land at the top and keep moving.

Inside, he paused to catch his breath and savor to cool of the building out of the sun. He walked as calmly as his shaking frame would allow him.

"Captain Norwood is in, Joe." Mrs. Blankenship indicated one of the chairs and went into the office. She returned with Major Jackson.

"After you, Mister Lockhart." The Executive Officer held the door.

"Midshipman Lockhart, sir." He stood at attention because no one had made any move for him to do otherwise.

"At ease." The CO smiled and handed him a package of papers. "Your orders arrived, and they are different. Still a third-class cruise, but different from the others."

Scanning the orders, Joe saw a set for air transport to Rota, Spain, then to Naples, Italy. Report to *USS Point Defiance* (LSD-31) in Naples. Debark in Naples on or about 10 July, subject to ship's operations. Report to Naval Air Facility Capodichino NLT [no later than] 21 August for return transportation to McGuire Air Force Base, NJ.

"An amphib, sir?" Amphibious ship.

"Disappointed?"

"No. Surprised – and excited. How did they find out that I wanted to go on leave in Italy after the cruise?"

"Maybe they didn't. Perhaps the MEDTRAMID cruise puts you where they need you."

"Sir?"

"It's not an NROTC cruise. Mediterranean Training for Midshipmen is a program for top-performing Academy midshipmen, embarking them in Sixth Fleet ships in the Med. They will get off in Naples, too, but they'll fly home as a group to start their summer leave Stateside." He paused. "It won't be a party. You'll still be a third-class midshipman, living as an enlisted man."

"I heard some of the horror stories, sir."

"On top of that, you'll be the only NROTC bunking with prospective ring-knockers." The nickname for Naval Academy midshipmen and graduates, known for their very large class rings.

"Annapolis midshipmen are supposed to be the cream of the crop."

"Don't tell them that," said Major Jackson. "Their heads are already swollen. You may not be all that impressed."

"They'll take the same grief below decks, won't they?"

"Maybe more. See what you can make of it, Mister Lockhart."

Joe sensed a challenge. Not knowing what the major meant, he changed the subject.

"Any reason for an amphib instead of a destroyer or cruiser?"

"Space. The Academy can put more men in an amphib than one of the others. More chiefs, petty officers and officers, so the supervision is better. You'll see what I mean." Major Jackson and Captain Norwood exchanged knowing smiles. They were both Academy graduates.

"Is this still secret, sir?"

"It never was. We were just being discreet. My suspicion is that someone wants you to be over there for some reason. Nothing may come of it; however, don't be surprised if you get sudden orders to leave the ship. I hope you'll be back here on Move-in Day to help us out."

"Me, too, sir."

Captain Norwood extended his hand. Joe shook it and the Major's.

"Good luck, Joe."

"Thank you, sir."

Diego and Annabelle Ardwood were in the secretary's office. He briefed them on their way to the car.

🙦🙦🙦

The next morning, Joe went out to the porch when the newspaper hit the front door. The others were at the breakfast table. He picked up the *Richmond Times-Dispatch* and came back in. As he walked toward the dining room, he unfolded the paper and gasped.

AMERICAN EXECUTIVE WOUNDED IN ATTACK IN ROME.

Nancy Lockhart, the well-known Vice President of Operations of Smithson Italia, narrowly escaped death in a brazen attack outside the company's headquarters on the Via Arenula.

Unknown gunmen fired shotguns from a black Mercedes-Benz and sped off. Doctor Lockhart dropped to the pavement so that most of the shot passed over her, making two large holes in the plaster of the building.

She was treated for minor injuries at the emergency clinic and released. Officials at the US Embassy and the Italian State Police are investigating.

Doctor Lockhart has been the target of a particularly vicious publicity campaign, with posters and leaflets distributed in major Italian cities. They appear to come from Communists and other left-wing groups, but the left-wing parties deny having anything to do with targeting the popular American businesswoman.

This is the first incident using mafia-style methods. Authorities refused to comment on involvement by new players in the campaign or to answer speculation that the pharmaceutical executive may be engaged in illegal activities.

A Smithson Group spokesman in Richmond had no comment pending receipt of new information…

He ran into the dining room. "Grandpa! They attacked Mom. This is what Agent Redwood was telling me about." He gave his grandfather the paper.

Annabelle rose and read over his shoulder.

General Ardwood read quickly. "This is a direct assassination attempt, not a bombing with unknown victims. Let's call your mother now. She should be home, being the day after."

Joe paced like a tethered bulldog in the hall, holding the handset to his head, listening to the switches close in Richmond, New York, Penmarch, and Rome. The others gathered around him.

"*Pronto?*"

"Mom!"

"Hi, Joe. How are you doing?" She sounded so calm.

"I'm okay, but what's happening there? I just read about an attack in the *Times-Dispatch*."

"Yes. Lucky that I didn't have any meetings scheduled yesterday."

"Are you hurt?"

"I'm fine. Well, almost. Ruined a new pair of hose, and my jacket has holes in the elbows now. I rolled, so there wasn't any bruising to speak of."

"The newspaper said they shot you."

"Shot *at* me. I was able to drop to the sidewalk behind parked cars."

Joe held his breath. He needed to calm down. "We're all worried. Here, talk to Grandpa."

He gave the phone to Matthew.

"Hello, Nancy? Are you causing a ruckus again?" He smiled, knowing she could feel it.

"Sorry, Dad, but I guess I am."

"Worse than it was at Christmas, I take it."

"I may not be able to function here much longer."

"Weren't you working on finding your own relief?"

"We've identified three people, but the only one who speaks any Italian can't rotate in before July."

"What will you do?"

"If there's no job at Smithson for me, I'll retire. I can find a lot of things I'd rather do than dodge bullets and buckshot."

"I think Joe wants to talk to you again. Here. Love you, dear." He gave the phone to Joe.

"Mom, do you know who's behind this?"

"Yes. I got word from Doug's dad through an acquaintance here." Jim Redwood's son Doug was Joe's classmate from high school in Rome.

"Hey, I wrote to you. My summer leave starts in Naples in July."

"That's great. You can help load boxes."

"Yeah. Here's Grandmaman."

Annabelle and her daughter talked in French for a minute, then rang off.

Matthew put his hand on Joe's shoulder.

"Better?"

"Yes, sir. Much."

"She's tough stuff, your mother. Now that she's older, I'm glad she was so headstrong and focused as a child. She should be fine."

"I hope so. May I call Special Agent Redwood? I want to make sure he got the news."

"Certainly. Do you think he's home or at work now?"

"Home. At least I'll try there first."

The FBI agent picked up.

"Just about to leave for work. The report was in the *Washington Post* this morning, but I got a call yesterday right after it happened."

"Anything I should know or do?"

"Nothing I can talk about on the phone. I know where you're going, and we'll be in touch."

"Thank you, sir."

They hung up.

"Breakfast may be getting cold," said his grandfather. "Let's finish it, then take you to the station."

18. MEDITERRANEAN CRUISE

NOISE. SO MUCH NOISE. Joe wiggled the "Mickey Mouse" noise suppression headgear for the thousandth time, but it was already as close to his ears as he could get it.

At Union Station in Washington, he had boarded the gray school bus that was carrying midshipmen from Annapolis to McGuire Air Force Base in New Jersey. That ride had been as uncomfortable as any he had ever experienced. Watching the scenery zip past on Interstate Highway 95 at least held his interest, but his back and butt complained as they debarked the bus. Less than an hour later, they had filed out to a Trans World Airlines Boeing 707 chartered by the military to carry troops and other personnel back and forth over the Atlantic. It earned its nickname as a "red-eye" flight. He had slept neither well nor long.

When the aircraft had begun to bank repeatedly, Joe recognized a landing pattern. He guessed that the city on the coast was Cadiz. On the third turn, he made out the Naval Air Station at Rota, sticking out into the ocean.

"No weekend pass here, gentlemen," said the lieutenant who met them in the terminal. "Your flight to Naples is on the tarmac and ready to leave." They had climbed up the ramp protruding behind the aircraft. So far, Joe had eaten only airline food since leaving Charlottesville.

The C-130 four-engine cargo plane that took off from NAS Rota made the bus sound like a quiet limousine. There was no escape from the vibrating of the big turboprop engines shaking the fuselage. The midshipmen and a half-dozen marines tried to get comfortable in the webbing that passed for seats along the outer wall of the cargo bay. Pallets of supplies hid the passengers on either side from each other.

One passenger fascinated Joe. A wiry man who might have been as old as Joe's grandfather, he sported short-cropped gray hair, was clean-shaven, and wore civilian clothes: polo shirt, bomber jacket, jeans, and hiking boots. While Joe and his companions stared glassily around, unable to relax or read or talk, the stranger slept soundly, leaning back into the webbing. Joe wondered if hidden hooks held him in place.

The trip was long enough that Joe's eyes drooped, and his head kept falling forward. After studying the sleeping man, Joe tried to imitate his angle. He found a position that would allow his head to rest against the vertical straps behind him.

The thump as the plane hit the runway woke him suddenly. The deceleration ensured that he was fully awake as he checked his watch. He had slept for three hours.

Looking to the end of the row, he saw the civilian looking at him. The deep-set eyes were gray and penetrated whatever they looked at. The man gave him a thumbs-up. Joe smiled and returned the gesture. Apparently, they were the only two passengers who had taken a nap.

When the plane stopped and the engines idled, the loadmaster ordered everyone to remain seated until the cargo bay was clear. They watched a pair of forklifts roll up the ramp and disappear with the high-priority pallets. The loadmaster gave them a wave, and they stood and stretched.

As Joe reached onto the pallet of personal luggage to retrieve his seabag, the older man caught up with him, carrying a small duffel.

"You're either a quick study or a natural soldier," he said as they walked into the sunlight.

"Sir?"

"First thing you learn in combat: eat and sleep whenever and wherever you can." He peered at Joe's nametag and extended his free hand. "Marty MacKenzie, Mister Lockhart."

"Joe. Thanks for the advice, but I've only ever fired a rifle on the training range."

"Anyway, nothing makes the trip shorter than sleeping through it."

"True."

They walked through a room for a perfunctory customs check. The finance guards put an "X" in chalk on Joe's seabag and waved him through.

"This doesn't feel like Italy at all. Everything's in English."

"Well, it is a US Naval Air Facility. This corner of the airfield is a little piece of America." MacKenzie pointed across open space. "That's the civilian terminal, and over there is the Italian air base."

"Like Ciampino, except for this right here."

"You've been there?"

"I'm from Rome. Until this year, Ciampino was the only airport I'd ever flown from."

They stepped outside.

"There's your ride." A chartered tour bus was waiting at the curb, a hand-made sign "LSD-31" taped to the right windshield. They shook hands, and Joe joined the other midshipmen.

ଌଌଌ

"Hey, Lockhart, you're a pretty one." Joe heard the guffaws behind him and turned to face the four boiler technicians on the lower level of the fireroom. Thanks to a radarman in CIC, the Combat Information Center, who had befriended him two weeks before, he expected rougher harassment in the Engineering Department. He had mentally practiced some attitude, remembering what Tony had taught him.

"I'm not pretty, Taylor, but a rusty bollard would look good standing next to you." Three of them guffawed even louder. Taylor, a little shorter than Joe but maybe twenty pounds heavier, scowled, then sneered.

"You need an attitude adjustment, Lockhart. I'm the petty officer here, and you just volunteered to rebrick the floor of this here boiler. In you go."

The other three covered their giggling with grins and sparkling eyes. Earlier, Joe had loaded the refractory bricks into the boiler, standing for hours inside the dark, hot, airless chamber, receiving the bricks that they passed to him through the hole for the fuel atomizer assembly. *Someone is about to pull something,* he thought.

Joe climbed over the pile of atomizer barrels on the deck plates. As he clambered head-first into the opening in the boiler, he felt a hard, metal shaft slide up between his legs. Just before it reached his butt, he jumped into the boiler, rolled quickly to put his hands out and grab the atomizer barrel.

Surprised by the sudden move, Taylor let go, but not before Joe caught his wrist and pulled him in. His face struck the boiler, and he fell into the space between the walkway and the boiler front. Joe held on until the bully grabbed the edge of the hole with his other hand. His nose was bloody from a cut, and he had a bruise on his cheek.

Grabbing the boiler technician by the front of his shirt and using the rim of the opening as a fulcrum for his forearms, Joe lifted the other man to sit on the deck plates of the walkway.

"I told you I wasn't pretty. Go cornhole someone who is."

"You son of a bitch. I'll get you for this."

"No, you won't. I'll rebrick this floor, just as you ordered, *Petty Officer* Taylor. But try any shit on me again, and I won't mind spending time in the brig for the pleasure of breaking something in your body."

Taylor started to say something, but one of the other three swatted him on the back of the head. "Let it go, Bubba." He hauled himself up and went to the paper towel dispenser by the control board to tend his bleeding cut.

When Joe came out two hours later, the next watch was on, and Taylor was nowhere to be seen. The petty officer who inspected Joe's work complimented him on it and told him to go get some chow.

NFSO, the thick, black Navy Special Fuel Oil that coated the atomizer barrel, had left tell-tale stripes along the inside of his dungaree trousers. *That will never come out.* He wondered if it was worth it to buy a new pair at the Navy Exchange.

❧❧❧

Joe's radarman friend joined the mess line at the same time. Unlike most immigrants from Southern Italy, the Rispoli family spoke Italian at home. Marcantonio's father worked as a lab technician at Columbia University. More head-strong than his siblings, young Marcantonio had enlisted in the Navy rather than go to college. Both his brothers were drafted upon graduation. One died in Vietnam, and the other came back disabled by Agent Orange.

The two friends chatted privately in Italian when they could, and the radarman helped Joe avoid many of the embarrassing scrapes that befell the Academy mid-shipmen. Joe knew Naples and showed Marcantonio the neighborhood where his parents had grown up.

Rotating through the different departments had exposed Joe to the signal bridge, which he enjoyed, the navigation bridge, CIC, and the Gunnery Department, such as it was. As an "amphib," *Point Defiance* carried only small guns for self-defense. Her main armament was the Marine Expeditionary Group and the landing craft in the well deck, which conveyed the marines ashore. In addition to the crew, the ship accommodated three hundred marines, as well as the dozen midshipmen learning about the life of a sailor at sea.

Well, they were *supposed* to be learning. Joe's Academy shipmates seemed to think that they already knew everything. Jason Lockhart senior may have been a Navy surgeon, but at least he had told little Joe about the snipe-in-a-box trick and other hazing activities. Being naturally curious, Joe soaked up as much as he could about the minutiae of every job. The others seemed to dodge as much work as possible.

There were plenty of opportunities to go ashore. Most of Joe's shipmates headed for the neighborhoods near the Fleet Landing, where the brothels and bars were. With no taste for that, Joe tended to go alone, against the standard advice.

On a tip from Marcantonio, he did not volunteer his language services and spoke only English when in earshot of others.

"When they need to know, you can offer, but being invisible is a good policy." Joe could appreciate the wisdom of that.

The ship spent two longer visits in Naples because that was where much of the maintenance work was done. On liberty ashore, Joe usually took a book or some stationery, so he could read or write letters.

He had received a letter from his grandparents and one from his mother. Nothing from Sandra, probably because she would not have his address. For that matter, he did not know what she was doing or where. She had mentioned a summer program at the American Academy in Rome, but she had not applied by the time he stormed out of her apartment. When he remembered that scene, he felt a knife twisting in his soul. He hoped that they could make up sooner rather than later, but not knowing made it worse.

Sometimes he went ashore with Marcantonio, who was enthusiastic about seeing his parents' former hometown. They visited the Duomo, the National

Archeological Museum, the Posillipo and Vomero hills, and took a hydrofoil to Capri.

One evening when the radarman was on duty back at the ship, Joe went ashore for supper. His short haircut and black Oxford shoes marked him as an American sailor. He enjoyed eavesdropping on locals who did not expect him to understand them. It had been a favorite pastime as a young boy, riding the buses and trolleys around Rome.

As he finished his first course in a trattoria not far from the port, the conversation at the next table caught his attention. Four men were discussing a plan to detonate an explosive device the following week at the Fleet Landing, where small craft shuttled the American sailors to their ships anchored in the Bay of Naples.

As he listened, Joe pretended to focus on his book. Accents from Turin or Milan. The men had drunk another two liters of wine by the time Joe reached the fruit course at the end of his meal. One of them got louder as the wine flowed, but they hushed their discussion whenever the server came around.

After paying his bill, Joe made a show of asking the waiter in English where the Londres Hotel was, then leaving quietly. The server barely lowered his eyebrow to signal his understanding. He would not give Joe away.

Back on the ship, Joe went up to the Flag area, where the Admiral, the Marine commander, and their staffs worked. He sought out the Staff Duty Officer, who gave him the name of the Intelligence Officer (N-2), a Lieutenant Briggs, who happened to be on board that night. He escorted Joe to the wardroom, where the officers ate and relaxed.

"Have a seat, Mister Lockhart," Briggs indicated the sofa and laid a yellow legal pad on the coffee table. "Go through this from the beginning, so I can get my notes straight."

A half hour later, Joe returned to his berthing compartment three decks below the wardroom and turned in. He hoped he had made a difference.

19. Enemies Close In

FOR THE NEXT FIVE NIGHTS, Joe fell asleep exhausted and sore. He had rebricked boilers, packed steam valves, helped reassemble a forced draft blower, and carried hundreds of pounds of heavy metal parts, asbestos lagging pads, refractory bricks, and other paraphernalia up and down the three levels of the boiler room of *Point Defiance.*

While Taylor avoided him, the others accepted him cheerfully enough. It was more than Joe had hoped for. Not only did he quietly enjoy their acceptance, but he acquired a deep respect for the hard, thankless work the engineers did below decks. No one knew or cared what happened in "the holes" (the engine rooms and boiler rooms) unless the lights went out, the screws stopped turning, or the ship ran out of fresh water. Then they blamed the "snipes," the engineers.

On the other hand, Joe thought, *no one bothers the engineering officers or chiefs.* Everyone was a self-appointed expert on gunnery, painting, signaling, navigation, data science, and even food service. But he never saw anyone not from the Engineering Department climb into their dark, steamy, smelly world.

On the sixth day, Marcantonio came back from an errand ashore with a copy of *Il Mattino,* the daily newspaper in Naples. Joe was relaxing on a bollard not far from the quarterdeck.

"*Guarda.*" Look. He passed the paper to his friend. The headline announced that the carabinieri military police had arrested four men in the act of planting explosives at Fleet Landing. "Getting close and personal, man." Marcantonio shook his shoulders.

"Anyone else find out about this?" asked Joe, swinging his head to indicate the ship.

The radarman shrugged. "Unless it gets on AFN, no one will." The American Armed Forces Network had a radio station in Naples, broadcasting in English.

"Scary, huh?"

"You still going out tomorrow?"

"Of course. It's our last night before the amphibious exercise in the Aegean. You have duty, don't you?"

"*Sì. Fai attenzione, amico.*" Be careful, friend.

The next night, Joe walked to the shopping district between the Via Toledo and the Riviera di Chiaia. He admired the displays in the high-end shops, then purchased a cameo brooch for his mother. It cost less south of the city, where the factories and workshops were, but he could afford it, and he didn't have a means of getting out there.

After eating in a pizzeria (*when will I enjoy real Neapolitan pizza again?*), he made his way back to the Fleet Landing, which was inside the main gate of the Stazione Marittima, the passenger port of Naples.

As he approached the gate, a group of four men closed in on him from three sides. He moved to the side, but they moved with him. He stopped. They stopped.

"He said to kill this one," one of the two in front of him said in Italian. "He's dangerous."

Joe gave them what he hoped was his blankest stare.

"Seems like another stupid American sailor," said the one on Joe's left. "Are we supposed to get something from him?"

"No, make it look like a street mugging and leave him to die. No guns or knives."

"Not just mess him up?"

"Not good enough. I don't know what he did, but the general wants him dead."

Joe focused on the two directly in front of him.

In his peripheral vision, he sensed something coming toward him from the right. He grabbed the stick, pulled it to the left, and shouldered the attacker into the two facing him. The man on the left swung something at him. Joe felt the pain and heard the cracking as he bent sideways. He went down and rolled away toward the other three. As he reached to grab the legs of the fourth man, something crashed into the back of his head and in his chest on the other side from what already hurt. Then nothing…

ଷଷଷ

Lying with his eyes closed, Joe knew he was at sea. The gentle rolling of the big ship was as familiar as his bunk.

But this was not his bunk. He opened his eyes.

Sick bay. He had never seen this place, but a hospital ward anywhere looks the same. There were four beds, but only one other patient in the room. Bandages obscured his face, and he had more bags hanging on the stand near his bed than Joe did.

Joe's ribs hurt terribly if he tried to take a deep breath. He hoped they were cracked and not broken. His arms were yellow with bruising, making him wonder what the rest of him looked like.

"Good morning, Lockhart. I hope you slept well." The corpsman came in bearing a bedpan, which he set on the chair next to the other patient. "I'll get Doctor Minehart." He left.

The medical officer could not have been more than thirty years old, but Joe recognized the kind of M.D. who takes himself seriously. Nancy Lockhart had pointed out the type often enough. The physician paused at the bedside.

"I'm Doctor Minehart. How do you feel?" He checked Joe's eyes and ran his hands along Joe's arms and legs.

"Not sure. I haven't tried to move anything yet. How long have I been here, and what happened?"

"About eighteen hours. You should know what happened, Lockhart. It took six shore patrolmen to subdue the riot that you and your marine buddies started. You injured Italians, and your friend next door has been unconscious longer than you now." He pulled back the sheet to check Joe's chest.

"What riot? What marines?"

"The amnesia act won't fool me." Minehart stopped and looked sternly at Joe.

Joe stared into the doctor's eyes until the latter blinked.

"Doctor Minehart. I don't have amnesia, but something is very off here. Where are these marines?"

"In the brig, of course. Their commanding officer will decide whether to hold mast or a court-martial after the police report arrives."

Joe reached out and took Minehart's arm, pushing against the pain it caused him.

"Please ask Lieutenant Briggs on the staff to come here. He understands the background. I know what the thugs were there for."

The doctor appeared offended and surprised and opened his mouth to protest.

"Please do it, Doctor. Trust me. I'll explain it to the Marine CO too, but let me talk to Mister Briggs."

Joe let go. The physician left, shaking his head.

Twenty minutes later, the N-2 came in.

"You look terrible, but not as bad as the others."

"Someone knocked me unconscious almost immediately. What happened while I was out?"

"Four of our marines, including your roommate here, said they observed a scuffle at the main gate and that you were on the ground. Four Italians were kicking you and beating you with bats and brass knuckles. The marines weighed into the scene and beat up the locals."

"They recognized me?"

"No. They said they were only trying to pull them off you, that the Italians were killing you."

"So why are they in the brig?"

"The Italian police at the gate responded and called in the Shore Patrol. The Italians claimed that you and the marines started the fight. Because the ship had to sail, the police let the Shore Patrol bring you aboard, but they will investigate and call you in when we return to Naples next month."

"And the locals?"

"I assume they made their statements to the police."

"You want to know what was really happened?"

"Yes."

Joe recounted the events up to the point he passed out. "Those marines were right. They saved my life."

"I'll go see the Captain and the CO of the Marine unit right away." He stood and began to leave.

"Mister Briggs?"

The N-2 stopped.

"Remember they mentioned a general who wanted me killed?"

"Yes. Well?"

"He's tried before. The FBI liaison in Rome needs this information as soon as possible."

"Are you sure?"

"Absolutely, sir. If you go back-channel to AMEMBASSY Rome, the FBI agent there will recognize my name and follow up on this. It's part of a much bigger scheme." Back-channel communications meant an encrypted network used by the intelligence agencies.

"Want to tell me about it?"

"You're not cleared, if you can believe it. Someone else will have to brief you in."

"You get some rest. I'll be back after I check this out."

ଊଊଊ

"Nancy, please," Sandro Moretti said firmly. "This is not optional. We have to make it hard for them – whoever they are."

"I understand, but I've taken the bus for twelve years, and no one bothers me on the bicycle."

"That's the problem, according to the police inspector. You need to stop traveling predictably. The company's insurance policy requires that we act on suggestions from the police and other security experts."

"Okay. I guess I can drive, much as I hate it."

"No. A company car will pick you up each day and take you home."

"Like some kind of Mafia don?"

"It makes it harder to attack you or whatever."

"All right, but only until we find out who is behind all this trouble, or I leave. Is that satisfactory?"

"Of course. Speaking of leaving, the Board took your recommendation and voted to offer the job to *Dottoressa* Grimaldi."

"Good. Madeleine will be top-notch."

"On the phone, she surprised me. Her Italian is excellent."

"Her first language is French."

The president smiled. "She does sound like she's from Torino. They all speak French up there."

"She speaks German, too, which will please our partners in Cologne."

"It will be hard to follow you, Nancy."

"By September, no one will remember me, Sandro. She's that good."

❧❧❧

Joe paced in the six feet of open deck in sick bay, willing his cracked ribs to heal faster. The bruises had started clearing up, and only small pangs reminded him that he wasn't going back to full duty yet.

"Lockhart, would you get back in bed, please?" Doctor Minehart stood at the door.

"Gee, doc, I need *some* exercise. And this doesn't hurt."

"At least sit on the bed for your visitors." Joe thought that the doctor had acted differently since the N-2 walked out to check on Joe's story.

The major commanding the marines appeared, with the Chief Engineer and the Main Propulsion Assistant. The latter two were Joe's department head and division officer while he was in Engineering. Joe slid from the bed and stood at attention.

The major put out his hand.

"I owe you an apology and my thanks, Mister Lockhart."

Joe shook his hand. "Sir?"

"You just sprang four of my best marines from disciplinary proceedings that would have been a miscarriage of justice, but which we would never have detected."

"Corporal Gomez hasn't sprung yet, sir." Joe nodded to the bed next to his, where the marine was now awake but not moving much.

"Maybe he'll heal faster, now that he's not going to the brig." The major looked at Gomez, who smiled.

"I'd like to thank them, sir."

"I'll send them up later. I wanted to see how you two were doing first."

"The doctor here doesn't want me running around, but I feel okay, except for an occasional twinge in the ribs."

The doctor said, "I apologize, too, for jumping to conclusions before hearing the whole story. But you still must take it easy." He looked at the MPA. "Probably light duty starting the day after tomorrow, but nothing before that. If he runs into a valve handle or a feed pump before his ribs heal, he could break them."

"I understand, Doc," said the engineer. "We can find some paperwork for him."

Joe sighed. "Just as I was getting used to the holes."

With another handshake and some words with Gomez, the four officers left. Joe walked to the other bed.

"How are you feeling now?" He put out his hand. "I'm Joe."

Gomez tried to lift his arm from under the sheets, winced, and let his hand fall back. "Peter. I hurt all over, but that means I'm alive."

"I almost wasn't. Thanks."

"So I hear. If they wanted to kill you, why didn't they stab you or shoot you?"

"Their boss told them to make it look like a street mugging. No knives or guns."

"Weird."

A loud noise in the passageway outside announced the arrival of three marines. Each sported cuts or bruises on their faces, and one of them was limping.

"You must be Midshipman Lockhart," said the oldest one, a sergeant. "Only a middie would be dumb enough to hang around with Gomez." They laughed and gathered around their friend's bed.

"Guilty as charged. I owe you my life."

"And we owe you our freedom." The sergeant shook hands. "Mike Shaffer. This is Randy Hall and Rick Williams." More handshakes. "We owe you a beer for springing us. As soon as Gomez here can move, we'll each buy you one."

"Then we'll carry you back to the ship," said Hall.

"Let's make it dinner – on me. Saving my life is a big deal to me."

"Let's argue about it later," said the sergeant. "Meanwhile, when are you gonna stop goofing off in here, Gomez?"

"Doc isn't taking bets yet. No fun in the sandbox next week, and I might not go ashore in Piraeus after the exercise."

"Well, we'll see."

"Where are you guys stationed?"

"Camp LeJeune, North Carolina."

"I'm in Virginia. If Pete here can't join us before I leave, I'll come find you."

"Hear that? We're in trouble now!" The four marines laughed. Before they left, they exchanged addresses stateside with Joe.

☙☙☙

"Dottoressa, do you know that man outside your building?" asked the driver as they pulled away from the curb.

"I didn't notice, Adriano."

"He has been watching the last three mornings. And there is someone else in the evening when we come back."

A cold chill gripped her stomach.

"I guess I should be paying attention."

"Under the circumstances, signora, it would be wise. I'll tell the police. He could be one of theirs."

"Thank you. Should I be carrying something?"

"Without a permit and training, a gun would be more dangerous to you than anyone else." He glanced at her in the rear-view mirror. "But perhaps a knife in your purse or somewhere else would be useful. The worst that can happen is they take it away from you."

"That's a thought."

"Of course, considering your backhand and your serve, you might consider carrying your tennis racket or affecting a cane." He smiled in the mirror; she smiled back.

233

When she walked into the reception area, she stopped halfway to her door. Maria Grazia stood behind her desk, looking as fresh as a super-model on a cover shoot.

"*Buon giorno, dottoressa.*" She smiled, but then her expression darkened. "Are you all right?"

"I'm not sure. The extra measures for my security are making me more worried than I was before."

"Can I help?"

"My building may be under surveillance. Adriano was sharp enough to spot the men watching. Do you have the name of the new FBI liaison, the one who replaced Jim Redwood?"

"Special Agent Pietrowitz. Mark Pietrowitz."

"Would you call to see if he can talk to me about this?"

"Certainly." She reached for her telephone and dialed as Nancy went into her office. Maria Grazia buzzed her as soon as she hung her coat and walked to her desk. "Agent Pietrowitz, signora."

"Grazie. Hello?"

"Hello, Doctor Lockhart. What can I do for you today?"

"I wanted to tell you that Smithson is making me commute by company car now."

"Good. The Polizia have asked about doing that for weeks now."

"Oh. No one told me about that. Anyway, the driver noticed that the same man has been outside my apartment building every morning and a different one in the evening. I thought you should know."

"The police want to keep an eye out for you, but I'll contact them. If it's not their surveillance, they will definitely want to check on it."

"Thank you. Is there anything I should be doing?"

"No. Being aware of unusual people or things and reporting it is important. So is varying your routine. For example, not going to the same restaurant at the same time, or not taking your coffee break at the same time each day."

"The caffè is a tradition here."

"Yes, but it makes you predictable. Have them deliver to the office often enough that anyone watching can't count on when you'll be walking to the bar."

"I understand. I will be so glad when —"

"We will, too, Doctor Lockhart. Believe me." Nancy realized why he cut her off and felt embarrassed.

"Thank you, Agent Pietrowitz."

"You're welcome, ma'am. Let's stay in touch."

After she cradled the handset, she sat in her chair and stared out the window for a while. Then she let out a breath and went to discuss the day with Maria Grazia…

ଛଛଛ

After work, Nancy changed at home and walked to the Cavalieri Hilton Hotel across the street. She had a reservation for an hour of tennis with the pro, something she very much looked forward to each day. Since the trouble with General Arcibaldo and his people had escalated last December, the tennis court was the only place left where she enjoyed some control.

Unknown to her, the two young professionals at the courts had a bet to see who would beat her first. They knew that Nancy Ardwood had been an American champion after the war. Both men had been on the Italian Olympic team, and they liked not having to back off for her as they did for other guests. She was improving their game.

But still, they should be able to beat a woman with a grown son! Neither would admit it aloud, but it was embarrassing.

An hour later, Nancy walked across the parking lot of the hotel, her racket on her shoulder and a towel around her neck. She planned to shower at home.

As she neared the gate, the doors on a dark Mercedes-Benz to her right opened. Two men jumped out and ran toward her. Spreading her feet, she hit the driver with her racket in the side of the head. He crumpled to the ground, forcing his passenger to jump around him. Her famous backhand came up, and something cracked when her racket went into his ribs. As the racket bounced, she swung it quickly as the man's head came forward. He staggered when his head snapped back. Blood spurted from his nose.

Nancy ran, dodging behind the number 96 bus that was crossing in front of the hotel.

The man who seemed to watch her house in the evenings was running toward her. She fled into the building and took the stairs to the back door rather than stop at the front door.

While she pulled her keys in her pocket, she heard the man running up the stairs. She got the door open, jumped in, and slammed it in his face. The man crashed against the door as she threw the deadbolt.

His footsteps faded. Gathering her breath, she ran to the front door and slid that deadbolt. Then she went to the phone and dialed 112.

By the time the police rang her doorbell, the men in the Mercedes-Benz had fled the scene. However, the police interviewed the doorman at the hotel, who had seen the scuffle. She let them scrape a sample of the nose blood on her arm and borrow her racket to remove the skin and hair for analysis. She promised to come to the *commissariato* police station down the street as soon as she showered and changed.

Two hours later, she had signed her statement, reclaimed her racket, and walked to the *rosticceria* next door, where she and Joe liked to eat when neither wanted to cook.

After a filling meal of roast pork, potatoes and artichokes, she sat for a while, finishing her wine. An American man walked in. About six foot two, athletic figure, crew-cut black hair, clean-shaven, wearing a gray suit that screamed "FBI."

"Doctor Lockhart, I'm Mark Pietrowitz."

"Of course. The reception for the new consul last month." She indicated the other chair at the table. He sat.

"Yes. I wish this were as pleasant. I stopped by the commissariato to get the details."

"Is this who I think it is?"

"Probably."

"This is what happened to Joe last year."

"Jim Redwood briefed me on that, and I went back over the file. Then I got a call as I was leaving to come here. I have news about your son too."

"Oh my God. What?"

Agent Pietrowitz looked around the restaurant.

"I think we should take the conversation outside. May I walk you home?"

"Thanks." She drank the last swallow of her wine.

He walked on the street side of her as they returned to her building.

"Two days ago, Joe was assaulted outside the port on his way back to the ship. Four marines saw the attack and fell on the assailants, beating them up badly. He is in sick bay in *USS Point Defiance*, which sailed the next day."

"Two days ago? Why —?"

"The newspapers reported it as a brawl between the marines and some locals, so no one here paid attention. This evening, I got a call from the Intelligence Officer on board the ship. When Joe came to, he explained that the thugs had orders from the general to kill him and make it look like a mugging. They were almost successful."

"How is he?"

"Cracked ribs and some bad bruising, but he'll heal. One of the marines was still unconscious when he woke up."

"Were the marine friends of his?"

"No. Total strangers. They saw what they thought were thugs beating a sailor and stepped in to help him. The locals claimed that Joe and the marines started the fight, so the marines ended up in the brig. The officers on board are sorting that out now."

"How did Joe know what really happened?"

"He listened to them arguing about the general's order before they attacked him."

"He is good at eavesdropping and looking dumb."

"That's what the Intel Officer said. Apparently, Joe is the one who alerted him to the bombing attempt in Naples that was in the papers last week. He overheard the conspirators at the table next to him."

Nancy walked silently for a while.

"What about the man who tried to follow me into the apartment today?"

"Sorry, I should have mentioned that. Police protection detail. He is doubly embarrassed not to have moved on your assailants before they struck and for the broken nose he got on your door."

"Oh no! I injured a policeman?"

"One of the dangers of plainclothes work. Don't worry about it. The *commissario* sends his compliments on your athletic skill and speed."

At the stairs to her building, she said, "Would you like to come in for some coffee?"

"Thank you, but I can just make my daughter's recital if I hurry. Maybe another time."

"Yes. Thank you again."

"You're welcome. Call me if you have any questions."

Inside, she sat at the kitchen table for an hour, staring out the window into the night. Four more weeks. Would they leave Madeleine and the company alone after Nancy left? *Will I make it that long?*

20. Summer School

THE DAY AFTER READING Joe's letter, Sandra found a note in her student mailbox to go to the School of Graduate Studies. She found the office, where a pleasant secretary greeted her. Sandra read the nameplate on her desk: Eleanor Ritchards.

"Congratulations, Miss Billingsley. The American Academy accepted your application."

"Wonderful! Where do I go?"

"Wait here a minute. Dean Anderson wants to meet you. We've never had an undergraduate apply for this program. In fact, few graduate students make it."

"Oh. The materials didn't appear to restrict applications like that."

"They don't. Please, sit down." Mrs. Ritchards picked up her phone and pressed a button.

The dean opened his door. Sandra recognized him from some of the assemblies. He waved her in and introduced himself.

"I hope you don't mind, but when the letter arrived, I was curious. Your file and portfolio are most impressive."

"Thank you, sir. Do I need to do anything here?"

"Only take this, and show up by the end of May." He handed her an envelope. "You spent a year in Rome already at our program, I see."

"Yes, sir. I'm familiar with the place."

"Have you ever done conservation work?"

"No, but it fascinates me, so I've been studying."

"Even though you're an undergraduate, there should be no reason why you could not do well in the course."

"I hope so."

"Do you need any funds for travel? The scholarship includes housing, with a stipend for subsistence."

"I saved for the round trip for personal reasons already, so I'll be fine. You must have needier students than I."

"Thank you. Would you mind making a presentation to my graduate classes when you return? I try to encourage them to look into conservation as a way of supporting their art, and this would help."

"Of course, sir. I'll be back next semester."

"Good. Mrs. Ritchards will contact you."

℞℞℞

"Agent Redwood, it's Sandra."

"Where are you?"

"At home. The conservation program at the American Academy this summer accepted me. It runs from the first of June until the end of July."

"Excellent! Congratulations. Could we meet at the coffee shop in about an hour?"

"Yes, sir."

She put away her books, changed into her sweats for the dojo, and went to the diner on Dupont Circle. It was too early for the evening crowd, so she and Darlene chatted at the counter.

"Gonna be boring around here this summer without you and your friends. How's Joe?"

"Okay, I guess. We keep playing phone tag. Final exams start soon, so we're both busy. After that, he has his cruise somewhere."

"There's your other friend."

Redwood nodded to the back wall. Sandra took her coffee to the table while Darlene carried a carafe to the table and poured him a mug of coffee. Then she left them.

"About this summer," he said.

"I still don't know where I'm supposed to intern or for how long. The staff at Quantico say that they don't know either."

"That's because Vasari's project is coming to a head. Did you tell me that this school is to become a conservator?"

"Yes. I don't think one comes out qualified and ready to work in the field, but certainly it should qualify me for an apprenticeship at a museum."

"Sandra, I can't believe this serendipity. You are turning yourself into a serious asset. A conservation school would be ideal, considering what you are doing for the Bureau now."

"You mean this will be my summer training?"

"Not quite. The others will be going to FBI field offices, but we can't do that with you. Instead, we were thinking of sending you to Rome to help the Art Crimes Division and Interpol from that end. Would you mind staying on after the school?"

"How long? Last time you offered me an internship, I stayed for a year and a half."

They both chuckled at that.

"Yeah, well this time it would only be the rest of the summer, long enough to count it as your Field Office tour. Ever come across the name Mark Pietrowitz?"

"SAC in Los Angeles. He called you a couple of times before I left."

"Last December, he took over from me in Rome. It happens that he started out in Art Crimes. So, he understands what you and Vasari are doing."

"Should I look him up?"

"Let him reach out to you. For now, we still want your involvement to stay secret."

"This is becoming very exciting."

"But also dangerous, Sandra. You may need those nastier skills we taught you before the summer is over."

"Have the forgers or their patrons gotten wind?"

"We don't think so, but guess what else is coming to a head?" He paused to sip his coffee. She gasped.

"Not Arcibaldo!"

"The same. The hate campaign against Nancy could get worse."

"Do you need me to do anything?"

"Not yet, but Mark or I may bring you in. Joe plans to take his summer leave in Italy, so he'll be there too." Sandra's eyes shone. He smiled. "I think that's all for now. Send me your travel plans for summer school when you can. You'll receive your assignment with everyone else at the end of your two-week campout in the swamp. Yours will be to New York. Bob Worthman knows that you will be in Rome. The New York Office will reimburse your airfare. Any questions?"

"Do I contact you or Agent Pietrowitz when I find out my address and phone number?"

"Yes. Tell Maria." Maria Williams had taken over the FBI office the year before when Sandra returned to GW. "And open a PO Box at the APO in the Annex." The Army Post Office.

"That will be helpful." She paused. "Just curious, but where's Agent Vasari in all this?"

"For one thing, assigning you to New York makes you his office colleague. If this comes together as I think it will, he will be flying between Rome, Cologne, Paris and London like a jet setter for about a month. You may see him in Rome, but I can't guess when or how."

"Fair enough."

"Good luck on your exams."

"Thanks. Give my best to Arlene."

He dropped a five-dollar bill on the table and waved to Darlene as he left. Sandra finished her coffee, then jogged to the dojo.

&&&

By the beginning of May, Sandra was sure that her letter to Joe had crossed his. She called every night that week, but he was never in his room. Both universities went into final exams. Between the last exam and graduation, she packed and shipped her things, then gave a set of keys to the classmate who would sublet her apartment for the summer.

Finally, she called Richmond.

"Madame Ardwood, this is Sandra."

"What a pleasure! Are you looking for Joe?"

"Yes, ma'am. We keep missing each other."

"Well, you missed him again, and he will be heartbroken. He has been trying to call you too. We will go to

Charlottesville to pick him up tomorrow. I'll have him call when we return. We don't have a queue at the phone here."

"That won't work. My weekend class is going into the field. I'll try later."

"Okay, Sandra. I will tell him. And I hope you will visit us again soon."

"Me, too. Please give my best to General Ardwood and Mary."

"I will. Au revoir."

The next morning, Roy Yu picked her up to go to Quantico.

21. ALL ROADS LEAD TO ROME

THE BOATSWAIN'S PIPE blasted its shrill whistle over the noise of the machinery in the fireroom. Joe winced. The boatswain's voice came over the loud-speaker, almost as loud.

"Now secure the special sea detail. Set the watch. On deck section one." *Point Defiance* had anchored in the Bay of Naples.

Throughout the ship, officers, sailors, and marines left their positions and headed either to their at-anchor duty stations or to their berthing spaces to change for liberty ashore.

In the engine rooms, the machinist's mates were shutting down the propulsion engines. On watch in the fireroom, Joe saw the steam pressure rise. He tapped the fuel control handle down a bit. The fire in the boilers settled to a low heat, enough to keep steam to the evaporators and electrical generators.

"Not bad, Lockhart," said a voice behind him. "You might make a decent snipe someday."

"Thanks, Chief. I like it down here. No outside interference, if you know what I mean."

The boatswain came on the loudspeaker again.

"Midshipman Lockhart to the bridge!" Normally, the bridge would send a messenger to call someone.

"What the hell? Lockhart, get outta here!"

The chief beckoned the fireroom petty officer in charge, who moved to the control panel while Joe ran up the three sets of ladders to the main deck. Three more decks and he reached the bridge.

"Over here, Mister Lockhart." The Commanding Officer waved him to the bridge wing, outside and away from the others. Lieutenant Briggs was there. "Go with Mister Briggs."

Briggs led him to a door behind CIC. Special clearances restricted access to the N-2 spaces. Inside, the room looked much like CIC: a plotting table in the center, some status boards around the sides, radar repeaters, telex printers, and a half dozen radio handsets of different colors. Leaning against the table was a familiar figure.

"Hello, Joe." Marty Mackenzie held out his hand. Joe opened his own palm, black with grease and NSFO. Marty shook it anyway. "How fast can you pack?"

"Just need to throw my toilet kit in my seabag." He looked at his stained, smelly dungarees. "And change, of course."

"Forget changing. There's a helo turning over on the flight deck. Grab your gear and meet me there."

The N-2 went to one of the telex machines and tore off a page as soon as it stopped printing.

"New orders, Lockhart." Briggs handed him the message. "They'll brief you in Gaeta. Right now, we need you out of here before anyone notices you're gone. No farewells."

"I have duty tonight."

"We know," said Marty. "Your friends will hit the beach without looking for you. Go. Now. See you at the helo."

Joe said to Briggs, "Thank you for everything." Then he ran to his berthing compartment.

Three minutes later, he dashed across the flight deck, passed his bag to the crewman inside and climbed in. He almost did not strap in before the aircraft took off like a rocket and flew straight and low up the coast.

Staring in amazement at the familiar countryside from a new angle, Joe recognized the ancient Roman highways snaking among the volcanoes around the NATO base. Fifteen minutes later, the helicopter landed gently in what looked like a parking lot inside the Italian Navy fuel depot in Gaeta, halfway between Rome and Naples. Gaeta was the homeport of the Sixth Fleet Commander and his flagship.

He followed Marty to a long jetty, alongside which *USS Springfield* had moored. Not having been so close to a real cruiser before, Joe gawked. The missile launcher behind the superstructure towered over him as he walked up the pier. The barrels of the big guns on the foredeck pointed to starboard. The crew must be doing some maintenance.

Conscious of his filthy appearance, Joe climbed the ladder to the quarterdeck. He saluted the flag at the stern, then the Officer of the Deck, who returned his salute. Marty walked along the main deck and turned into one of the watertight doors. Inside, he opened the door to a stateroom and held it for Joe.

"My humble abode, Joe. Welcome."

The room featured two bunks and two small foldout desks in a tall drawer unit. A washbasin with a mirror and a closet with some empty hangers. Two plain chairs.

"You have questions, but you also want to shower and change. Now that we have you off the map, we can take our time. First, I haven't introduced myself properly." He showed Joe his credential pack.

"Naval Investigative Service."

"Yes. Most people know that we coordinate drug busts, but we also investigate other crimes. And we do counterespionage." He motioned around the room. "The top rack is yours, and the unit on that side. The head and showers are at the end of the passageway."

Joe opened his bag and got out some fresh underwear and a clean dungaree uniform.

"You can stow the dungarees. The cruise is over." Marty turned to the door. "Want some coffee? I'll get it while you clean up."

The khaki uniforms were at the bottom. Joe stowed the clothes in drawers as he emptied his sea bag. By the time he got back from the shower, Marty had come back from the mess decks with two mugs of hot coffee.

"I didn't ask if you took cream or sugar."

"Black is fine."

The khakis felt strange after two months in blue dungarees.

"Now, that looks like Mister Midshipman Lockhart!" He smiled. "How do you feel?"

"Good, but still confused." Joe picked up the message that he had only glanced at. "It says here that I am assigned to Commander, US Sixth Fleet, for duties to be determined. What the hell?"

Marty laughed. "I've seen some vaguely worded orders in my day, but those take the cake!"

Joe checked himself in the mirror and put the stuff on the little desk into his pockets. "Well?"

"Jim Redwood was here yesterday." His expression was serious.

"Something with my mother?"

The NIS agent nodded. "Smithson increased security after the attack before you and I flew that C-130 to Naples. Two weeks ago, they started making her ride a company car to and from work and sending out for coffee instead of walking to the bar next to the office."

"She must hate that."

"She does, but she's gone along with it. Her replacement is due in mid-August. Three days ago, they tried another assault, this time to kidnap her, apparently."

"It failed, I take it."

"Yes. Your mother was crossing the parking lot at the Hilton on her way back from tennis. She disabled both men with her racket and ran to her apartment."

Joe let out a breath of relief, then smiled. "Last time she used that backhand on me, I slammed into a wall and broke a Greek statue."

"Is she a bodybuilder or something?"

"No, but she was a tennis champion. It doesn't show in most clothing."

"Redwood said you're no slouch on the courts yourself."

"Maybe, but I can't beat her or my grandparents yet." He sipped his coffee and sat. "So, why am I here?"

"Partly to hide you, partly to position you for the operation that Redwood told you about."

"When I saw him, there were two operations, and if the one using only the Italian Police worked out, they wouldn't need me for the other."

"Things are more urgent now. Arcibaldo's people discovered the plant this week and eliminated him. The only thing we got before that was that Arcibaldo found out that you were on a Med cruise but wasn't sure which ship. Figuring that all the ships go to Naples, he put a lookout at the Fleet Landing. He found out where you were only the day before he sent those goons to kill you."

"So, get me out of sight."

Marty nodded. "Redwood has been working on the decoy idea with the defense intelligence people and the police. Then this latest attempt on your mother came up. We're hoping the analysis on the skin and blood your mother collected will point to the general's associates."

"Then you'll go after him."

"Not immediately. After they arrest the two thugs, they can start countering the disinformation about the left-wing groups being behind the hate campaign."

"Will that protect her?"

"Not from a direct assault, but they also need to prevent an attack by left-wing actors believing the lies."

"The Communists and the Socialists have been saying all along that they had nothing to do with it."

"Fortunately, there is a lot of sympathy for your mother in this country. The Interior Ministry does not think it will be a hard sell."

"How do I help?"

"We're working on that. We want to be sure to reveal your presence in such a way that we catch Arcibaldo, not just his flunkies."

"Meanwhile, I'm on the staff here."

"Yes. The N-2 is setting up a cover assignment for you to work as a translator. You'll be a new gumshoe as far as the rest of the officers and crew are concerned."

"I can handle that. Anything real to translate?"

"How about preparing a daily briefing of the European press?"

"Can you get me the Spanish, Italian, French and German papers every day? I could give you a list."

"That would be perfect."

Marty walked him to the various offices and introduced him to the Chief of Staff, the Commanding Officer, and the N-2. They had supper in the wardroom, then went up to the Intelligence spaces to discuss his "duties to be determined" as a press briefer.

ౠౠౠ

"Sandy, it's for you!" Lucy held the handset while Sandra dried her hands.

"Thanks. *Pronto?*"

"*Buona sera, signorina.* Are you free tonight?"

"David! Of course! Where are you?"

"At the Annex, but I can sneak out for a couple of hours later. Where would you like to dine?"

"There's a trattoria halfway down the hill from here. Good food, cheap, and some privacy if you want to talk."

"Sounds wonderful. How about seven?"

"Great." She gave him the address, phone number and directions from the bus stop. "You don't want to try to park around here."

When he walked up the street, she came out of the doorway of the restaurant and met him with the traditional double-kiss. "Been wanting to do that since the trip to New York."

"Me too. Hungry?"

"Yes." She led him to a table in the back of the little eatery. During dinner, he wanted to find out as much as he could about the course.

"My father went to Rome one summer on what I thought was a consulting assignment here. I wonder if he was teaching this class."

"Maybe he did. We've had several professional conservators work with us from Europe, America, and even Korea. They are unbelievably specialized."

"Often only one artist or the studio of a single master. Did you learn anything that you can relate to our case?"

"Yes. I know why the reds on the lady's sleeve were different and what the forger should have done."

"Impressive. Can you show me?"

"At the school?"

"Sure. Part of my cover in Rome is to visit that course and interview two of your instructors, Mattei and Alberini."

"When?"

"Alberini first, the day after tomorrow."

"I'll be in Mattei's class in the afternoon, but in the morning, I could show you what I discovered."

Over the fruit course, he asked her if she would like to be more involved in the case.

"I've been grinding my teeth keeping out of it."

He cut a slice of apple and speared it with his fork. Then he paused before looking at her.

"Would you be willing to work with us on actual paintings?"

"Not photos?"

"No. We're close to making a series of raids, and we hope to arrest all the principals at once. We may need your help to sort out the forgeries from the originals. At least the *Dama con Liocorno,* the other two Raffaellos you helped us with, and a Caravaggio."

"Oh my God. Where? When? How?"

He put his hand on hers.

"The case is still coming together, but very fast. Surprise: the biggest cache is here in Rome."

"How can I help?"

"We want to use you on whatever we confiscate, but we don't want to endanger you."

"Have you run this by Agent Redwood?"

"I was going to call him after I talked to you."

"Do that. I'll be ready. I'm also looking forward to showing you what we're doing in the conservation course."

He insisted on picking up the check, with a crack about her taxes paying for it. They walked to her apartment building, but he declined to come in.

"I'd love to, but I am still keeping my profile as low as possible."

"Well, thank you. Good night."

She walked up the stairs and let herself in.

"Sandy, who's the hunk?" Lucy was still standing at the front window watching David walk down the street.

"A friend from New York."

"Why didn't you bring him up?"

"He didn't want to come, but he'll be in the lab on Friday morning. He has some meetings at the Academy."

"He looks like that portrait of Giorgio Vasari."

"Yeah. He gets that a lot." Sandra smiled and went to her room feeling very lucky.

ଔଔଔ

The next morning, Sandra had finished washing her breakfast dishes when the phone rang. Lucy and Melanie were still asleep.

"Hello, Sandra?"

"Maria! How are you?"

"I didn't think you'd remember me."

"Of course! Are you still at my old desk?"

"Yes, and that's why I'm calling. Could you come down here to meet with Special Agent Pietrowitz?"

"Sure. When?"

"Three o'clock?"

"No afternoon classes today. I'll be there."

After lunch, Sandra caught the number 60 bus to Piazza Barberini and walked up the Via Veneto. Located in a palazzo across the street from the American Embassy, the Annex housed the hundreds of military and civilian personnel who worked for the Military Advisory Assistance Group (MAAG) administering the Marshall Plan that had rebuilt Western Europe after World War II. They were not part of the normal diplomatic corps but interacted directly with their counterparts in Italy. The agencies represented included the FBI, the Coast Guard, the Commerce Department, the Department of Agriculture and all the armed forces. Though most of the recovery work had been accomplished, the MAAG was still active.

When Sandra had first arrived, she had checked in with the Civilian Personnel Office and set up her post office box, but the FBI office had been closed. She had left her contact information on a card in Maria's PO box. Now it felt weird to be called in for what must be Bureau business.

Maria looked the same. In her forties, with black hair and blue eyes, she disarmed men and women alike with her cheerful perkiness. Only the slight lines in her face betrayed the loss of her childhood sweetheart, who fathered and helped raise their children before dying in Libya in an oil field accident. Her Italian was flawless, if slightly accented. A first-generation American, her parents had emigrated from Ireland, which gave a pleasant lilt to her English. The apartment in Rome was paid off, so she stayed on when the boys grew up and moved to the States.

The two women exchanged hugs before the secretary buzzed her boss. Mark Pietrowitz came out.

"So, this is the amazing Sandra Billingsley," he said with a broad smile and a firm handshake. "Agent Redwood warned me about you."

"Oh?"

"Yes. Maria, may I borrow her?"

"Of course. Do you want me to hold your calls?"

"Please. And some coffee if you would? Come in, Miss Billingsley."

Inside, Sandra stopped in her tracks.

"Hello, Sandra." Jim Redwood stood. "Good to see you."

"Is this about Joe or David?"

"Both, I think," he said. "Shall we sit down?"

While they sat at the table, Maria brought in a tray with a coffee carafe and mugs.

"For starters, Vasari tried to call me this morning, but I was already landing at Fiumicino. We had lunch, and he asked me about you."

"Well?"

"How involved do you want to be?"

"Is that even a valid question, sir? Whatever you need."

"The Art Crimes Division may be participating in raids with the finance guards and the police."

"It's what I trained for. Are you worried?"

Pietrowitz raised his eyebrows at that. Jim noticed.

"Sandra has been through Quantico, but obviously we can't give her a badge."

"Can she work in the field?"

"Don't cross her in a dark alley, Mark. Trust me."

She blushed but smiled.

"I thought she was an art consultant."

"That too." He looked at her. "Vasari says he's going to the American Academy tomorrow."

"Yes. He wants to see what I learned that the forger of the *Dama* did not."

Pietrowitz asked, "the conservation course?"

"Yes, I really am a full-time student at George Washington. The FBI is a side-gig for now, isn't it, sir?"

Redwood chuckled. "True enough."

"You told me not to tell Agent Vasari about Quantico. Is that still the case?"

"I briefed him. There are now six people who know about it."

"That makes things easier, sir."

"What kind of a program is this, Jim?" asked Pietrowitz.

The head of Special Projects looked from him to Sandra, then sighed.

"Seven." He explained the secret training at the FBI Academy. "No one at Quantico ever brought her to the mat, and she was the best shot in her cohort."

Pietrowicz thought about that as they refilled their mugs from the carafe.

"I can see why you wanted her here."

"It really is about her ability to detect forgeries," said Jim.

"Please, sir. I can spot differences but not tell you which one is authentic."

"Good enough, Sandra. Anyway, I am glad you won't need protection if the raids don't go peacefully."

"Did I understand that this was also about Joe?"

"Yes. You know about Nancy?"

"I know about the bombing at the Aprilia plant, and I read about the attempted assassination in May."

"Are you still in touch with Joe?"

"No, but not for lack of trying. We played phone tag after spring break but left for our summer programs without exchanging addresses. I don't think he knows I'm here. Diego and he expected to be on a ship in the Caribbean."

"We arranged for the Navy to send him to the Med. Last week, we cut his cruise short. He's in Italy."

"That's great! Can I see him?"

"Probably, but not right away. Remember the operation he volunteered for?"

"Yes." Sandra's expression went from happiness to concern.

"Well, the one mounted by the police without Joe fell through when Arcibaldo's people killed the informer."

"So, you're setting him up as a decoy." She struggled to keep the anger out of her voice.

"Not until we can figure out how to do it safely and still catch the general."

"What about Nancy?"

"That is getting worse. Two of the general's men tried to kidnap her in the Cavalieri Hilton parking lot the other day. She got away, but so did they."

"How can I help?"

"You two got along pretty well last year, didn't you?"

"Yes."

"Mind giving her a call? She probably feels besieged and lonely right now."

"I'd be happy to. Is she in the same apartment?"

"She is."

"How much can I tell her besides the conservator course?"

"Nothing yet. Joe hasn't had any mail from you and only one letter from her, forwarded from the university."

"I'll call her from home. She's probably at work now."

❦❦❦

"This is a fantastic setup," said Vasari, as Sandra opened the door to the conservation lab. "It looks like the one my father had at the Metropolitan before they got gas spectrometers and an electron microscope."

"That might be a weak point," she said, "but it means that we learn the principles and basic techniques solidly without relying on machinery."

"Good idea. No wonder museums want Italian-trained conservators."

"Hello? Sandy?" A knock on the door preceded the two wide-eyed graduate students coming into the room. "Hi, I'm Lucy." She walked over to David with her hand out. Sandra almost rolled her eyes but introduced Melanie instead.

"Are you a conservator?" Lucy didn't have to bat her eyelashes; Sandra figured her voice did that for her.

"No. I'm with the FBI. Art Crimes Division."

"Really? Wow! Have we done something illegal here?" They both looked at Sandra.

"No, ladies," said Vasari, laughing. "I know her from New York. I'm here to discuss techniques we use back in the office. We often work with conservation schools on unusual challenges." He put a hand on Sandra's shoulder. "For example, she was going to show me something you all learned this week." He asked Sandra. "Does it need to be a particular color?"

"No. We had green in class. Let's use that."

When her roommates were not staring at David, they appeared surprised as Sandra stepped through the paint mixing process and showed him how changing one of the oxides in a step would cause the slightest difference in matching the colors. The three cans all contained the same oxide.

They stood around the four swatches of green for a while, thinking.

"Why did you make three different batches?" asked Melanie. "Professor Alberini only had us use that one." She pointed to the perfect match.

Sandra looked at him. "Go ahead," he said. "I think I get it."

"Agent Vasari is in Art Crimes, right?" Her classmates nodded. "Our instructions only listed the ingredients and the order to use them, right?" They nodded again.

"Our logs make us note not only each ingredient but its date and place of origin. We used an oxide made in Florence in 1956. These other two came from Freiburg in the fourteenth century and Milan in 1845."

"Where did you find them?" Lucy asked.

"They were all on the shelf over there. I saw them when I got my can. So, I ran all three."

"Why would you use an outdated oxide?"

"David is looking for forgeries, aren't you?" She turned to him.

"Yes. And you just told me two things: a reason why some restorations might never match and another way to date the work, because today we can run laboratory tests to identify the exact oxide. I knew this would be interesting, but not that it would be so helpful. Thank you."

"You're welcome." The three women said together, then laughed.

David looked at the clock. "Do you ladies have plans for lunch? I don't see Doctor Alberini until three. I feel like celebrating this."

He winked at Sandra as they cleaned up the experiment and put everything away. They ate at a trattoria in the piazza near the Academy. The detective entertained them with background stories about well-known forgeries, but mostly he showed a deep interest in their course, their studies, and how they had come to be in Rome. Sandra watched him charm them, remembering what Redwood had said about putting people at ease. Her roommates would not suspect anything about her after a couple of hours with David.

He walked them back to the Academy and said goodbye at the door to the library. Sandra thought she heard Lucy sigh as David pulled on Sandra's hand and led her toward the faculty offices.

"Well-handled today, Sandra."

"I wanted to say the same to you. I nearly died when they showed up."

"To make sure I understand. What does this tell us about the red on the lady's sleeve?"

"You'll have to run analyses on all the paintings. I don't know which *Dama* is the original, but one of them has paint mixed after 1956, or the forger needed an eye exam."

"Wouldn't it be weird if they got shuffled?"

"There were two restorations in this century, but those conservators should have recorded what they used. This case is becoming even more interesting."

"Indeed. Thanks."

After a double-kiss, he knocked on Professor Alberini's door and walked in.

After class, Sandra returned to the apartment to check her laundry. Nancy had invited her to supper in Trastevere, which was across the river from the Smithson building. Not one to worry about "not having a thing to wear," Sandra usually didn't care what was ready or not. But she had been a fan of the trail-blazing executive since long before meeting Joe or his mother. If something needed cleaning, she would pay extra for one-hour service at the *lavanderia*.

Just as she got back from picking up her rush laundry, the phone rang.

"Hello, Sandra. It's Nancy."

"Seven thirty, right?"

"That's right, but we have a problem. Smithson security does not want me taking my meals where they can't arrange protection, and I didn't warn them about tonight. Frankly, I didn't think of it."

"So, another time?"

"I have a better idea. Let's make supper at my place. I'd rather kick off my shoes to sit with you."

"That's great. If I remember correctly, the number 96 goes up there."

"Yes, but let me pick you up on the way home."

"Okay. What time?"

"How about six? Bring something to stay overnight, so you don't have to go back right away."

"I'll be ready. Thank you!"

"Thank *you*! See you this evening."

22. SANDRA AND NANCY

NANCY TASTED THE RIGATONI and pronounced them al dente. She cut all the flames on the stove and carried the boiling pot to the sink to decant the pasta into the colander. Sandra was putting olive oil and red wine vinegar on the table. Then she put the salad bowl in the center, so they could serve themselves.

"Won't the fish dry out?" Sandra asked as she filled the carafe with water.

"Modern magic: aluminum foil and a low flame on the oven. Do you drink white with seafood?"

"I like to sip white, but I prefer red with all food."

"There's a Grottaferrata in the cabinet by your right elbow and glasses above."

Sandra poured the wine while Nancy doled out the pasta, applied the sauce, and put out the pecorino with a grater on the table. They sat together.

"This is wonderful!" said Nancy. "I haven't had supper here with someone since Joe left. Thank you again."

"Thank *you*! Each week last year, I made a Roman meal for one in my apartment and turned over a glass for him. I can't believe I'm here again."

Nancy raised her glass. "Here's to Joe – wherever the hell he is."

"To Joe – wherever the hell he is."

"You know that he's in the Med somewhere, don't you?"

Sandra caught herself. "Last I knew, he and Diego were going to the Caribbean."

"I got a phone call the day after the shooting in May. He had orders to a ship in the Sixth Fleet. *Point Defiance.* He should leave at the end of July in Naples."

"That's fantastic! I wish I had known."

"You two can make that up when he gets here to help me move."

"He'll be overjoyed to be back home."

Nancy's face darkened. "Funny you should say that. Twelve years here, and this apartment has not felt like home since the day he left – until you walked in."

They ate in companionable silence for a while.

"Did you say Doctor Grimaldi would be here soon?"

"Around *Ferragosto.*"

"There won't be anyone around to interrupt you." They both had experienced Rome devoid of its citizens for the traditional mid-August holiday. "Do you know her?"

"Oh yes. Madeleine and I go way back. I was working on my doctorate in pharmacology at the MCV when she joined the staff as a clinical researcher. She had just come back from World War II."

"Before Joe."

"Before Joe's father too. She was at our wedding, then followed me to Smithson in 1950."

"I'm sure you'll be glad to turn over. Do you ever miss Richmond?"

"Not until Joe left. After that, I began to miss our home, my parents, and the friends that are still there."

She took a sip of wine. "Then all this trouble with the hate campaign started, and I'm holding on by my fingernails, hoping to get out of here alive."

"I would be terrified, I think."

"Well, it keeps me up at night. Do you remember that our house was burglarized when you worked for Jim Redwood?"

"Yes."

"It taught me how easy it is to get into the house. Maybe not sneak in, but break down a door or the kitchen window."

"I didn't realize you were so vulnerable here. Why don't you move?"

"I'm almost ready to leave. I guess if anything more happens, the company will put me up at the Cavalieri Hilton across the street, but that's crazy."

"Now I wish I had a scooter or a bicycle. I could zip over here after class more easily."

Nancy put down her fork.

"Would you like to borrow the Vespa or the bike? The Fiat 1500 works too. I only need one of them to get around."

"That would be fantastic. I could shop at the Trionfale market again like before and bring it here."

"Try all three tomorrow and pick one."

"You ride Joe's bike up this hill?"

"Until Sandro Moretti put his foot down and insisted on my commuting with a driver." She smiled at Sandra's surprised expression. "I confess that I pushed it the first few times. How did he zip up and down this mountain all those years?"

"Maybe he weighed less then."

The whitefish had not dried out. They sprinkled it and the cold greens liberally with lemon juice and dug in. Conversation slowed as bone-picking required their attention.

Nancy put the *Symphonie Fantastique* on the record player while they had coffee in Nancy's office, the most comfortable room in the apartment. Sandra admired the Old Masters prints on the wall.

"I have this Piranesi in Washington."

"I remember when Joe said you bought it. Something about no meat for a month."

"No new shoes. The FBI job made it possible."

"Ever see Jim Redwood? Just before he left, he told me he was going to DC."

"I ran into him in January on my way to the National Gallery of Art. Arlene and he had me over a couple of times. I can walk to their place."

"Good for you. How different is it being here this time?"

"Trastevere and the Academy feel the same. The conservation course and the people are new, and, of course, Joe isn't here."

They both yawned at the same time and apologized.

"Do you need to be back at school tomorrow?"

"No. Saturdays are free."

"Joe wrote that you learned tennis last winter. Would you like to play in the morning?"

"I don't have a tennis outfit or a racket."

"I have extras of both. We're about the same size."

"I'd love to."

The next morning, they played at the Cavalieri Hilton, which they enjoyed enormously. It took Nancy back to her days as the pro at the Richmond Lawn Tennis Association and to the year she and Luke taught Joe the game.

"I can't believe that you only started playing last Thanksgiving."

"GW has courts, but I haven't found a regular partner yet."

"You're a quick study. I would invest some effort in finding someone. What about the Redwoods?"

"I'll ask them. Thanks."

After changing in the apartment, Sandra tried the bicycle and the Vespa and chose the scooter. Keeping it parked inside the American Academy rather than on the street should be safe enough.

They walked back to the hotel for lunch. Sandra noticed how alert Nancy was crossing the street, but so was she.

They found a table near the garden outdoors. A soft breeze, typical for the top of the Monte Mario, kept the summer sun under control. Behind Nancy's shoulder, the city shimmered in the heat.

Sandra's gaze switched back to Nancy. She understood why strangers thought she was Joe's sister. The resemblance was more than striking. They had similar mannerisms, the same athletic stride and posture, and the same gentle eyes. Only a close friend or coworker would know what steel flashed behind them.

"Nancy, I am still blown away to be able to borrow the scooter. I have hardly gone anywhere but school because the bus takes so long."

The older woman chewed her bite of sandwich and swallowed it with some Pinot Grigio.

"I have another idea if you want to think about it," she said. "Why not stay here at least until Joe gets back, and commute to school? Come and go as you like."

Sandra thought for only a moment. "Oh, Nancy, I would absolutely rather room with you than Lucy and Melanie. It's a deal!"

"I have a washer and dryer too."

"Thank you! This is marvelous."

"Shall we take the car and move what you need now?"

They drove to Trastevere, and Sandra moved into Joe's room.

֍֍֍

The next morning, they took the Fiat to Saint Paul's-within-the-Walls. The long bus ride had made going there impractical. Sandra had attended Mass near the Academy twice, but it lacked the singing and participation she liked. Moving through the familiar service with others made her aware of how much she missed having her emotional state reset each week in church.

The two women quickly found a pleasant routine. Every morning, Sandra took the Vespa to school after Adriano left with Nancy. On her way home, she did the shopping. Each of them had work to do after supper, sometimes in different rooms, but often in Nancy's study. Sandra slept better without the partying, and Nancy slept better with someone in the house.

On Tuesday, Sandra called Agent Pietrowitz between classes.

"You're living with Doctor Lockhart?"

"Yes. Is it okay with you?"

"Not a problem. Does she know that you are working with us?"

"Not from me."

"For your safety, I'll make sure that the police protection detail knows about you."

"I've seen them. Always the same two men."

"Anything else?"

"Maria has the number here. Will you let Agent Vasari know how to find me?"

"Yes. We'll take care of it. Be careful."

That evening while Nancy worked at her desk, Sandra sat by the coffee table with her books and her sketch pad. She sketched out portraits of Nancy working intently in her study, playing tennis, sitting at the kitchen table, and riding behind Joe on the Vespa. She put them away to paint later. Preparing Christmas presents in the summer and fall was something she learned to do in Rome before. This year, she hoped to present them in person.

23. Sixth Fleet

VICE ADMIRAL NELSON PORTAGUE was a portrait in contrasts. Sandra would have loved to capture him in a painting. He stood erect and perfectly plumb with the horizon, which meant that he let the ship roll under him without seeming to move a muscle, while others were struggling to hold onto railings and furniture. No one had spent as much time at sea as he had, at least no one above the rank of commander.

He had a reputation as a crusty bastard, with a terrifying scowl he rarely dropped. Those who worked closely with him knew better. Still, he was not one to pass out compliments lightly or to thank a man for doing his job.

After Joe delivered the first typed précis, the N-2 invited him to the daily briefing with the Admiral. Joe stood against the back wall with the other junior officers. Everyone seemed very attentive both to the briefers and to the Admiral, but they did not seem terrified. Joe was terrified, though, until the old salt cracked a joke about the Soviet Squadron Commander at the anchorage off Kithira Island. Then he saw the smile lines and the crow's feet. After the laughter subsided, the Admiral resumed his intimidating scowl.

The N-2 called Joe into his office that same afternoon.

"The Chief of Staff wants you in the lineup for the briefing starting tomorrow."

"I typed up my summary. Does he want me to read it?"

"No. I can't guess who else will have gotten it out of the in-box, but the Admiral will have read it, and he'll have questions. He grilled the Chief of Staff and me about you for a half-hour today."

"What will he ask me?"

"About your process. He'll probably want to clarify little things. It won't take much time. By the way, do *not* read what you typed. Prepare a card of headlines perhaps or a short summary of what you thought was most interesting, and let him take it from there."

Despite the frigid air conditioning in the room, Joe felt a trickle of sweat run down his back.

"Do I look at him or around the room?"

"At him unless something is going on that draws his attention too. Sometimes three-way conversations start up with one or more of the staff. Usually, the Admiral lets it go on until they digress, or it looks like something we need to discuss offline. Don't worry about it. Just take your cue from the Admiral or the Chief of Staff. I'll be there too."

The next morning after the intelligence portion of the briefing, Joe walked to the podium. He kept his hands inside the lectern, so no one could see how white his knuckles were.

"Good morning, Admiral. Yesterday's news from around Europe —"

"Just a minute, Lockhart, isn't it?"

"Yes, sir."

"Relax, young man. I eat captains and majors for breakfast, nothing younger than that." A few of the senior staffers chuckled. "Now that we've introduced ourselves, we can start the briefing, but first –" he swung around. "Who else read the European press briefing?" He held up Joe's typewritten report.

A lieutenant junior grade from the Strike Warfare section held up his copy. The Chief of Staff and the N-2 raised their hands. An embarrassed silence fell on the room. Joe heard the blowers in the ventilation system and a pair of deckhands shouting outside.

"Next time, I expect that many hands from people who have *not* read it." He scowled at the Chief of Staff, who nodded. "Continue, Mister Lockhart. Don't repeat the whole thing. They'll catch up."

"Yes, sir. Yesterday, the German press reported that three missile battalions left Dresden headed toward the Austrian border. The Naples newspaper noted that Colonel Ghedaffi cut the ribbon on a new oil rig in Cyrenaica, the closest ever to the Egyptian border, and the first by the new joint venture with an American company." A murmur came from the back of the room.

"Silence in the peanut gallery!" the Admiral growled. "Anything else catch your interest, Mister Lockhart?"

"Only that the French Mediterranean fleet left its base at Toulon two weeks early for Exercise Île-d'Or. *Il Mattino* carried a story about an explosion at the ENI oil field near the Algerian border that killed three Italian engineers. The timing is curious." ENI was the Italian state oil company.

The Admiral stared at Joe for almost a full minute. In the back of the room, some junior officers crammed together, trying to read the one copy of the news summary.

"Thank you. I see you're a Midshipman Third Class. You must be a rising youngster." Joe knew the Academy called its sophomores youngsters.

"Yes, sir."

"What company?" Thirty-six companies formed the Brigade of Midshipmen at the Academy.

"NROTC, sir."

The Admiral did not contain his surprise. "And you're on the MEDTRAMID cruise?"

"I was, sir, but not now. I'm in N-2." Joe nodded toward the Intelligence Officer.

"Chief of Staff, I want to see Mister Lockhart after the briefing."

"Yes, sir. N-2, send him down, please." *Oh God,* Joe thought. *I'm done for.*

"Meanwhile," the Admiral said, raising his voice, "the rest of you take note of what you can extract from completely unclassified sources if you just pay attention to what you're reading." He turned to Joe. "Well done, Mister Lockhart. I'm looking forward to tomorrow's report." He rolled his hand for the next briefer.

As Joe walked back to his place against the back wall, he saw Marty smiling from the side of the room.

ଛଛଛ

One day, the N-2 beckoned Joe into his office when he came up from breakfast.

"We just got a call from London on the secure phone." "London" meant CINCUSNAVEUR, the Commander of

US Naval Forces in Europe, which included the Sixth Fleet. "Washington wants to know how we find out so much about movements in East Germany, Algeria and Libya." Colonel Ghedaffi had expelled all Americans from the North African country. Joe's little summaries must be going up the line.

"Something wrong with my reports, sir?"

"Not at all. Satellite imagery confirmed all of them – the next time the birds could take a pass and look. Your reports are two or three days ahead of the satellites. Very embarrassing."

"But it's in the papers. Not even classified."

The N-2 grinned. "Just keep translating." He waved for him to go to work.

જ્જ્જ

Two days later, Joe sat on a hose cabinet on the starboard side, enjoying some sunshine, as the waves rushed down the side of the ship. He watched the seabirds dive on the garbage in the ship's wake. This half-hour after lunch was a precious break from the hours he spent in a windowless room, scanning a dozen newspapers as quickly as possible and typing up his summaries.

The French Navy suddenly canceled the Allied exercise for "operational requirements." Inside the "N-2 shop," they knew that the oil field explosions were part of some cross-border fighting. Algeria had only been independent for a few years, and the new government faced challenges from within and from its neighbors on all sides. Sometimes, the threat of a return of the French kept a lid on things and forced the warring sides to talk to each other. Joe had learned all this from the Toulon and Marseilles newspapers, which regularly covered events in Algeria, and from the Naples paper. Many of their readers had come from North Africa. For them, it was local news.

Some of what he read did not make it into the summaries. By comparing articles in the neofascist *Il Secolo d'Italia,* the leftist *Paese Sera* and *La Stampa,* and the Communist *L'Unità,* Joe could make sense of General Arcibaldo's campaign against his mother. The public prosecutors had made a sensational display of the two thugs who attacked Nancy in the parking lot, emphasizing their connections to the general's party. Attention was quickly shifting away from the left-wing parties, and the affair was turning into a scandal for the general and his friends. There was even speculation that he might lose his seat in Parliament. He had already lost his Army pension for abusing government vehicles (the public reason for his arrest after the coup attempt that Joe helped foil), but those misdemeanors were not enough to keep him from political office.

Marty startled him out of his musings with a tap on the back.

"You're a hit, Joe." They both looked at the bird-feast following the ship.

"Yeah, but what happens later? I do have to go back at some point."

"The Admiral has the Chief of Staff working on that."

"I have another mission. I'm only supposed to be stashed here."

"This is not about keeping you. He wants more linguistic expertise at hand. Problem is, no one ever tried systematically to inventory the language talent in the Navy outside the CT rating." The cryptographic technicians were the linguists who listened to foreign radio signals and wiretaps. "Now there's a move at the Bureau of Personnel to identify officers with your kind of experience. They'll be called Country Area Regional Specialists. Once they're identified, their knowledge can be considered when making assignments. For now, the Chief of Staff put BuPers to work finding people like you to detail to the flagship."

"That's good, I guess."

"It's great, but not why I came looking for you. You need to pack your seabag again."

"Back to Italy?"

"I'm not sure, but things are serious in Rome. The people trying to stop Arcibaldo need you on-site. You'll be flown out as soon as we're close enough to Sicily. The Admiral's helo will take you to Syracuse. The Italian Air Force will fly you to Ciampino."

"Does my mother know?"

"No. We're still hiding you, but Redwood said that you would be happy with the bodyguard in the house now. One Sandra Billingsley."

"You're kidding! Sandra?" Joe leaped off the cabinet and grabbed the agent by the arms. "She's in Rome?"

"Taking a conservation course at the American Academy."

"She mentioned that, but I didn't know she got in. This is wonderful! I can't wait to see her – them."

"Easy, Joe. Not at first. She is there for school and some other thing that I'm not cleared for. Your mother invited her to move in when they met. Apparently, her roommates were driving her nuts, so she accepted willingly."

"So, my mother doesn't know about Sandra and the FBI?"

"Not yet, but she's there whenever your mother is not in the office."

"That is a relief. So where am I going?"

"I don't know. Redwood and the SAC in Rome, Mark Pietrowitz, will take it from here."

The next morning, Joe checked out with the Admiral and the others, and boarded the helo for Syracuse. Publicly, he was on leave, but a secret set of orders in the N-2 spaces, at CINCUSNAVEUR in London, and at the American Embassy in Rome detailed him to the "FBI Liaison Office, MAAG ROME, for temporary duties to be determined."

24. Sandra Comes Clean

SANDRA WALKED WITH NANCY to the car and closed the door behind her.

"Ciao, Adriano," Sandra said to the driver as she scanned the street and the windows of the hotel.

"You don't have to walk me to the car every day, Sandra."

"*Ma mi piace salutare 'sto fusto.*" But I like to say hello to this hunk. The man blushed as the two women laughed.

As he put the car in gear, Sandra walked back into the building. She collected her purse and her book bag, and carried them to the basement garage. On her way out, she slowed Joe's Vespa in front of the morning plain-clothes man. She winked and gave him a small wave. He smiled quickly and nodded. She drove off. It gave Sandra a feeling of usefulness and pride to be Nancy's protection detail. *I trained for this,* she thought.

Her last class ended about four, so even stopping at the Trionfale market for fresh produce, meat and bread, she was waiting on the sidewalk each night when Adriano brought the executive home. After the second day, Joe's mother stopped protesting.

Wednesday evening, the wall of the hotel reflected the orange sky and clouds as Sandra opened the car door. As Nancy swung out, an open window created a black square that caught Sandra's attention. A bright spot appeared in the black area. She focused. A barrel emerged and settled in position.

Sandra pushed Nancy to the ground as the bullet ripped into the wall beyond them, exploding chips in all directions. Then they heard the shot.

"Stay down behind the car!" Sandra rose to the window and caught the eye of the plainclothes policeman, who was already running toward the gate. He disappeared, heading into the hotel entrance, shouting into a small radio handset.

"*Adriano, giù!*" she shouted. He dove down across the front seat.

A second round creased the roof of the car and fell with a splat on the sidewalk.

The rifle pulled back into the window. Sirens came from the police station at Piazza delle Medaglie d'Oro.

Sandra scanned up and down the street. It seemed empty. She put a hand on Nancy's shoulder.

"Let's go. If anyone else is coming, they're not here yet." She called into the open rear door in Italian. "Adriano, you come too. Leave the car!"

They ran up the stairs and into the building. Just as they shut the big outer door, a bullet pierced the heavy wood. A large splinter tore into Adriano's right arm. With a loud groan, he twisted and fell into Sandra. She caught him.

Nancy let them into the apartment. They sighed after the door closed, and Sandra threw the deadbolt. She helped Adriano into the kitchen while Nancy went for the first aid kit in the bathroom. He was bleeding through his sleeves. Sandra took off his coat and cut his shirt sleeve open with kitchen scissors. Nancy came in and took over.

While Nancy checked Adriano's arm and extracted the splinter, Sandra answered the doorbell. It was the police lieutenant from the station, with another officer. After ascertaining that Adriano was in good hands with a medical doctor and that no one else was hurt, he questioned them about the attack.

"Our man out front saw the whole thing, and his account matches yours."

"Were you able to catch the sniper?" asked Sandra.

"No. Apparently, they had taken two rooms, so he took that third shot from a different room while we were rushing to the first one."

"That was a well-organized effort," said Nancy.

"Yes, signora. We will find out who."

"I think we know who, Lieutenant, but proving it will be difficult."

"High-powered sniper ammunition is not common. We will trace those bullets." He turned to Sandra. "Congratulations, signorina. I am impressed that you were able to push Doctor Lockhart out of the line of fire. How did you do that?"

Sandra considered her answer.

"I was admiring the sky reflected in the windows. The open window made a hole in the reflection, which caught my eye." She shrugged and dropped her gaze.

"Impressive reactions. You can take the car after the crime scene investigators collect the evidence." He nodded at Adriano's arm in a sling. "You may not be driving right away."

"We'll take him home," said Nancy. "With an antibiotic at the urgent care clinic, he should heal enough to drive in just a couple of days."

"Let us take him home, signora."

She turned to the driver.

"Sandra can take the company car into work tomorrow. It should take them a while to organize something else."

"Grazie, dottoressa." Adriano went with the policeman.

"I'll bring the car back," said Sandra. "It would be safer in the garage downstairs."

The lieutenant said, "If you stop by the station in the morning, we'll have your statements ready to sign."

"Thank you, lieutenant," said Nancy. She accompanied them to the door.

When Sandra came back up from parking the company car, Nancy was staring out the kitchen window, shivering slightly. The younger woman drew up a chair silently and put her arm around Nancy's shoulder. Joe's mother stopped quivering. They sat there until the sun dropped behind the pines in the yard next door.

ᘒᘒᘒ

The next morning, they signed their statements at the police station. Sandra left the company car at the garage on Via Arenula. Nancy walked upstairs while Sandra crossed the river and took the bus up the hill to school. She could use the trolley to get back to the Smithson building to bring Nancy home in a different company car.

That day, the newspapers and broadcast media overflowed with sensational reports of yet another attack on the popular executive. This time, however, most newspaper pundits suggested that it might be the work of the neofascists. The first editorials appeared, praising the courageous doctor for standing up to the bullies who had tried to kill her and to frame their opponents for the deeds.

In a press conference two days later, the general in charge of the State Police announced that they had traced the bullets to a lot that had been stolen two years earlier from the army munitions depot near Modena. The police had arrested the soldiers involved, but not before they had turned over most of the ammunition to neofascist extremists. Many boxes of bullets were still unaccounted for.

❦❦❦

"Excuse me, Dottoressa." Nancy looked up at her secretary standing at the door. "Agent Pietrowitz on the phone. I think it's urgent, by the edge to his voice."

"Thank you, Maria Grazia." She picked up the handset and pressed the blinking button. "Hello, Special Agent Pietrowitz. How can I help you this morning?"

"Could you spare a couple of hours? I would like to brief you here in our offices. It's classified."

"Just me? When?"

"Just you, but you know the others. If you could come now, we could have you back at your desk by lunch."

"It will take me a half hour to call the car around."

"Don't bother. We have a car waiting by the Caffé

Arenula. It should be time for the coffee break. Just walk there like you usually do. You'll recognize the car. Get in the passenger's side."

"Well, okay. See you soon." She cradled the telephone. "Maria Grazia, did you hear that?"

"*Sì, dottoressa.* I take it you won't be back from your coffee break?"

"I have a hunch about this. Do I have any meetings this afternoon?"

"No, signora."

"Good. Don't book anything new. If anyone asks, tell them I am running some errands before Doctor Grimaldi gets here. I also need to buy some things for Joe."

"I understand. I'll close up if you don't make it back, but I'll call you at home tonight to check on you."

"Probably wise. Thanks."

After packing her purse and her briefcase, Nancy walked downstairs and out to the café. She almost tripped when she saw her own car parked outside. The visor was down, obscuring the driver's face. She took a deep breath and slipped into the seat. The driver put the car in gear as she closed the door.

"Sandra! What the hell?"

"Surprise: I'm your duty driver today."

"Don't you have class?"

"No. The course wrapped up yesterday. I'm full-time on my other summer assignment now."

"What's that?"

"Please wait until —" She slammed on the brakes, downshifted, and spun to the left behind the Fiat 600 that ran the red light in front of her. "*Glimmortaccitua, cretino!*"

Nancy's shock instantly melted. "Was that on the Ohio driving test?"

Sandra gave her a quick smile. "No. Evasive driver training. Don't worry: I'll get you there."

"I was referring to the advanced Roman dialect. Did Joe teach you?"

"Sorry about that. I did hear that one first from him on the scooter, but I've picked up a few of my own since."

Nancy chuckled, then gasped as Sandra did an illegal U-turn on the Via Veneto and slid into a no-parking space immediately in front of the Annex. A marine who had been standing there to keep it free opened the passenger door. He saluted, closed the car door and held the Annex door for them. Inside, Nancy stopped.

"Sandra, what is this all about?"

"Oh that? Special Agent Pietrowitz did not want us delayed by parking problems, and you *are* exposed out there. He asked the Marine CO for help."

"I could get used to this."

"Third floor. Do you prefer the elevator?"

"Let's admire these beautiful stairs."

They walked up to Room 335.

"Nancy Lockhart, this is Maria Williams, who relieved me last year."

The door to the agent's office opened. "I thought I heard Sandra's voice. Please, come in."

"Hello, Nancy." Jim Redwood stood by the conference table.

"This is a big surprise. I thought this young lady was a precocious undergrad. Now I'm in a sealed room with two senior FBI agents. And I don't know *what* she is."

The two men looked at each other, then her.

"You're in for more surprises," said Mark, "but let's take this in order. Please, have a seat."

While they settled and passed around the vacuum carafe of coffee, he put his head out the door and exchanged remarks with Maria.

"Ten minutes to Ciampino," he said to Jim. "He should be here in time to join us."

Nancy resisted the temptation to ask questions. Instead, she switched her gaze to each in turn.

Mark sat. "Nancy, you are the only one in the room who needs to be briefed, and that is why we are here. It's about our friend Ettore Arcibaldo."

"I figured as much. The other day Sandra saved my life. His people are getting too close." She squeezed Sandra's hand. "Thank you again."

"All in a day's work." Sandra smiled then nodded to Redwood. "Maybe you should explain me to her."

"Right. Nancy, Sandra here is an undergraduate at GW, and she did come here for the conservator course at the American Academy.

"She is also an employee of the Federal Bureau of Investigation and a graduate of the FBI Academy at Quantico."

"An FBI agent?"

"No, but only because of her sex." Jim went on to explain her unusual situation and how she was continuing her academic career while waiting for a permanent assignment or a badge.

"School ended," said Nancy to Sandra. "Is this why you haven't gone home?"

"No. I was hoping to see Joe when he comes home on leave, but I do have another assignment from the Bureau, unrelated to the Arcibaldo case."

"What does my son have to do with this?"

Redwood answered. "Joe is the target. The general is not the type to kill blindly for revenge. He wants it to further his cause. While discrediting his political enemies by framing them for the hate campaign against you, he hoped it would cause Joe to suffer."

"But I expect Joe to come here! He'll be a target."

"Actually, we pulled him off his cruise three weeks ago. He is on his way here to join the operation against Arcibaldo."

"You're using him as a decoy." Nancy's eyes flashed. Barely restrained anger boiled under the accusation.

"His idea, Nancy. We tried another plan, but the informant was uncovered and eliminated. I promised Joe not to bring him in unless that failed. He was right about one thing: he is the only decoy capable of drawing Arcibaldo out."

"Isn't his campaign starting to crack? The press pinned the latest two attacks on his people."

"Yes, but that is making him more desperate. Setting up a sniper was a big step, done too hastily to frame the left wing. The people privy to the coup attempt last year know that it was his people who got those stolen munitions."

"I thought we couldn't talk about that."

"Everyone here has been briefed."

For a few moments, no one spoke while Nancy digested the details of what she had just learned. She blinked and sighed.

"I'm not happy about this, but at least I'm not being surprised after the fact like last year. Let's have it."

For the next forty-five minutes, they outlined a plan to draw the politician into a public confrontation. They would fine-tune it after Joe arrived.

After a short break, they reconvened in the secure room.

"Where is Arcibaldo now?"

Mark said, "In Rome most of the time. He lives in an apartment around the corner from Party headquarters."

"Is he still using Army vehicles?"

"No. Bullet-proof Mercedes-Benz sedans."

"I thought his financing dried up after the coup attempt."

"The four investors in New York were not his only source. We are still trying to identify some deep pockets that became active only since then."

Redwood said, "Some of the cash is coming from numbered Swiss accounts through his contacts in Northern Italy, the rest from Germany and Abu Dhabi."

Sandra perked up. "Is there a pattern to these transfers? Do we have dates or approximate times?"

"I don't know, but I am sure we can find out. What are you thinking?"

"Oh, just the accounting major in me coming out. I thought we might compare them to other investigations to look for overlap. I don't know, like some of the money laundering schemes the new RICO unit is working on, or the other case I'm here for." Racketeer Influenced and Corrupt Organizations Act.

Redwood raised his eyebrows and wrote down some notes. "Good idea. We'll run it by some of the major cases that could use the data. I'll make sure Vasari gets it too."

"Who's Vasari?" Nancy asked.

"The agent I report to for my original assignment here."

"Is he likely to call you?"

"Yes. His name is David Vasari, and he looks like the Giorgio Vasari you've seen pictures of." Nancy nodded.

A knock on the door. Maria stuck her head in. "He's here."

Still in his khakis and well-tanned, Joe entered the room. Both Nancy and Sandra jumped up, but Sandra was closer.

As they squeezed each other, they began to cry, muttering, "I'm sorry, so sorry."

The adults watched with confused expressions as the two young lovers exhausted themselves with apologies.

Finally, they stepped back, smiling weakly at the others. He went into his mother's arms. Neither said anything, but they hugged long and hard.

"I guess that's enough PDA," he said. "Midshipman Lockhart reporting for duty, sir." He faced the two FBI agents.

"PDA?" asked Mark.

"Public Display of Affection. Something I learned from the Annapolis midshipmen on cruise." He smiled. "The NIS agent on the flagship said you are ready for the decoy operation."

They sat around the table, with Joe between the two women.

"How up to date are you, Joe?"

"Everything in the Italian press up to forty-eight hours ago. It takes a day for them to fly the newspapers out to the ship."

"Not the attempted assassination the day before yesterday, then?"

"No." Joe quelled the leap in his throat and forced himself to speak steadily. "I could tell something was brewing from letters in *Il Secolo d'Italia.* The general needs something dramatic to help his position in the party debate scheduled for next Friday. Three days ago, he wrote a letter to the editor warning that the Communists would probably assassinate an American public figure and that the nation needed him and the MSI to restore order. On the surface, it looked like standard political speechmaking, but when I looked at his other speeches and letters, I could see him setting the stage for another apparent anti-American hit, which we know he would carry out with his own goons."

"You're reading all that?" Mark sounded surprised. Joe explained his briefing project on the Sixth Fleet staff and how he was able to match hints in the opposing Party organs.

"What's this latest attack?"

They briefed him on the sniper, on Sandra coming to Rome for school and to help Vasari and how she wound up in Joe's room. Then they went through the plan again.

They took another break. When they gathered again, Jim Redwood noticed Joe and Sandra staring at each other and holding hands.

"In case you two lovebirds were wondering, the plan does not include Joe's going back to the apartment on Monte Mario until we arrest or neutralize the general. We'd like Sandra to stay put if you don't mind."

"I wondered how to bring that up," said Nancy. "And after?"

"I still have the Vasari mission," said Sandra. "I can move closer to wherever his team is based if Joe comes home before we make that round of raids."

Nancy said, "Raids? I'm looking forward to learning about this other mission."

"We'll get to that, I promise. Meanwhile, Joe will stay in a guest apartment the Embassy maintains near here. The Polizia is lending us a Vespa 125, so he doesn't have to use any family vehicles."

"Any questions?" Redwood looked around the room.

Joe spoke. "You have all the planning done and a lot of resources set aside for this, but I think we may be overlooking something."

"What's that?"

"Arcibaldo's state of mind. Did you say he rushed the last attack?"

"A little."

"I've read everything he's written in the various newspapers for two months. I think I can feel him between the lines. He is becoming very perturbed, but he may still need something to tip him to move rashly into the open."

"Why?"

"Unless we force his hand, so he becomes enraged and careless, I'll graduate and be a full commander before he exposes himself. Look how carefully he organized the coup."

"What do you suggest?"

Joe's idea did not sit well with the agents – at first. After a half-hour, they started adding some supporting features to reduce the risk.

After explaining Sandra's work with Vasari to Joe and Nancy, they decamped to the grill in the basement for lunch so that the young Lockhart would not be seen on the street.

25. Tickle the Tiger

OUTSIDE THE BUILDING on Via della Scrofa, two men chatted casually. The skinny one looked perpetually hungry. The bulkier one occasionally touched a nasty scar in front of his ear. He also was missing a front tooth. Both men sported black mustaches and short hair.

They smoked as they watched the street. Local pedestrians found reasons to go past the entrance on the other side of the road. Even without uniforms, the two men were sentries in any sense of the word.

The building they guarded housed the headquarters of the *Movimento Sociale Italiano*, the Italian Social Movement, as well as the editorial offices of its party newspaper, *Il Secolo d'Italia*. The MSI was the last vestige of the Social Republic of Salò, which the dictator Benito Mussolini established in 1943 after the King fired him, and Italy switched sides in World War II. The Party tried to maintain the Fascist ideal in a hostile government and enjoyed a sizeable following with its nationalistic and racist rhetoric. At the edges of the Party, violent extremists could find support and shelter, but the same could be said for the Socialist and Communist parties. The political parties on the extremes needed to walk a fine line not to run afoul of the relatively new Constitution of the

Italian Republic. No one was more adept at walking that line than Ettore Arcibaldo, retired Commander of the Carabinieri Corps, Italy's military police.

Joe recognized the two men as he drove up and parked the scooter a few meters from the door. His heart pounded in his ears as he mustered his best acting demeanor. Wiping his hands on his new cotton slacks, he walked to them with a smile.

"*Salve, ragazzi. Ci incontriamo ancora, eh?*" Hello, guys. We meet again, eh?

Their cigarettes fell from their mouths, and they looked at each other. Should they grab him or not? They also were surprised that Joe spoke Italian. He had not spoken to them when they kidnapped him and left him bound in a villa off the Via Aurelia Antica. Joe's escape was the first thread to unravel in the general's plan for a coup d'état.

"Tell you what. Either let me in to visit the editorial offices or take a message to General Arcibaldo. I'm sure you don't want to leave your post."

The heavy one waved his hand. With a light step, Joe walked past them and took the stairs to the next floor. He paused in the hallway to make sure everything matched the layout he had memorized from the newspaper articles about the renovations. After a few deep breaths, he stepped into the office.

"Hello. May I help you?" the secretary at the counter asked. He was Roman, with clear skin, slick black hair and perfect teeth.

"I'm here for *dottor* Ricci." In Italy, the honorific applied to anyone with a university degree, not just physicians.

"The subject of your visit?"

"It's confidential, but it involves the general, who would rather talk to the editor about it than me."

"Your name?"

"Also confidential. Just mention dottoressa Lockhart of Smithson Italia. He'll see me."

The secretary seemed perturbed for a moment. He picked up the phone, thought better of it, and walked to the editor's door. He came back almost immediately.

"Dottor Ricci will see you."

"Thank you." Joe took long steps to reach the door just ahead of the secretary and let himself in.

The man sitting in his shirtsleeves put his cigarette in the ashtray and looked up through wire-rimmed glasses.

"Who are you?"

"I'm Joe Lockhart, Doctor Ricci." He crossed the room and offered his hand. "I think your party leader is looking for me."

Ricci paled, but he stood and shook Joe's hand.

"You seem rather older than I imagined."

"Just a boy, my mother's only son."

"What do you want, young man?"

"A message for General Arcibaldo and another for your newspaper. First, tell him that he is to stop the campaign against my mother now. I'm in town, and he does not need to attack me through her anymore."

"Your mother is the target of the Communists and the anarchists, not us."

"Please don't insult my intelligence, sir. I've read everything you've published for some time now. Even a superficial analysis of the material shows that writers here at *Il Secolo* wrote the copy, some of it by the general and yourself. A laboratory comparison of the hate campaign materials and MSI party publications revealed that they came from the same printshop and paper stock."

Joe watched the emotions race across the editor's face: offense, defensiveness, insult, anger, resignation.

"We retain nothing but the greatest respect for Doctor Lockhart. We —"

"Good." He took an envelope from his jacket pocket and set it on the desk. "Then you should be delighted to run the contents of this letter in your newspaper, acknowledging that dottoressa Lockhart has been a friend to Italy, and thanking her for the many jobs she brought to the country and for her contribution to Italy's reputation as a provider of generic medicines to the world."

"Are you asking for some kind of retraction?"

"No, not at all. That would be admitting publicly to the general's hate campaign. Your newspaper never accused her of anything specific. The only one with a problem saying something nice about a Lockhart is General Arcibaldo himself."

"Why should we do this?"

"Because the center newspapers and the Socialist and Communist papers are coming out with something similar. *Il Secolo d'Italia farà brutta figura.*" *Il Secolo d'Italia* will lose face, badly.

The editor frowned. "Is that all?"

"For now. Just be sure also to tell the general that it will not go well for him if he tries anything else on my mother."

"You are threatening a national hero and a member of our Parliament."

"Not a threat. A promise. Just leave us alone."

Joe turned to the door. "Have a nice day, dottore." He let himself out and walked swiftly down to the street.

He heard someone shouting at the two guards as he cranked the scooter into life and sped away. Only when he cleared the corner did he let out a breath and realize that his back was soaking wet.

ʘʘʘ

In the morning, Sandra drove Nancy to work. Moretti agreed to let her use the Fiat while Adriano healed and the body shop fixed the company car. After the commute, Sandra took the car to the Campo de' Fiori for canvas, brushes, and other supplies. She hoped to start one of the portraits before Vasari called.

After losing a half hour looking for a parking place, she also decided that she would return the Fiat to the house during the day and use the scooter or the bicycle until it was time to pick up Nancy again.

As she walked to the kitchen from Joe's room, the phone rang. She picked it up in the hall.

"Hello, Sandra. It seems you took on another assignment while I was gone."

"David! Are you in Rome?"

"Yes, and I need to introduce you to the rest of the team. Do you have class today?"

"No. The course is over. But I am driving Nancy Lockhart to and from work while her driver recovers. You know about that, don't you?"

"After your brilliant suggestion the other day, Redwood called me in and briefed me about the case involving Joe."

"I need to do some shopping for supper about five and pick her up at six. What do you need today?"

"A meeting at eleven with the Italian police agencies, Interpol and the Ministry of Cultural Assets."

"I can do that. Where?"

"At the Ministry off the Via del Corso. Do you know where it is?"

"I think so, but I'll look it up to be sure."

"Shall I pick you up?"

"No. I'll take Joe's Vespa."

"Excellent. If you don't see me, go to the Fine Arts Division, and ask for Major De Santis of the Finance Guard. They'll point you to the right place."

"Got it. Arrivederci."

It was already ten o'clock. She looked in the kitchen to see if she needed any staples at the market. After putting on a little mascara and a light lipstick, she checked her dress for stains and retied her ponytail. Then she ran down to the garage and drove downtown on the scooter.

David was waiting at the main door to the Ministry. Sandra noted with some pleasure how he did not stand out as an American at all, in his light blue linen sport coat and tailored trousers. He smiled and waved when she approached, then led her upstairs.

I should not be surprised, she thought as she admired how the statues, paintings and even the frieze work in the halls and rooms gleamed with cleanliness and care. This was a building full of people who cared deeply for the art of their country.

In the meeting room behind the Fine Arts Division, a diverse collection of men had gathered around a large oak table, mostly near the tray of aperitifs and fruit juices.

David did the introductions: officers from the Finance Guard, two museum curators, investigators from the Carabinieri and the Italian State Police, as well as Scotland Yard and the Sûreté Française. Professor Alberini waved after an initial shock of seeing Sandra in the company of the lead investigator.

The deputy minister in charge of the Fine Arts Division, a young man for the job, seemed slightly intimidated by the room of art experts and law enforcement. He welcomed them, assured them of the full support of the Ministry, and left.

David stood and walked to the easel with a chalkboard at the end of the room. "For the sake of those who have not been privy to the entire operation, let me summarize it briefly." He smiled at the Scotland Yard inspector and the French officer. "Bear with me." They nodded for him to continue.

"Over the last seven months, this team assembled the evidence needed to obtain warrants to seize more than two dozen Renaissance paintings in four cities. Each of these was cleverly switched with an excellent forgery during shipment from its home museum on tour. That more than thirty museums and a like number of insurance appraisers did not spot these substitutions speaks to the skill of the forgers and the thieves' attention to detail. In fact, we are not sure we can catch the thieves, but we can arrest the patrons who bought or sold the stolen originals and the copies, and if we can carry this all the way through, catch the forgers, if they are alive. Some of the forgeries have circulated for more than fifteen years." He began listing the works on the blackboard. "For security, there is no complete list on paper. Each of you has a partial list. Please remember your part as we discuss what I put on the board."

Sandra felt dizzy as David wrote the names of the artwork that they hoped to recover. The list read like the index of one of her art history texts. As he wrote, he answered questions about individual pieces from the men who had those on their lists or who had collaborated in the investigation.

"Yesterday, we had a new development, which may identify a new player, responsible possibly for many of the thefts here in Italy. I ask you to extend your stay in Rome by at least another day because we may need to change parts of this briefing depending on that information."

He explained where they expected to find each of the paintings and pointed out which team members would lead the raids on those locations. More than two hundred police, carabinieri, and finance guards were standing by to help. The magistrates at the Palace of Justice had issued sealed warrants the week before.

"Questions?"

A carabiniere major raised his hand. "Will the raids be simultaneous? If not, what is the, the *temporizzazione* —"

"The timing, sir," said Sandra.

"Yes, the timing." He smiled at her. "Grazie."

Vasari smiled too. "We are hoping for simultaneous operations, or as close to that as possible. However, the new information may affect that. We'll know more this afternoon. Also, each of your teams should be able to make your arrests and confiscations without help from the others. No matter what happens, we should not come away empty-handed."

There was some nodding and smiling at that. Sandra guessed that hundreds of professionals had been working long hours to put this together.

A finance guard major asked, "What is this new information, Agent Vasari?"

"I am embarrassed to say, but only yesterday did one of us think to cross-reference major financial transfers from cases *not* involving art dealing. For us Americans, for example, there are a handful of transactions reported by our money laundering investigators, which do not track with the other flows they follow. Likewise, some money moving from Switzerland to Italy only started in the last year, to someone we thought lacked access to that kind of cash."

"Interesting. You will know something after lunch?"

"It may be nothing, but if it isn't, it might point us to these three missing pieces." Vasari drew a circle around the *Dama con Liocorno* and two other paintings, all from the Borghese Gallery. Sandra stifled a gasp. "More questions?"

Sandra took a breath and raised her hand. "I know I am probably the newest person on this investigation, but I want to be sure about that list. Is each of these the original, or are we also going after the forgeries? Especially those three in the circle."

"Good question, Miss Billingsley. Some are known forgeries, which have been sold or displayed as originals, and that will be the grounds for the arrest. We also hope to find originals at the locations we assigned. Almost all the warrants will be served on collectors or dealers, a few on wealthy secret collectors."

He pointed to his circle. "These three are question marks. We are almost positive that they are in Rome or nearby, but they are on this list by elimination. We accounted for copies or originals of each of them, but we are not sure whether we will find the originals or the copies when we get them together. The lab analyses will help."

"Thank you, Agent Vasari," said one of the curators. "I had not understood why we had multiple instances of the same work."

The carabiniere who asked about timing waved. "I think I have worked with everyone in the room over the last few months. Could you tell us what the young lady's role here is, apart from serving as my interpreter, of course?" He smiled and gave her a small bow.

"Thank you, Major. Miss Billingsley is assigned to the FBI Art Crimes Division. She launched this entire operation last winter by noticing differences between the *Dama con Liocorno* at the Borghese Gallery and the painting on tour at the National Gallery of Art in Washington. After that, she has pointed out details in almost all the paintings that we then identified as forged. She graduated from Professor Alberini's course at the American Academy, and I brought her in to help us with identification and comparisons.

"Yesterday, she was the one in an FBI meeting on a different case who suggested comparing the dates of financial transactions in that case with the movement of art in this case. That may expose another player."

"Remarkable," said the Carabiniere major. "*Complimenti, signorina.*" Congratulations.

"*Grazie, maggiore.*" Sandra blushed under the intense stares of the two dozen men in the room.

Vasari began to erase the board. "Let's gather here at nine tomorrow morning to find out about the possible new information and agree on the timing of the raids."

David and Sandra walked to lunch at Il Barroccio around the corner from the Ministry. Hearty Roman fare put them in a pleasant mood. After the meal, they walked back to the Ministry, where David borrowed a phone in the office of the deputy minister. Redwood was in. It was a short call.

"You scored again, Sandra."

"How?"

"Each of the transfers of cash to the general's accounts here in Rome occurred almost exactly one month after one of the movements of the missing artwork."

"Forgeries or originals?"

"Both. When one of them moved, he got money. Mind you, those are just the titles of the pieces. We are tracking at least three versions of each."

"They're all in Rome?"

"Yes, but I don't expect them to be at Arcibaldo's apartment. More likely a villa somewhere remote. Do you know anything about him?"

"No. Joe might, and I'm sure Agent Redwood knows when the general changes his underwear."

"I'm going to the Annex to meet him. I may call a meeting with the team that was going to focus on those paintings. Will you be home?"

"Until five, then shopping and commuting. We should be back by six-forty-five."

"Are you staying in?"

"Oh yes. Nancy is almost under house arrest until this case is over, and I'm her bodyguard."

"You are an amazing woman, Sandra. I sure hope you get that badge sooner rather than later. I want you in Art Crimes."

"Relax, David. I need to finish school." They reached Joe's scooter outside.

"We'll wait for you." He squeezed her hand. "See you tomorrow."

She drove back to the apartment, humming happy songs to herself.

ଷଷଷ

Nancy looked over the kitchen table at her houseguest. They each speared a big pasta shell and chewed slowly.

"I like Grottaferrata," said Sandra after a sip of her wine, "but my favorite is this Montepulciano d'Abruzzo."

"Me, too, I think. Almost criminal how inexpensive it is."

"Yeah."

Nancy put her fork down. "Sandra, I really miss having Joe home, but I don't want you to leave when he comes back."

"It should only be a few days more. The newspapers and radio news reports all changed tone, have you noticed?"

"That's not the point. I assume you two are lovers, and I don't want to push it. But I wonder if I could make something of that dining room I never use, at least until I leave in August. If I outfitted it as a bedroom, do you think you could stay until we all go back to the States?"

Sandra tried to think of a downside.

"I'd love to. Would Joe have a problem with it?"

Nancy smirked. "Right. I shouldn't talk so loudly. He might knock down the door."

The phone rang. Nancy went to her study. She came right back.

304

"Agent Pietrowitz for you." Sandra went to the phone.

"Sandra, Vasari confirmed that they've narrowed down the three circled items to a villa in the Castelli Romani belonging to our friend's cousin. The cousin died two years ago, and Joe's buddy uses the place as if it were his. Get this: his cousin was an art dealer until he retired about ten years ago."

"Can they confirm that the items are there?"

"Almost sure, from the shipping company receipts the finance guards examined. Not every guy with a pickup truck can move pieces like that over international borders."

"Interesting. How does this tie to our friend? I thought he lived in Rome."

"He does, but he often isn't home. Now we know why."

"You said the place belongs to his dead cousin. Whose is it now?"

"We're in Italy, Sandra. He only died two years ago, so it's nobody's and everyone's until the heirs accept the inheritance. In a well-off family with assets but also debts, it could take years to sort out."

"So, if he is using the place, he must have been working with the cousin before he died."

"My guess."

"What about the transactions matching?"

"Let's not discuss that over the phone. Redwood or I will be at the meeting tomorrow."

"I'll save my questions for then."

"You keep safe – and Sandra?"

"Sir?"

"Have you had evasive driver training?"

"Yes."

"Including vehicle inspection?"

"Yes."

"Good. Be extra careful. Joe's buddy stormed out in a rage no one had ever seen in public before. Go into max bodyguard mode until we see who he calls in."

"Got it, sir. Thanks."

She returned the handset to the telephone cradle and walked back to the kitchen with a clenching feeling in her stomach.

"Everything okay?"

"So far," Sandra said.

"You look like you need more of this." Nancy topped off her wineglass.

Lying awake in bed, Sandra reviewed what she had learned at Quantico about car bombs, vehicle attacks and tampering. Then she pictured Joe's smooth skin next to hers and imagined it in Joe's own bed. That helped her relax.

❧❧❧

The next morning, they walked down to the garage. Sandra had insisted on not leaving the car in the street overnight.

"Watching you crawl around that car is making me nervous."

"Sorry, Nancy, but that call last night was to warn us that the general may escalate and do something drastic without trying to set up his opponents."

"Like a car bomb?"

"Like a car bomb."

"What are you majoring in? This is crazy."

"Accounting and art history. This is part of my FBI training. There!" She closed the hood, tossed the flashlight in the back seat and opened the door for Nancy.

Nancy rolled her eyes and got in. Sandra slid behind the wheel.

As they turned down to the Viale delle Medaglie d'Oro, Sandra saw a familiar figure in her rear-view mirror, but before she could focus, the man on the scooter dropped out of sight.

There did not appear to be anyone following them. At the last intersection before the Lungotevere along the river, a large truck stood crosswise to their street, blocking traffic. Two cars stopped in front of Nancy's car, and two men got out of a parked car near the truck.

Sandra cut right into the alley that led to Viale della Conciliazione. Accelerating down the narrow road, she forced a skid to the right onto the main street.

A bullet crazed the glass in the rear window, followed by the sound of the gunshot and Nancy's surprised shriek.

Nancy ducked, then sat back slowly.

"Let me guess. Ambush?"

"Yes."

Sandra pulled to the left and passed the other cars on the wide street at high speed, turning quickly into the alley leading to the narrow Borgo Santo Spirito. This took them around the columns of Saint Peter's Square and the Holy Office. In less than a minute, they were climbing the Janiculum Hill, past the statue of Garibaldi and the stately pines that looked out over the city.

Watching the young woman drive, Nancy felt herself relax. *That is confidence under pressure,* she thought. They dropped into Trastevere and crossed to Nancy's office three bridges downstream from the attempted ambush.

At the Smithson building, Adriano came out of the main door.

"I can start driving you tomorrow, dottoressa." He eyed the shattered rear window with surprise as Nancy emerged from the car. She motioned for Sandra to join them on the sidewalk.

"We were ambushed today – well, almost. Signorina Billingsley dodged the ambush. Could you show her wherever it is you have glass work done? Also, things have become more dangerous. Are you ready for possible car bombs and ambushes?"

Adriano smiled. "Now you understand why Smithson hires retired police and military chauffeurs. And why I never leave the car when you ask me to wait. The signorina obviously has fine skills, so it looks like you are doubly covered."

"Sandra, would you tell Agent Pietrowitz that we'll return to using the company car? Then you can get on with your other work."

"Sure. After I take this car to be repaired."

Nancy went in. Adriano showed Sandra where the auto glass shop was and followed her there. By eight thirty, she was back at the house picking up the Vespa. She would ride in with Adriano and Nancy the next day to bring the Fiat back to the apartment building.

Several times, she thought Joe was following her on a heavier Vespa, but she could never take a second look before he vanished. *Love-sick wishing,* she thought. *I will be so glad when this is over.*

She was barely in time for the meeting at the Ministry of Cultural Assets.

Special Agent Redwood was in the room. Vasari introduced him to the few people who had not met him, then gave him the floor. The FBI agent reported that the financial transactions had confirmed that the unknown party holding the three missing titles (nine pieces) was the retired general, Ettore Arcibaldo.

When the exclamations subsided, he continued.

"This will cause a public scandal, but it should take some of the attention – and the pressure – off the other teams. However, the general has considerable resources at his disposal. He keeps the art at his cousin's villa in the Castelli Romani. The cousin died recently, so ownership of the villa and its contents will be fuzzy. From the documents that the Finance Guard tracked," he nodded to the two officers, "we know that he ordered the forgeries, traded in the art with his cousin, and owns the nine pieces we are seeking.

"But if we don't capture him personally at the villa, we won't be able to prove that the paintings are his because of where they are located."

Vasari asked, "Where he is now?"

"Just returned to MSI headquarters. Surveillance reported that he had parked across the river, watching an incident with a stalled truck. After the truck moved, he left."

Sandra raised her hand. "If so, sir, he just became directly involved. That truck was an ambush for Doctor Lockhart."

More exclamations from the men.

"Is she okay?"

"Yes, sir. I took an alley to Conciliazione and over the Janiculum to get her to work. The car needs a new rear window."

"Thank you, Miss Billingsley." Redwood addressed the assembly. "For those who may not be familiar with the case, General Arcibaldo has conducted the hate campaign against Doctor Lockhart since last fall, not the Socialist and Communist Parties or far-left groups. He expected to discredit his political adversaries. Obviously, he is not happy that Doctor Lockhart evaded his last three assassination attempts. The team that goes to Castelli must be ready for a violent response, and he will attempt to flee. Thank you." He sat. "Agent Vasari?"

David outlined the latest information on the location of each suspect. All but three were at home.

"The other three are the general, the collector near Lake Bracciano, and the cardinal who lives near Villa Giulia. We expect them to arrive home tonight. To make this as close to simultaneous as possible, we will conduct the raids starting at sixteen hundred hours."

"Anything different about General Arcibaldo?" asked Major Mancini, the carabiniere.

"That team will assemble at the air base at Ciampino and stay ready to move. They must wait until he returns to the villa. Though he has done that every day, his behavior has been unpredictable of late." He paused, thinking. "Are you comfortable with this assignment, major? We can brief you to another team." Like US Marines, the carabinieri were famous for their loyalty to the Corps.

"He and I go way back, and not pleasantly." He leaned over to Redwood and lowered his voice. "I was in

SIFAR two years ago, in the room with you and young Lockhart." Italy's military intelligence service.

Forty-five minutes later, there were no more questions, and the teams had planned smaller meetings. Radio checks would start at 14:00. Sandra noticed that Redwood and Vasari both wore ear pieces with the distinctive curly wires into their jackets. She guessed that Mark Pietrowitz and Maria Williams were on that link too.

As the meeting broke up, Vasari and Redwood approached Sandra.

"Ready?"

"Not sure where you want me, but yes, I'll be ready. I think I should leave dinner and a note on the kitchen table for Nancy." She looked at her dress. "And maybe find something more rugged to wear."

"How is Nancy getting back from work?" Redwood asked. "We can pick her up."

"No need. Adriano is back on duty, so the company will shuttle her. Assuming I go home tonight, I'll go in with her tomorrow and bring her car back from the auto glass shop."

"Right. Tell us what happened."

Sandra described the ambush and how she got to Smithson. She told them about Adriano's experience.

"When shall I report to Ciampino, and where?"

Vasari answered. "I'll pick you up at one because I want you in with the team when we start radio checks. The general will attend a ribbon-cutting at three. I want you close by for this, so we can put your eyes on the art right away."

"I won't need a radio, then?"

"Probably not, but I'll bring an extra set in case we change our minds."

"Can I get a vest before we go in?"

"Good point. I think we can find your size back at the office."

"Okay. See you at one."

Outside, she cranked the Vespa and drove to the Trionfale Market. She left the ingredients for supper in the refrigerator and the table and wrote a note for Nancy that she might be home late.

She fixed herself a salad for an early lunch, wondering where Joe was and what his part was in all this, besides annoying Arcibaldo.

❖❖❖

From the Via della Scrofa, Joe returned to the Via Veneto by weaving through traffic for a mile up the river and approaching the Embassy from the north. He parked the scooter in the Embassy lot and walked across the street to the Annex. Maria waved for him to go into the inner office.

"You stirred up a hornet's nest, Joe," said Mark Pietrowitz, seated behind his desk. He had a radio set over his shirt, with the curly wire going to his ear. "After you left, surveillance reported a lot of scrambling and people racing after you."

"I went upstream and lost them on the Lungotevere."

"How did you do that?"

"Easy compared to last time: I have a more powerful Vespa, and they don't have siren-equipped Carabinieri cars." Pietrowitz nodded his understanding.

"Are you ready for Phase Two?"

"Sure. May I ask what's happening with Sandra and the art operation at this point?"

The FBI man looked at the clock. "She should be headed to a meeting at the Ministry of Cultural Assets with the leaders of the teams that will make the arrests."

"With Agent Redwood?"

"No. David Vasari is our lead investigator for this. Jim is working with RICO and Washington to gather the data for the Finance Guard this afternoon. Sandra's hunch about matching cash transfers caused quite a stir. This may be a new SOP for the Bureau." Standard Operating Procedure. "Are you alright?"

Joe realized that Vasari's name had caused his expression to darken. "Fine, sir. So, who will be working with me on the next phase?"

"An old friend, I think. Do you know where the police headquarters is?"

"Which one?" All the law enforcement agencies in the country had headquarters in the capital. Pietrowitz chuckled.

"The Questura."

"Via San Vitale near the Quattro Fontane."

"You really do know this city, don't you?"

"It's my hometown."

"Right. They're expecting you. Park in the courtyard. Officer Proietti should be sitting on his motorcycle – or whatever he is riding these days."

"Maurizio?" The motorcycle officer had shadowed him on a Vespa and deliberately caused a collision, which allowed Joe to escape his second kidnapping.

"Have fun, you two, but remember, we are trying not to get you killed. Just shake up the general."

"I understand, sir."

"We told them that you'd be there at thirteen-hundred, so eat lunch first."

"Yes, sir." Joe opted for a cheeseburger and fries at the American grill in the basement again. He couldn't order those anywhere else.

Exactly at one o'clock, Joe rolled up to the guards at the gate of the Questura and held out his Navy ID card. One of them pointed to the parking area for motorcycles across from the entrance and motioned him in.

The Questura, headquarters of the State Police, occupied a full city block, but it was a rectangle with a large area inside. Opposite the gate, Maurizio's familiar figure sat on a police-equipped Ducati 250. He wore blue jeans and a leather jacket, even in the summer heat. He waved and swung off his motorcycle as Joe approached.

"*Ben tornato!*" Welcome back. After a hearty handshake, he showed Joe where to park.

"It's good to be home. Driving a regular motorcycle, now?"

"Not for this job. How do you like the little 125 we gave you?"

"Little? It has twice the power of my Vespa 50. I can ride to Milano on the *autostrada* with it."

"I'm glad you're happy. I suggested the larger size when I heard the request come down to the motor pool. We may need to outrun Mercedes-Benz machines this time."

"How do we want to do this?"

"Come inside. We'll have a caffè in front of the wall map and discuss it."

They spent a half-hour reviewing the general's usual movements. Except for political appearances with the public, he rarely went anywhere besides party headquarters, his apartment, and the villa outside Rome. Maurizio showed Joe the file with photographs of Arcibaldo's different cars and the chase cars that carried his escorts. In some of the photos, he could see the rifle held by a passenger.

"I need to look out for these guys."

"Yes. I will be looking for them too. His driver will always act to remove him from the scene unless the general orders otherwise." Maurizio tapped the photos of the chase cars. "But these guys can be called up by radio instantly. They would do anything to take you out."

"Let me guess. Don't approach him until I first know where one or more of these three are."

"That's the idea. If they take you down by running into you or shooting, the best I can do is call for backup."

"I'm only supposed to worry him, not start something with his crew."

"Okay. Let's see if we can pull this off without starting a fight."

They walked back to the parking area. Maurizio held out a helmet for Joe, then took it back. "I guess they need to see who you are, don't they?"

"Yes. Let's not provoke a high-speed chase."

"If one starts, I'll move in front of them and force them to slow."

Maurizio hung the helmet on his motorcycle and walked to a plain white Vespa 150. "Did you check the card inside the compartment of your Vespa?" It identified the vehicle as belonging to the State Police and authorized the operator to use restricted lanes and no-parking zones. Joe nodded.

"Haven't used it yet. Let's go."

"He's having lunch at Alfredo's near his apartment. You know it?"

"Everyone knows Alfredo's."

They left the Questura and rode easily down the Quirinal Hill past the presidential palace to the Piazza Venezia. Riding in the trolley and bus lanes, they zoomed along the Corso Vittorio Emanuele, slowing when they turned into the narrow, cobblestoned street near the Via della Scrofa. Maurizio fell back out of sight, but Joe knew he was there.

Passing the MSI headquarters, Joe waved at the two sentries, who were turning over to the afternoon shift. They started to run after him, but the new guards called them back. Joe took the corner, then slowed as he turned the next corner toward the restaurant.

Outside, some tourists were enjoying the creamy pasta dish that Alfredo had made famous. Arcibaldo sat at the last table, sipping some water and listening to Ricci, the editor of *Il Secolo d'Italia*. The water carafe was holding down some bills, so they were about to leave. Joe spotted one of the three chase cars he had studied, an Alfa Romeo Giulia, parked across the street from the restaurant. No one was in it.

He cruised past the restaurant until he caught the general's eye. He tapped his forehead in a cocky salute and grinned. Then he waved as he sped down the street. In his rear-view mirror, he saw no reaction, but he did not expect one.

The two Vespa riders returned to the Questura, where they waited for updates from the surveillance team. When the politician left the party headquarters to go to a rally next to the Coliseum, Joe passed his car on the Viale dei Fori Imperiali and waved at the general through the window before speeding off.

After giving a speech at the hall near the Coliseum, the general rode out to his villa, followed by a gray Lancia sedan. As they passed the hippodrome on the Via Appia, Arcibaldo recognized Joe coming the other way on his scooter, waving at him with a stupid grin. He scowled, but there was nothing he could do. The cheeky American boy zipped by in a flash.

"*Basta.*" Enough, Joe said, as they parked in the Questura courtyard.

"That was fun," said Maurizio. "That last time, you finally got to him."

"I thought that was you between his car and the chase car."

"Yeah. I looked in the back window. He was shouting something at the guy in the front seat. When he stopped turning around to look for you, I peeled off to catch up with you."

"He'll probably be ready tomorrow. You want to come to the Embassy, or shall I come here again?"

"The general's men staked out the Embassy. Come here."

"Okay. Ciao."

Back at the Annex, Maria was packing up for the day. Agent Pietrowitz beckoned him into the office.

"I'd say that was very effective harassment, Joe. He's been screaming at his people on the phone since he got to the villa."

"Knowing which cars to look for helped. Tomorrow, though, he'll be ready."

"He is probably planning now. Why else have his security detail come out? He doesn't usually meet them there."

"Should I annoy him on his return to the city or later in the day?"

"Let's stick with the plan for now. The ribbon-cutting at the new MSI Youth Center. He may be in a more relaxed mood leaving that."

"It is his last event of the day. Do we expect him to go to Via della Scrofa or the villa?"

"Lately, he's been going to the Castelli after the last commitment. I would set up for that."

"Okay. Will someone tell Maurizio – Officer Proietti – when to expect me?"

"Yes. The ceremony starts at three, so you don't need to roll before that."

"Two thirty at the Questura should give us time to figure out an approach."

"Sounds like a plan. This may all be over in the next twenty-four hours. Hang in there."

"Is he planning something we can catch him on?"

"He already has. Remember Sandra's comment about matching financial flows with the dates that paintings moved?"

"Yes?"

"She was right. Ettore Arcibaldo has the missing art. The Art Crimes task force will include him in the sweep. Let's hope he doesn't give us the slip."

"When?"

"They'll decide that at a meeting in the morning. It's news to the others, so they will do some last-minute planning for the raid."

"Good luck, sir. You and Agent Redwood worked for a long time on this."

"Thanks. Good night, Joe."

ಙಙಙ

A block from the new MSI Youth Center, Joe stopped for a red light. In his rear-view mirror, he saw a sedan turn left in front of oncoming traffic, and he heard the crunch of a collision. He lifted his foot from the ground and gunned the Vespa. He felt himself falling to the left as the car next to him at the light accelerated and cut into his path. He rolled as he hit the pavement and came up as a third car turned in front of him and braked hard. The rear doors opened, and men from the last two cars ran toward him.

Joe stood to face them but felt his hands pulled behind him, and a gun barrel pushed into his side. With his hands tied, he was dragged into the car blocking the Vespa. A man sat on either side of him. One of the men in the street righted the scooter and walked it to the curb, locking it there.

"What —" Something struck the back of his head. His vision faded in and out as he struggled not to faint. The man on his right slapped a blackjack against the palm of his hand.

"Shut up, or we'll gag you."

The three cars formed a convoy speeding out of town. Joe recognized the Via Appia, so he guessed that they were going to the general's villa. As he nursed his headache and watched the pines zoom by on either side of the long, narrow highway, he realized that they had swapped out all three chase cars.

He wondered how Maurizio was and felt a deep pain for the gutsy motorcycle cop who had gotten into two crashes, trying to protect him.

26. LADY WITH AN ATTITUDE

AT EXACTLY ONE in the afternoon, Sandra stood on the sidewalk outside the apartment building. A navy-blue carabinieri Alfa Romeo turned the corner from down the hill and pulled in front of her. David Vasari opened the door, and she slipped in. The driver used the hotel's circular driveway to turn around, which allowed Sandra to wave to the protection detail. She saw him walk to his car as they returned to the street to head the other way.

"Who was that?"

"The policeman detailed to watch our building when someone is there."

"I didn't know how important the case with the general was until this morning."

"Yeah. I only found out when I started staying with Nancy. I knew who he was, but not that he was behind the hate campaign."

"Got a radio and a vest for you."

"Thanks. Any news from Joe?"

"Not since yesterday. He buzzed Arcibaldo three times, which got the old man very angry. Today, they're supposed to make another pass when he comes out of the ribbon-cutting ceremony."

Forty-five minutes later, the driver pulled through the gates to the air base at Ciampino. The Italian Air Force and the international airlines shared the one runway.

They stopped outside a hangar. Vasari took his gear from the trunk and handed a vest and radio communications set to Sandra.

"You know how this works?"

"It looks like a standard comm kit. Who will be on it?"

"The FBI, the MarDet commander, and Marty McKenzie, the Sixth Fleet NIS agent." Marine Detachment.

"The Embassy guards?"

"Only as backup. They're close at hand, and bringing anyone else in would draw attention. You and I will go in with the Italian police and carabinieri. Pietrowitz and Redwood will go with the teams arresting the cardinal and the collector in Bracciano —"

Sandra whipped off her denim blouse and strapped on the armored vest. David and the driver gaped, but she was buttoning up before either could say anything.

"Thanks to the FBI Academy, I'm used to not having a lady's room around. Nothing you haven't seen on the beach, is it?"

"Uh, no. Do you want a weapon?"

"No. I haven't been to a practice range since I got here. If I need a gun, I'll borrow one from the general's men."

Vasari started to say something but realized that he did not have a comeback for that.

They walked into the hangar. Inside, about sixty police and carabinieri milled about six Army troop trucks. The troops were eating sandwiches and drinking from canteens and bottles of water. At two o'clock, everyone gathered near their vehicles while the radio circuits were tested. Vasari had a hand-held radio, but he was having trouble understanding the rapid talk from the other teams.

"Want me to carry that? Then you can concentrate on the arrests."

"Good idea. Thanks." He gave her the lightweight handset and told her the call signs for the other groups.

With the communications checked out, everyone stood down again to wait for the report that the general was moving. Technicians swapped out two radios that did not work right. David and Sandra went to a folding picnic table that had been set up in the hangar. The carabiniere major from the meeting waved for them to sit with him.

"*Ciao, Vasari,*" he said to the FBI agent. He shook hands with Sandra. "Miss Billingsley. I am Alcide Mancini."

"*Molto piacere, maggiore, mi chiami Sandra, la prego.*" Pleased to meet you, major. Please call me Sandra.

"*Alcide, allora.*" The carabiniere smiled. The conversation continued in Italian.

"Major Mancini is the commander of this mission," said David. "He will present the warrant and direct the men covering the exits of the villa, as well as the main house. We're there to take possession of the art, identify it if possible, and accompany it back to the Ministry of the Interior."

"Not Cultural Assets?"

"Actually, only Interior has a strong room big enough and secure enough. It used to be the holding tank for political prisoners in Mussolini's day. And Interior controls the State Police, of course."

"Ironic, isn't it?" said Sandra. "You and I will hold back, I take it."

"Yes. Our biggest problem should be staying out of a crossfire if it turns violent."

"I understand. I'm glad Joe is out of this, though."

"I agree. But he succeeded in distracting the general. That should help."

"Are you all sure that the general doesn't know about this operation?"

Alcide said, "Yes. Normally, he might have suspected something or put more resources into checking his tracks with the art, but he has had his hands full directing the secret campaign against the left using Doctor Lockhart and dealing with the challenge he faces inside his own party."

They nibbled on cheese and fruit and sipped bottled water while chatting about personal things. The major was surprised by Sandra's command of Italian, even with the two years she spent in Rome before.

At three-twenty, word arrived that the ribbon-cutting ceremony had ended. Arcibaldo was going to his car. The troops boarded their trucks. David escorted Sandra to a carabinieri cruiser and held the back door for her. He closed the door and walked around.

Alcide jumped in the front seat. *"Andiamo!"* Let's go!

The convoy rolled out of the hanger to the air base gates. The car stopped on the Via Appia with its blue light flashing, blocking traffic for the column to make a left turn. Then the driver sped up the oncoming lane with siren and light and took the lead again silently.

Sandra mentally walked through the plan of the house that the team had studied that morning. The carabinieri cruiser drove up to the main door and stopped. Alcide got out while the trucks continued around the villa. When they were in position, they disgorged their policemen and soldiers who ringed the house inside the walls. A state police captain joined Mancini. The carabiniere driver brought a crowbar with him. *He must keep that on the floor up front,* she thought.

Sandra and David waited behind the command car while the driver preceded Major Mancini and the captain to the door.

She studied the house. It could have served as the model for a half-dozen Hollywood versions of a sumptuous Italian villa. Some mold stained the yellow stucco and frieze work, window frames showed a little wear from the merciless Mediterranean sun, and the white marble decorative edging needed some in-depth cleaning. In this land of villas, it had probably been built as a simple, two-story country house for a well-off Roman family. A house with an absent landlord (*or disputed ownership*) and no on-site caretakers would look like this quickly. She was sure that the art inside was worth more than the house.

No one answered the doorbell. Mancini rang two more times. They could hear a scuffling noise, so they knew that someone was in there. As the driver was inserting the crowbar to force the door, it opened. One of the thugs that Sandra recognized from the FBI file on the general stood at the door.

The driver almost fell in. The thug brought his elbow down and decked the carabiniere.

27. Ladies and Massacres

THE DRIVER TOOK the Via Appia well above the speed limit, making Joe hope someone would pull them over. No such luck. In less than twenty minutes, the driver turned into the gates of a villa overlooking the Pontine Plain and stopped in front of the main house.

The three passengers pulled Joe out while the driver took the car away. The thugs dragged him up the stairs and into the house. When he paused in the darkness to let his eyes adjust, the blackjack smacked his buttocks.

"Move!"

They walked him to a sort of parlor to the left of the staircase. The one with the blackjack shoved him into a chair with armrests and upholstery. He was the guard with the missing tooth and the scar.

"I wanted to kill you before, but the boss didn't want you injured. Not to hurt your pretty face." He squeezed Joe's cheek until it would bruise. "He doesn't care now, but I promised not to let you die before he got here."

The blackjack cracked a rib on his left side. Joe struggled not to cry out. The pain made his vision narrow. It stabbed him worse when he tried to inhale.

"That was just a love-tap, asshole!"

"*Basta!*" Enough! The other guard grabbed Blackjack's arm. "Save it. The general will want to watch his last hours. Count on it."

Joe almost kicked out but caught himself. He did not want to give them a reason to bind his feet like last time. *Better not to move until I'm completely free.* He could run – kind of – and hide if left alone. He concentrated on breathing as slowly as necessary for his ribs not to make him gasp.

"I'm going to the kitchen," the thin one said. "You want something?"

The third man laughed. "You were right," he said to Blackjack. "He must have a tapeworm."

"*Vaffanculo.*" Fuck you. Skinny walked to the other side of the house.

The other two took positions in front of Joe, Blackjack on the sofa, the other in an armchair on Joe's other side. Blackjack took out his cigarettes.

"Not here. You know the general hates smoke."

"Shit. Yeah." He put away the cigarettes and took out the *Gazzetta dello Sport.* While he studied the racing pages, the third man settled himself comfortably in the chair and fixed his gaze on Joe.

The stare made Joe uncomfortable. The man was shorter than either of his companions, medium build, and clean-shaven. His dark eyes made Joe think of a cobra about to strike. Were it not for the distraction from his ribs, Joe might have been hypnotized like a mongoose. The man seemed never to blink, but after a while, Joe realized that he simply did not blink as often as most people.

Joe thought about what he should do first if freed for whatever reason. He reviewed a couple of moves he learned from Tony and one that Sergeant Henry taught them last summer. When he found a breathing rate that did not make his chest hurt, he settled in for a long wait.

Maybe he dozed because he was surprised when the driver walked in the door. "He's coming."

The third man, who apparently was in charge, moved his head toward the kitchen. The driver went to get Skinny.

When the general came in, he paused to let his eyes adjust, then saw the young American in the chair. Black-jack hit his arm. Joe got up, which made his ribs scream. He pressed the feeling down and stood up straight.

"Well, well, Mister Lockhart. I hope you have had fun because the only question now is how quickly you will die and what we will do with your remains. I'll give that some thought."

He walked upstairs while his driver and bodyguard joined the others in the parlor. Doors closed and opened, and a toilet flushed. Arcibaldo returned in his shirtsleeves without his tie.

"At this point, young man, you and your mother have exhausted any usefulness you might have had for me."

"Sorry to ruin your plans."

The general held out his right hand. His driver handed him a short whip made like a cat-o-nine-tails. He swung it across Joe's midsection. The rib flexed, and he bit his mouth to keep from screaming as the leather knots tore across his stomach.

"What were you trying to do?"

"Only get you to leave us alone. All this was unnecessary."

"But I have a score to settle with you."

Joe took a slow breath and looked directly at the retired officer.

"If you wanted was revenge, you could have had me killed in Virginia. We have bargain prices for hit men in America."

The whip came across his midsection in the other direction. Joe's vision narrowed again. He focused on the general's face until the blackness withdrew to the sides.

The doorbell rang. Skinny started to the door, but the general hissed at him to stop.

The bell rang again. Joe stood still while the other men silently put themselves between Arcibaldo and the door. They heard a crunch at the door. The general turned to the door and nodded to his driver, who opened the door.

A carabiniere with a crowbar almost fell into the room. The general's driver lowered his elbow on the back of the new man's neck, driving him to the floor. A carabiniere major and a Polizia captain stood at the door. The man on the floor swung the crowbar at the driver, cracking his knee and bringing him down too.

Joe reached up with his cuffed hands and lunged over Arcibaldo's head. He pulled back hard and twisted with all his might. Arcibaldo fell sideways, dragging Joe off his feet. The general struggled, but Joe held on.

He was choking the older man, but not well because the chain of the handcuff was pressing under the general's chin rather than his neck. Joe fought to overcome the pain in his side and to focus on twisting the general's neck.

Blackjack pulled a gun and fired at Joe. The bullet ricocheted off the marble floor and winged the driver of the kidnap car on the arm.

Before Blackjack could fire again, the carabiniere officer shot him.

The gunshots brought more people through the door. First, a man in civilian clothes leaped over the general's driver, diving to the right. Behind him came a woman in a denim shirt and jeans. She moved left in a crouch.

Sandra! Joe could not shout with the pain in his ribs and trying to hang on to the general.

Skinny shot at Sandra, who disappeared behind the men on the floor. Joe stared in horror, shaking with the effort to hold his position.

Skinny crumpled and fell back in front of the man who shot him. *Is that Vasari?* Joe wondered.

The general's driver and the third man lay down and put their hands out. The major motioned to the carabiniere driver and the captain, who proceeded to handcuff them.

The driver of the kidnap car kept still after he was hit by the ricocheting bullet, but as the policemen gathered the others, he looked back at Joe and the general. Joe saw the gun but could only stare at the weapon.

Leaping over the men on the floor, Sandra fell on the gunman. She wrapped her arms around his head and twisted. He spasmed, then lay still. Joe stared in amazement as she stood and picked up the pistol.

She smiled at her lover.

"Hi, Joe. I see you have things under control here."

"Ciao, bella. You think someone could take over? If I move, I'll break his neck."

"That would not be a loss. Agent Vasari! Mr. Lockhart has the general alive. Who wants to arrest him?"

"Major Mancini, do you mind?"

"*Con piacere.*" With pleasure. While more police-men came in to take away the general's security detail, Alcide read the warrant to the seething politician. The police captain handcuffed him, and led him to a truck.

The medic with the team patched up the wounded and called for ambulances to take them, Blackjack and the other dead gunman away. They insisted on taking Joe too, to have his ribs X-rayed and bandaged properly.

Sandra gave him a kiss as they loaded his stretcher into the ambulance.

ဒဒဒ

While Vasari, the major and the captain split up to direct the search for the missing art, Sandra quietly slipped up-stairs in the main house. She found the bathroom, closed the door, and threw up in the toilet until she had dry heaves. After she flushed twice, she knelt there, waiting for the spinning to stop. Her heart did not want to slow down and the blood rushing through her body made her faint.

At last, she was able to breathe slowly. Like a mantra, she kept reminding herself that she had used the mini-mum force necessary. She had saved the general's life as much as Joe's. She rested for a while longer. Then she stood, went to the basin and washed up. In the mirror, she expected to see anything except her own normal face. But there it was, the same face she had that morning.

Then she looked deeply into her own eyes.

And knew that she was changed.

Forever.

Soon the team found the underground room where Arcibaldo had stored the paintings. All nine pieces were in the cache, along with two copies of Rubens' *Massacre of the Holy Innocents*.

There were still three hours of daylight left, so Vasari and Mancini had tables set up outside and had the policemen and soldiers carry the art up from the room. Sandra forced herself to calm down first, then examined the versions of *Dama con Liocorno*, moving deliberately over them in turn.

"Can't tell you which is the original, David, but these two were probably done by the same artist. Not that it isn't the original and the best damn forgery in the world. The lab may find differences."

"And the third one?"

"Just not by the same artist as these two. Let me finish looking at the others for anything obvious."

Versions of the *Massacre* were not supposed to be in Europe at all, so she examined them closely.

"I never studied this piece as much as the Italian ones, but they are by two different artists, so either one of these or one of the known pieces is the original."

"Amazing, Sandra. I absolutely cannot see the difference."

"We'll know more when the lab goes over them."

She took a similar look at the other pieces before the shadows began to lengthen. By then, the team had closed the house. Only the command car, the truck with the art, and an escort car of guards remained.

An hour later, the three vehicles rolled into the courtyard of the Ministry of the Interior. The trucks from the other two locations were there, and lab technicians and policemen were carrying the paintings into the strong room. Armed soldiers formed a gauntlet on either side of their path.

Sandra watched while Mancini, Vasari, Pietrowitz, and Redwood discussed the schedule for meetings for the next few days. They had a protocol worked out, but she figured that none of them expected to wrap up identification on three dozen paintings at once.

David waved for her to join them.

"Sandra, I'd like you to be present when the art experts arrive next week."

"You're kidding!"

"No. I don't intend to pit you against them, but I – no, we – want you to look at what they are doing." He tilted his head toward the other two FBI agents. "Partly, I think this is a rare chance for you to see so many top experts at work, and, partly, I expect that you may notice something that escapes them or that sounds off to you."

"Your ability to explain what you see is part of what makes you so valuable," said Redwood. "It makes people go back and check their assumptions. That way, we can all feel better about the findings."

An hour later, the meeting broke up. Sandra would be going to the Ministry of the Interior every day starting next week. She would also need to leave a deposition before returning to the US because there would be an inquest and a finding in the death of the security guard she had killed.

28. THE END OF AN ERA

DAVID DROVE HER BACK to the apartment building. Sandra assured him that she would be fine and that Nancy should be home. He drove away. She walked up the stairs and let herself in.

"Nancy? Oh good. I'm back."

"Just got back myself. Joe's not here yet."

"He's in the Salvator Mundi Hospital. The general's men nabbed him again."

"Oh my God!"

"He'll be okay. I'll tell you about it on the way."

"But the car is still —" She grinned. "The Vespa key is in the hall. Do you want to drive?"

❧❧❧

The two women walked into Joe's room to find him dozing in front of the TV news. The arrest of the general and the biggest art recovery haul in history filled the reports.

"Am I ever glad to see you two!" They engaged in a three-way hug, twice making Joe's ribs protest. Nancy stood back to let them share a long kiss, tears welling in her own eyes, knowing what it must mean for the two of them.

"Well, what did they find?" Sandra asked finally.

"Cracked rib. Some bruising. They want me here for concussion observation overnight."

"Routine," said Nancy. "I can have them release you to me for that. I am licensed, you know."

"Thanks, Mom," he looked at Sandra, "but it might be more trouble just now. All my stuff is at the Embassy apartment."

"I'll come for you with the car after I pick it up tomorrow," said Sandra. "We can move your things in the afternoon."

"What about your work?"

Sandra pointed at the television. "It's over. They don't need me until Monday when the experts start inspecting the pieces. Redwood and Vasari want me to watch."

Joe grinned. "This is the first time I've heard his name without feeling negative. I'm glad you two were able to work so well together."

Sandra put her hand behind his head and kissed his forehead. "Well, he *is* tall, dark and handsome." He gave her a playful swat.

Nancy spoke. "I'm only getting the TV news. Do you two want to tell me what happened?"

They pulled up chairs next to the bed, and each told their side of the story. The nurse kicked the visitors out after an hour, but he confirmed that the hospital would release Joe about nine or ten in the morning if nothing developed during the night.

Neither Sandra nor Nancy felt like cooking, so they left the Vespa in the garage downstairs and walked to the rosticceria at Piazzale delle Medaglie d'Oro for supper.

"Busy day tomorrow," said Sandra over their platters of roast chicken and greens. "Get the car. Pick up Joe.

Collect his seabag. Then I need to go back to the FBI office to see if they want me to find my own place or if they want me to swap with him."

"Hold it right there. You don't have to leave."

"But —" Sandra dropped her jaw, and she blushed.

Nancy laughed. "Easy, girl. I had Maria Grazia checking on things for me while you two were chasing bad guys. The movers arrive in the morning to replace the dining set with a bedroom suite. They gave me a big discount on the rental because I let them add my furniture to their inventory."

"She does everything for you, doesn't she?"

"You're not surprised, are you? Jim Redwood told me what he thinks of you."

"Still, she is amazing."

"That's why I hired her. We were the only women in the building for the longest time, a support group of two." Nancy smiled. "She had great fun, choosing furniture and bedding."

"I'm sure I'll like it. Doctor Grimaldi arrives next week."

"Yes. Thanks to you and Joe, I can concentrate on that and the move back to Richmond."

"I'm glad I'll be here. Joe won't be much use, for a while."

"There's that too."

They rose and walked out into the night. Silently, each pondered the enormity of that day. It was the end of an era, the end of a nightmare, and the dawn of a new life.

the end

AUTHOR'S NOTE

This is a work of fiction, not a historical novel. As far as I know, no program existed like the one I created to put Sandra in the FBI, although the timing coincides roughly with the recruiting of the first female special agents in 1972.

I have not quoted Edgar Shannon, though his presidency and the work of Paul Saunier are matters of record. Except for these two, the resemblance of any character to a real person is coincidental.

If you enjoyed the book, please leave a review with the retailer of your choice. If you spotted errors, I would welcome an email (jt@jthine.com). You may also send me a comment privately through my website (https://jthine.com/contact/).

Thank you in advance.

JT Hine